Foreign Object

Ron Base

1986
Doubleday Canada Limited, Toronto, Canada
Doubleday & Company Inc., Garden City, New York

Foreign Object

ISBN 0-385-25103-3
Library of Congress Catalog Card Number

First Edition

Cover design by Don Fernley
Foreign Object was produced on the Macintosh Plus™
using Microsoft Word™ and Pagemaker™,
and output in pages on the LaserWriter Plus™
by McCutcheon Graphics Inc., Toronto, Ontario
Printed and bound in Canada by John Deyell Company

Canadian Cataloguing in Publication Data

Base, Ron, 1948-
Foreign Object

ISBN 0-385-25103-3
I. Title.
PS8553.A83F67 1986 C813'.54 C86-094038-1
PR9199.3.B37F67 1986

Library of Congress Cataloging-in-Publication Data

Base, Ron
Foreign object.

I. Title.
PR9199.3.B3757F6 1986 813'.54 86-16653
ISBN 0-385-25103-3

For my mother, Jean Base,
with great love and affection.

Acknowledgements

To Dusty and Joan Cohl who guided me through the vagaries of the Carlton terrace and introduced the delights of the Hotel du Cap; to the Toronto Star for sending me each year to the Cannes Film Festival and never asking too many questions; to my wonderful editor, Jennifer Glossop, who asks many questions, and always the right ones; and finally, most importantly, to Lynda Ruddy – *je t'aime.*

We dance in a ring and suppose,
But the Secret sits in the middle and knows.

— Robert Frost

Man wishes woman to be peaceable,
but in fact she is essentially warlike,
like the cat.

— Friedrich Wilhelm Nietzsche

PROLOGUE

Cairo, 1975

For a long time there was only the blackness.

Then the blackness disappeared. What a good place to die, she thought. She sat cross-legged on the desert floor, her naked body washed by the light from the full moon. The moon was just above her. She could reach out and touch it with the tip of her finger. The moon turned the sphinx in the distance into an evil presence. In daylight it was another tourist trap in a world where everything, even history, was a tourist trap. Camel drivers pestered you to have your picture taken atop their animal. The ranks of folding chairs for the nightly *Son et Lumière* show made the area around the pyramids look disconcertingly like a drive-in. The desert was covered with the detritus of the world traveler: empty cardboard cartons, discarded Styrofoam cups. The tackiness of it surprised her. And saddened her. At night, however, the tourists were gone, and the moon and its ghosts reclaimed the ground. The sphinx was a fearsome thing, transformed to *Abu el Hui* – the father of terror. And it was a good place to die.

The thought of death warmed her in the chill air. It was so easy, really. Once you eased across the line in the consciousness, once you allowed yourself to accept the prospect of death, it became a welcoming thing. Lately, the consideration of death, its real possibility, had become a constant companion, like a book kept by the bedside that she could pick up and browse through casually. Death had taken on its own inescapable logic. If one was not happy with life, then the single alternative was death.

Irony lurked under the huge moon. She had come to Cairo not to die, but to be reborn. At least that's how she had thought of it. She was going to be with a special man; with him she was going to begin the journey into a new life. That was the irony – and the joke. She should have known better. She was by nature a pessimist. When you were down, life always gave you a kick, just for good measure. Life was shit; death was an old pal, waiting quietly a few feet away.

Death in the moonlight was hazy and difficult to define. She heard death's footsteps crunching on the sand. She swayed slightly, shivered in the cold night air and thought of Frankfurt. It seemed so long ago. She remembered the day, cool and crisp and gray. She had taken the train in from the airport at nine o'clock in the morning. When she saw what was playing at one of the cinemas just off the Elbestrasse, she smiled inwardly, and thought, Oh, go in, just out of curiosity. Besides, what else was there to do in Frankfurt at nine o'clock in the morning while you awaited your connecting flight to Cairo? She paid ten marks to a cashier then went up a steep flight of wide stairs. On the landing there was a bar, and a friendly grandmotherly type, all smiles and welcome. She spoke excellent English. What would she like? Scotch or cognac? The drink was included with the price of admission. She asked for cognac. Why not? Cognac and a movie at nine o'clock in the morning. What could be more natural? Lately her life had been like that. Everything out of kilter.

She went into the darkened theater. It was all quite civilized, unlike American movie houses, which always gave off an air of sleaziness. Here the seats were like easy chairs, plushly upholstered and tilting to accommodate each patron. There was even a holder for her drink attached to the back of the seat in front of her. There were perhaps a dozen other patrons, men of course, each one sitting alone, blank-faced, staring up at the screen.

On the screen, ludicrously enough, there was a documentary from Canada's National Film Board about the buffalo. It was in black and white, and the print was terribly scratchy. The sound wavered and gurgled as though coming from underwater. The buffalo were dying. Poor buffalo. The only exposure they received these days was in German movie theaters.

Finally the documentary ended. There was a short intermission. Then came the main feature, *Raunchy Housewife.* It was one of her earliest films, made when she was still telling herself that she was doing this because her mother, her silly, tiresome, flighty mother, was dead, and there was a younger sister to care for, and the money was so easy. Later, she gave up the excuses, and realized she was doing it for a myriad of complex reasons, the simplest and most irksome of them being that she liked the limelight and the money.

Anyhow, *Raunchy Housewife* was not very good. Certainly not like some of the recent ones. Everything was overlit and the sound quality was dreadful. She looked so skinny, she thought, as she watched herself on the screen removing her clothes. She was seducing the pool boy. What a plot. It took about five seconds to get the pool boy seduced. What was the kid's name? Duke? That was it, Duke. Not his real name, of course. No one used real names. Duke had pimples on his ass, and he had trouble keeping an erection. But from her reactions on the screen, you would have thought he was the sexiest stud who ever lived and that she was having the time of her life. But then that's where the acting came in. She was known for the emotional frenzy she brought to her work, how she really got into it. "Method fucking," they called it. Always teasing her. In real life, sex was between two people. In movies the sex was with the audience. It was a performance. You were too busy trying to communicate with the audience to get turned on. There were camera angles to worry about, and there were guys you never liked very much who always seemed to be having difficulties with their plumbing. It was an acting job. Jane Fonda did a sexy scene with Jon Voight in *Coming Home.* Well, didn't she? Okay, no penetration was shown. But it was still sex. You did a love scene and you kissed someone. Or you did a love scene, and you actually made love to someone. It was all performance. Everyone in the movies was selling fantasy. This was just another part of the fantasy.

She sat in the theater, watching herself with the pimply guy named Duke. She sat there with her cognac, and she began to cry. That surprised her. Why the hell was she crying? She had been doing a lot of that lately. She'd been drinking a lot and snorting too much coke and seeing the wrong type of guys who kept wanting the wrong kinds of things from her. She wiped angrily at the tears. This was nothing to be ashamed of. It was *acting,* for God's sake. You pretended, then you went home and got on with your life. Or you tried to get on with your life. Lately, she had not been very successful with the getting on. She was earning two thousand dollars a week for sucking guys off in front of a camera. And she was miserable. She was in a tailspin. None of it was fun any more. There was a deep, empty chasm in her. She could stand back and watch herself going out of control, and there did not seem to be a damned thing she could do about it.

She finished her drink and left the theater. The grandmotherly type looked concerned. She had not liked the feature? The girl in it was one of the big American stars. She looked like Grace Kelly. Everyone was crazy about her. She smiled wanly. No, no, she said reassuringly. The feature was fine. It was just that she had an appointment. The grandmother smiled brightly and wished her a good day.

She had taken the train back to the airport. Not to worry. Those movies were part of her past. The future was coming up. The future began in Cairo. Welles Carpenter was at its center. He was, he said, mad for her, absolutely stunned by her beauty and her talent. She was wasting her life in the adult-film industry. There was a future for her in mainstream movies. He would make her a star. She had laughed at that. She already was a star, she pointed out. Welles had frowned. He could make her a true star, he insisted. Yeah? she said, trying to act tough. How many other actresses had he said that to? His face was very serious when he replied. None. She was the first.

The plane, a DC 10, landed briefly in Munich. An Arab wearing a burnoose got on board with his three daughters. She was fascinated. She had never been farther from home than Los Angeles. The world, a place that until now had existed within narrow boundary lines, was opening up before her.

The flight took three hours and thirty minutes. As the plane approached Cairo, she was beside herself with excitement. The flight attendant announced they were about to land, and would everyone please fasten their seat belts. The red ball of the sun was disappearing into the western sky. Below, she spotted the three pyramids. From the air they looked like so many geometry-homework constructions. Beyond the homework the Nile was a jagged L running up to the

Mediterranean Sea. The Eastern Desert, ochre-colored at sunset, rushed into the sea.

She was disappointed that Welles did not meet her at the airport. But maybe he was filming. That was it, of course. How selfish of her. This was a very important movie for him. The most important movie of his life. His comeback, the evidence for what he called "those Hollywood assholes," that he was not washed up, that he could still deliver the goods.

Welles had sent his driver, a tall, good-looking Egyptian, who whisked her through customs in no time, everyone extremely polite, bowing. They drove into Cairo, through teeming streets, masses of humanity crowding everywhere. Everything was shadowy as the car sped through the city. She was not paying much attention, anyhow. She was preoccupied with Welles – and her future.

Future? Oh, Jesus. What future? There had been no future, not for her. She felt again the chill of the night. Not long now, she thought. Death was very close, taking its time, as death will. The warmth again flooded through her, protecting her from the cold. It was a good place to die.

There had been the welcoming fuck with Welles at the Mena House, in his suite with the Moorish vaulting, both of them excited and pawing away at each other. She worked all her little tricks, the ones he deplored when he was not loving them. He could not get enough of her, and his passion fueled her. It was one hell of a night. The next day, he said between bouts, they were shooting out by the pyramids. She would meet the producer. What was his name? God, she could not remember the bastard's name. But if the producer liked her, then she would play the part. Suddenly there was a shadow over everything. Wait a minute. She thought she already had the part. Yes, of course, Welles said. But the producer had the final word in these matters. There was no problem. Just turn on the charm. She would be fine.

The next day, under a languid early-morning sun, she accompanied Welles out to the set, driving up a winding road in one of the Jeeps. They were shooting at some ruins near the pyramids. The crew stripped to the waist, pushing reflectors and cameras into place as the sun heated everything. She met the producer on the set. God, what was his name? Small, constantly smiling. Not unattractive. And it was obvious he liked her. She saw the hungry look in his eyes, the look men tended to get when they were around her. She was used to it. She even found it reassuring. If she turned on the producer, then how could he say no to her?

That night, before dinner, she popped a few uppers to give her the charge she needed to get her through the evening. The three of them dined in the Indian restaurant at the Mena House, the producer full of charm and funny stories and exclamations about her beauty. She tried to bring up the subject of her part in the movie. That was brushed away with another story. There was lots of white wine and laughter to accompany the samosas, pakoras, pappadums, and the lamb pasanda.

They all stumbled back to Welles's suite. Like magic, the water pipe and the butane lighter appeared, and the producer showed them how to freebase cocaine. Then it really was a crazy time, a world-class rush, nearly orgasmic. She had to have more of that. Welles opened her blouse and caressed her breast. The producer's eyes glittered.

The first blackness.

When it began slowly to clear, she found she was naked, and so was Welles. The producer was down to his briefs. She was sitting on the bed. Welles kissed her breasts and murmured into her ear. The producer presented her with his best erection, and she automatically took it into her mouth, the obedient object of everyone's desires. The producer moaned. Welles continued to move his hands gently around on her breasts.

The producer tried to push her back on the bed. Abruptly she decided she didn't want any of this. She tried to pull away, and when the producer grabbed her arm, she lashed out angrily. The producer spun off her supine body, holding the side of his head, and Welles was no longer whispering but yelling at her, something about fucking up her future. And she could not stop screaming.

Another blackness.

The next thing she was in the producer's suite, and she was inspecting the ceiling while he churned away on top of her. She looked at him momentarily, saw the gritted teeth and the reddening face, thought of all the guys with pimply asses and trouble with their plumbing and went back to inspecting the ceiling. Afterward, the producer rolled off her and grumbled that she was like a sack of potatoes. And she laughed at that. Oh, Jesus, she thought. Men. Her life had been delineated by cheap, demanding, exploitive, insensitive men. God, where was someone with a kind word, a gentle touch? Where were those guys? Not here, that was for certain. Nothing here but a limp penis, a red face and a nasty voice. The voice cracked with laughter. The producer's voice. Did she really think she was going to play a part in his film? Her head throbbed and everything was gently spinning, as though the room had been placed atop a lazy Susan. That's what I'm here for, she said dully. That's why I came to Cairo. More laughter. She had come to Cairo to fuck, in case she didn't know it. And she wasn't even so great at that. Was she so gullible as to believe that with her background she would be allowed into an expensive production such as this? Oh, God, the producer laughed, that really was ridiculous. Funny, but ridiculous.

The blackness.

And now she was at the pyramids, sitting cross-legged, waiting for death. It was a good place to die. She looked around. Was that Welles lying on the ground? Was Welles Death? If he was, why did he not move? Never mind. Soon she would sleep with the Pharaohs. God knows she had slept with everyone else. Cheops. King Chephren. Tuthmosis. Good boys, all. She wondered if they might be interested in a screening of *Raunchy Housewife.* If they were like most men of her acquaintance, they would be very interested indeed.

Then Death stood under the moonlight. Here was the father of terror. Here was the end. One never knew about the beginning; it was, then, a curious feeling to know that now she was at the end, that it was all over. She heard a voice calling out for the end, begging for it. After a moment, she realized the voice was hers. But something was wrong. Death was turning, walking away. Even Death was rejecting her. She sprang to her feet and chased Death, confronted it in the desert night, swung and clawed at it in a frenzy. She must die tonight. There was no life, and now the possibility existed that there could be no death. She fought for death.

A single explosion shattered the darkness of the desert. The darkness absorbed the sound without difficulty, without so much as a shiver. It sent the sound thundering off across the desert toward the town of Saggara, knowing it would never reach that destination. Death was easily accommodated here, and the noise of it was soon swallowed up.

Death bent down and kissed the still warm lips. Kissed them lingeringly.

It was a good place to die.

1

Tom Coward arrived at the Hotel du Cap late one early May afternoon two days before the start of the Cannes Film Festival. He walked into the elegant, sun-drenched lobby, as warm and white and marbled as the inside of a rich man's dream. He wore a white fedora pitched down over his eyes. A faded Italian leather jacket was thrown over his shoulders. The white linen shirt was badly rumpled, and its tails flapped out of the waistband of the pale-green slacks. A three-day stubble dotted the paleness of his face, and his mustache needed a trim. He was jet lagged and hung over, conditions with which he was all too familiar. Edward, as usual, manned the front desk, guarding it with a cherubic Gallic face that radiated the expensive glow of a lifetime dedicated to the exercise of good and discreet taste. The welcoming smile Edward produced for Tom was ordinarily reserved for guests who were worth a lot of money, and who had reservations. Tom had neither.

Edward ran a manicured fingernail briskly down a sheet on which were laid out all of the hotel's one hundred rooms, and the large number of francs each would set back its occupants. There were small rooms that cost a great deal. And there were slightly larger rooms that cost a great deal more. When the finger completed its browse, it tapped against the paper. That signaled the arch of a brow. A ledger was consulted.

"There must be some mistake, *Monsieur* Tom." Edward looked at him helplessly. "We don't seem to have your reservation."

"That's because I don't have a reservation, Edward."

Edward was astonished at this news. His voice could not help but betray the shock. "You arrive at du Cap, *monsieur*, and you have no reservation? You arrive at du Cap just as the festival begins? And you have no reservation?"

"I don't know what got into me, Edward," Tom said. "I really don't. Perhaps it has something to do with the fact that I am here to interview Lacy Bergen."

Edward's eyes lit up. At last a name that bespoke the things with which he could deal – wealth and notoriety. "But of course, Lacy Bergen, the movie star." Edward sounded relieved. "Now, *she* has a reservation."

"There you go," Tom said. "I am with Miss Bergen. That is, I am with her party. I am not with Miss Bergen personally. I will not be staying in Miss Bergen's room, or anything like that."

The newly acquired calm began to slip off Edward's face. "But at this time of year, *monsieur*, just before the festival. My God! There are Americans who made their reservations a year ago."

"Those are not Americans, Edward," Tom assured him. "Those are Californians. There is a big difference. You don't let them in here on a moment's notice. Besides, they are not with Miss Bergen. I am with Miss Bergen."

There is an immutable law of French life: if you phone for anything, they will be booked up. If you just show up at the door, you can always talk your way in. The French do not appreciate much, Tom long ago had decided, but they do appreciate a little pushiness.

Thus, in the end, Tom got the room. His usual room. Ninety-nine. At the back of the hotel with the view of the rose gardens below, the Eden Roc pavilion at the end of the graveled roadway and the Mediterranean beyond.

Jean-Claude Irondelle, the hotel's gracious and elegant manager, looking very much like an aging French movie star, had magically appeared to adjudicate matters. Tom had known him for a long time, and that counted at the du Cap, at least for a room at the busiest time of the hotel's season. When Irondelle departed, having with his usual aplomb solved yet another of life's little problems, Louis, the hotel's long-suffering concierge, passed by. Louis, unlike Edward, did not look at all pleased to be serving the rich. He looked downright miserable at the prospect of serving Tom for two weeks.

"*Bonjour,* Louis," Tom said as he awaited the elevator. "Cheer up, the rich are dying out much faster than they can be replaced. Soon they'll turn this place into a Ramada Inn."

Louis grimaced with displeasure, as though he had just sipped a glass of Canadian champagne. "*Monsieur* Coward, I can only say that I hope we will not have a replay of your performance the last time you stayed with us."

"I'm a new man," Tom promised. "I've learned how to behave myself ."

"I doubt it, *monsieur,*" the concierge said acidly. "I very much doubt it."

Tom placed his luggage on the chintz sofa and threw open the shutters to clear out the sweet fragrance of the fresh roses that are placed each morning in the du Cap's rooms. The hotel smelled of roses, money and the Mediterranean. There are those who say that the Hotel du Cap is the finest in the world. The claim is made mostly by Americans. The Europeans tend to sniff a bit, and the sniffing has nothing to do with the roses. They grumble that the du Cap is a European hotel run for Americans. The waiters, they further complain, all have their hands out for a tip. And the Americans are only too willing to tip constantly, if only to demonstrate their ability to do so. If one is wealthy in Europe, the Europeans point out, one does not have to demonstrate wealth. Only the right people have money. In America, by contrast, all the wrong people seem to have it.

Whatever the arguments, the du Cap cannot be denied its exclusivity. Part of that exclusivity stems from its size. It is actually a converted mansion, built originally in the 1800s by a Russian prince. There are, therefore, only a hundred rooms, and the place gives off the feeling more of a private home, albeit a very expensive home, than of a hotel. The rooms are surprisingly small, and if the Belgian countess or the American movie star in the next room is being particularly well serviced by her lover, then what with the ancient acoustics, the entire floor is likely to hear about it.

The Russians discovered the place first, then the British, who were in the process of making the Riviera into a luxury resort, and finally the Americans, the Lost Generation, fresh from Paris in the twenties. F. Scott Fitzgerald wrote part of *Tender Is The Night* at the hotel, and set Dick and Nicole Diver loose here. Tom grew up reading the novel and fantasizing about "a large, proud rose-colored hotel." Now here he was, emerging dripping wet from the shower, deciding once again to shed the twenty extra pounds that gave him ungainly size. He knew damned well he should be *Gentleman's Quarterly* thin, square-jawed, long-necked and able to shrug into anything Italian and narrow cut. He wanted David Bowie grace, Mick Jagger insouciance. Instead, he had the beginnings of a Wallace Beery role. Life had a way of providing him with nothing but harsh truths. He was not skinny, and he was not rich. He would never be great. He longed to do something better than anyone else in the world, to be able to take people's breath away with his talent. But he was not the best. He took no one's breath away. God, he loved being in his thirties. He loved watching all the dreams play out, leaving him stripped bare of the long-held illusions, carrying only a grim knowledge of his failures and a lot of extra poundage. Ah, well. The pledge had been merely to get to du Cap someday, not to get there brilliant or skinny.

He once again inspected his phone messages. Alvin Jarvis, the producer of *Buns*, the freshly married and domesticated world traveler, had called from the Carlton, where he was staying with his lovely wife, Lea. There was a message to call Lacy Bergen, the famous movie star and model who kept making terrible movies that grossed a hundred million dollars. There was a message from his syndicate in New York, more than anxious to get the Lacy Bergen story. There was a message from his publisher. And there was a message from someone named Dieter Voss. Dieter Voss? Where had he heard that name? He thought about making phone calls. Then he thought about getting dressed, going down to the terrace and having Jacques, the bartender, pour him a glass of Mumm's. Much better idea.

He took the elevator to the lobby. The elevator was of glass and gold, and dropped slowly into the cool, marbled luxury of the lobby. As you descended, no matter what nastiness you had perpetrated in order to get here, you knew finally and irrevocably that you had arrived, and that you were experiencing a view offered to only a few hundred people in all the world. Of course, some interlopers were also able to gain access to that magical glass elevator: starlets with curves that got them into places their money never could, and certain journalists too naive to understand they were second-class citizens traveling in a first-class world. As the elevator descended into the lobby, Tom, of course, considered himself among the latter. People kept throwing him out of the best bars and telling him he could not check into the great hotels. But, by God, he kept doing it. Even if he could not quite get into the Italian clothes.

He went out on the terrace that overlooked grounds gently sloping off toward the pool. Jacques had the rough masculine face of a good-natured John Wayne. He presented Tom with a glass of Mumm's champagne, then embraced him.

"*Monsieur* Tommy, what with the hotel's new policy against allowing international riffraff, I didn't think you would be here this year."

Tom laughed. "I almost didn't make it this time, Jacques. They weren't going to give me a room. And I don't think Louis is all that glad to see me."

"Ah, *Monsieur* Tommy, Louis is, unfortunately, Louis. I don't think he has quite gotten over the unfortunate incident that occurred during your last visit with us. You need a sense of humor to be a great hotelier. Louis has no sense of humor. He will never be a great hotelier."

Tom raised the champagne glass. "*Salut*, Jacques. Always good to see the hired help."

"And it's a delight to have the riffraff back," Jacques said. "Enjoy your stay, *Monsieur* Tommy."

"I'm not allowed to do anything else."

Jacques started to turn away. "Incidentally, *Monsieur* Tommy, there was a gentleman here a few minutes ago looking for you. A *Monsieur* Voss. The last I saw of him, he was walking toward the pavilion."

"Do you know this *Monsieur* Voss, Jacques?"

"I know that he is a producer."

"Find me someone at this hotel who is not a producer. That's the guy I want to meet."

But he thought about it, finished his champagne and decided he needed the exercise. It was growing late in the day as he made his way down to the Eden Roc pavilion, where the hotel's restaurant was located. To the left as he strolled, beyond the flower gardens, tennis courts and cabanas were nestled among the pines. Here, the likes of Henry Kissinger could, if they so desired, safely sunbathe in the nude, away from prying eyes. In an upper corner of the garden stood the du Cap's one true oddity, a pet cemetery, where rich British dowagers once buried their doggies, brave little mutts tumbled into an early grave after two many bowls of caviar. Tom's favorite was the grave of little Dou-Dou, who had succumbed in March 1939 without, he imagined, ever being housebroken.

What impressed Tom about the du Cap was its constant sense of emptiness. Even when the hotel was full, which it soon would be, it seemed somehow empty – except for the help. The help was everywhere. There was no one on the upper terrace. A few people lingered on the lower deck adjacent to the pool. In the distance the Mediterranean was transforming itself from serene turquoise into morose taupe. As the wind rose, the sunbathers shivered and headed for a late-afternoon gin and tonic.

If there was anyone named Dieter Voss here, he did not immediately leap up and announce himself. A swarthy Arabic gentleman sporting a thick mustache and a gleaming gold bracelet glanced at Tom uninterestedly, then went back to trying to get the terrace and the pool into the viewfinder of his Nikon. A very prosperous-looking captain of British industry in white cap and red face clucked over the state of the market to a frail-looking gray-haired woman who did not seem at all interested.

Tom watched the sea crash against the rocks below for a few moments, then went back to the front desk. There was another message from Lacy Bergen. She was staying in a room on the second floor. Tom wondered if her mother was with her. Would Sacco turn up without Vanzetti? Bonnie without Clyde? Attila without the Huns? The orders, strict, firm orders emanating from the syndicate in New York, were to cover Lacy at the Cannes Film Festival. Well, the festival didn't start until the day after tomorrow. Until then, he was off duty. He decided to ignore the phone message.

Instead, he would drive into Cannes and have a drink. The madness would start soon enough. Besides, tonight he wanted to be alone. Outside, the sky suddenly growled and was pitched into blackness. The first splashes of the impending storm landed on the terrace. Was this a portent? he wondered. The prelude to something?

About nine o'clock that night, he drove his rented Renault toward Cannes. It had begun to pour, the rain lashing furiously at the weary little towns of Juan-les-Pins and Golfe-Juan, rendering them into unfocused blurs carelessly tossed at the side of the narrow, winding coastal road. On the radio Bob Dylan observed the "Tight Connection to My Heart." Dylan said he felt the breath of a storm. Tom Coward, on the other hand, felt nothing. The storms of his life were muted to a dull roar. Ennui and the next airline ticket were the order of the day. He was moving fast and going nowhere. The speed was beginning to scare him. So was the lack of destination. His book on the life of director Lex Madison and on his involvement in two notorious murders had been published a few months before. The reviewers were not particularly kind, but sales were terrific. For the first time in his life Tom did not have to worry about money. There were, however, other concerns. His ex-girlfriend, actress Stormy Willis, figured prominently in the book. Too prominently for her taste. She was furious with Tom and had sworn never to speak to him again.

Cannes slipped into view. The Dylan song came to an end. The melancholy he felt filled the car. He had spent much of his life alone, but never lonely. Tonight, driving through the rain, he was lonely. He needed a great love. An affair of the heart. Great love always took his mind off the nagging possibility that he was not exactly living up to his potential. What potential? In the parliament of his consciousness, that question was quickly ruled out of order. Better to think of Great Love. A couple of weeks of Great Love would make the world a better place. But as he turned left and drove down to the Boulevard de la Croisette, he realized he was aimlessly heading in the wrong direction if Great Love was what he was after. Lust occasionally shows up at the Cannes Film Festival, but never Great Love. Certainly not on empty, rainy nights.

The Hotel Carlton shone in the rain, an imposing white wedding cake, a grand joke of nobility, with cornices at either end and all sorts of intricate scalloping along its facade. He parked the Renault around the corner on Rue du Canada, noted that the prostitutes were already out, umbrellas up to ward off the rain.

The marquees and billboards that by tomorrow night would advertise the movies that would soon occupy dreams – and cinemas – around the world were at the moment grim iron skeletons in the rain. Workmen had nearly finished with the grandest of the marquees along la Croisette. It spread over the better part of a block, across the street from the Carlton. A huge curved scimitar was hung out in the darkness, its handle throbbing with thousands of jeweled lights, glittering red and gold. The movie's title, *Saudi*, was outlined in neon. "The Adventure of a Lifetime Is Now the Film Event of the Decade."

Tom hurried across the Carlton terrace. The wicker chairs and tables were piled together, waiting for the rain to stop and the movie producers to come. Be patient, Tom thought. They are about to arrive. Already present was the huge Rambo-like figure of international action star Touch Lathrop. He had taken his place to one side of the terrace, a huge cutout, stripped to the waist, angling the deadly snout of an automatic weapon at the world. If the Red hordes from the East attacked the terrace, then here was Touch to save capitalism. His face with those glittering blue eyes was oddly boyish. Tom was reminded of what John Huston once said about Audie Murphy, "a gentle little killer." Touch would be a gentle little killer.

The Carlton Bar was nearly empty. In a couple of days no one would be able to move in here, particularly if the rain kept up and the patrons could not sit on the terrace. For the moment, there was plenty of room. Henri, the white-haired bartender, was in a cheerful mood.

"You are early this year, Tom," he said, shaking the journalist's hand.

"I just couldn't stay away," Tom said. "Has Alvin been in?"

"*Monsieur* Jarvis? I haven't seen him yet. Can I get you a Pimms Royale?"

"The first one of the festival," Tom said.

Henri brought the drink quickly. Tom took a long sip. There were few things more satisfying than sitting in the Carlton bar at Cannes drinking Pimms. There were only a few of other patrons in the bar: an old man wearing a cravat and sipping Pernod and a couple of touristy-looking Americans drinking beer and waiting for the stars who, on this night, would not show. They stared at the bank of television monitors at the end of the room, the screens that would bring the festival to those too lazy or too drunk to venture out to find it for themselves.

"They say it will rain again this year for the festival," Henri said. "I hear the Americans are not coming. And the distributors are grumbling – they will not stay in the new Palais."

"It rains every year," Tom said, leaning against the bar. "And there are always rumors the Americans will not come. And the distributors always grumble about the new Palais."

"There is word that agitators will attempt to disrupt the festival with demonstrations," Henri continued. "There is a great deal of anti-American feeling this year, what with the American air attacks on Libya."

"Someone is always trying to disrupt the festival," Tom said.

Henri winked. "I hear it is the end of movies, the end of the world even."

"In short, it's the beginning of another festival."

"True enough," Henri said with a sad little smile. "And what of you, Tom?"

"Cheerfully gloomy," Tom said. "I'll feel much better once you get me another Pimms."

The coach lamps flickered and died. The room was plunged into blackness.

"*Merde*," Henri announced. "This has been happening on and off for the past two days. It's the rain." He hurriedly set candles on the bar and lit them. Then he took more candles to each of the two tables where customers sat. The room was cast in a yellowish, uncertain glow, shadows dancing off the stone walls and the vaulted ceilings.

At that moment that she came through the door, a woman of mystery, with the collar of her Burberry trench coat turned up and her long dark hair flecked with silver raindrops. Aha, Tom Coward thought. Here comes Great Love now, into a bar lit with candles and framed with dark shadows, a place where long-haired women were welcome and close inspections were not easy. He drew quick impressions: she was tallish, with long, slim legs showing below the hem of the raincoat. From where he stood, he could discern that her eyes were wide and dark. Even in the bad light you could see that she had the most beautiful mouth in the world. On a night like this, could a woman of mystery possibly have anything else? He was looking for trouble, and here was a woman who could get him into a lot of it.

She walked over to the bar and asked Henri for a cognac. Then she glanced at Tom.

"It's miserable out there," she said in lightly accented English. The most beautiful mouth in the world smiled slightly.

"Henri," Tom said, watching her, trying to bring her into focus, "put that on my tab, will you?"

"Certainly, *Monsieur* Tom," Henri said.

"*Merci*," she said. There was a second smile. No arguments about who would pay. Tom liked that. When Henri put the snifter of cognac down in front of her, she lifted it up toward Tom. "*Salut*," she said.

"To dark bars on rainy nights," Tom said.

She sipped on the cognac. "You are here for the festival?"

"I am here for the festival," he acknowledged.

"Then you are in the movie business."

"In a manner of speaking," Tom said. "How about you?"

"I am not in the movie business. Not even in a manner of speaking."

"Then you are not an actress or a model."

"Are all women at Cannes either actresses or models?"

"I used to think so."

"I'm sorry to disappoint you," she said.

"I'm not disappointed at all."

"But I do love the movies," she said. "When I was a little girl, I went constantly to the cinema. The lights would go down, and this tremendous feeling of well-being always flooded over me. At the movies, all your troubles disappear for a couple of hours."

"That's the movies," Tom said. "This is the Cannes Film Festival. There's lots of trouble at the Cannes Film Festival."

Her smile was tight. "I hope you're wrong about that."

But he wasn't.

Later, Tom would recall, it was at that moment that the tall man made his entrance. He seemed to slide into the bar on the coattails of Tom's worst nightmares. He was dressed from head to foot in leather. The leather offset the bizarrely outsize head that sat atop his body like an ill-considered afterthought. It was as though some explosion deep inside had created shock waves that caused the skull to distend into grotesque protrusions. The head was shaved except for a thin topknot of hair. It was colored in iridescent tones of pink and green and fell in a long fan down his back. Tom could not see his eyes for the cheap dark glasses. But he could note the thin cruel line of a mouth and the tiny white flecks of scar tissue that swam at the corners of it.

The man stopped just inside the door and glared at the woman. She jerked her head, and Tom could see her throat move as she swallowed. The man stared hard at her for a few moments then took a seat beneath the television monitors at the far end of the room. A waiter approached, but he waved him away.

Tom turned to the woman. "A friend of yours?"

"His name is Rakko," she said quietly. "You were right. This is not the movies. There is trouble at Cannes."

Abruptly, he was concerned. "Are you in any danger?"

"I'm not sure," she said quietly. "Do you have a car?"

"Yes," Tom said. "As a matter of fact, I do."

"This is an awful thing...you are a complete stranger. But I may need your help."

"All right," he said.

She stared at her cognac, and seemed to make a decision. "Please, wait here. I will be back in a moment."

She turned abruptly and walked out the glass doors that led into the lobby. The tall man jackknifed out of his chair and hurried after her.

Tom debated whether to follow. She said she might need his help. But perhaps this was a domestic thing. Maybe the guy was her boyfriend or her husband. That hardly seemed possible, though. The tall man looked more like a bad dream than like anyone's boyfriend.

The lights flashed back on. Then Tom heard the scream.

He raced out past the glass doors. Most of the furniture had been removed from the lobby for the duration of the festival. To the right was a corridor leading to the washrooms and a stairwell beyond. The tall man called Rakko was halfway down the hall in the process of giving Tom's woman of mystery a violent shove.

Tom rushed forward, grabbed a handful of leather and jerked Rakko away. He did not move very far. He turned slowly and looked at Tom. The dark glasses robbed his features of any emotion. He did not seem particularly upset by the unexpected interruption. Tom took the woman by the wrist. She was shaking.

"You had better leave," she said.

"Oh, come on," Tom said. "After I bought you a cognac and everything."

"No, please, *monsieur*."

Rakko then shoved Tom against the wall. The tremendous strength in that shove let Tom know immediately he didn't stand a chance against it. It made him realize his shortcomings when it came to doing anything physical.

The woman screamed something in French. Rakko said nothing, but he moved away a couple of feet. At that moment Tom sprang away from the wall and kneed his assailant in the groin. Rakko didn't make any sound, but he went down on the carpet very quickly on both knees.

Now the woman looked even more frightened. "You shouldn't have done that," he heard her say.

"I know, I should have slapped his face with a leather glove and challenged him to a duel. What can I tell you? I'm a dirty fighter."

Then they were racing back down the corridor, out through the lobby and into the night. It had stopped raining. The air was clear and full of the smell of the sea.

"My car is around the corner," he said.

"All right."

They hurried around to Rue du Canada. A couple of hookers eyed them uninterestedly. Tom and the woman clambered into the car and Tom started the engine.

"Where do you want to go?" he said.

"Please," she said, "just drive."

He steered the car out onto la Croisette, and they drove in silence along the empty rain-slicked boulevard. There was no sign of Rakko. The sand-colored fortress that was the Palais des Festivals loomed in the darkness ahead.

"There is a lot just to the left," she said suddenly. "Park there. We can walk along the beach."

The breeze had dropped off, and there was the hint of a warming wind. The lights from an American destroyer blinked in the Golfe de la Napoule. She shivered slightly as they walked along the thin ribbon of sand.

"You must think I am crazy," she said.

"Don't be ridiculous. He tried to hurt you."

"He would not have hurt me," she said in a voice full of certainty.

"I wouldn't be quite so sure about that," Tom said. "He's one of the most frightening men I've ever seen in my life."

"He does it to scare people. That's his job."

"He must be very successful."

"I'm afraid he is."

"Are you in danger?"

"I don't think so. Not really. I'm only sorry you got involved."

"But I had to get involved. It was inevitable."

"I'm afraid I don't understand," she said.

"I've been thinking about you all night."

"Me? How could you think about me? We've never met before."

"We've never met," Tom said. "But I've been waiting for you."

"For me? How could you have been waiting for me?"

"I was thinking it was about time a beautiful woman came running into my life. And in you came."

The most beautiful mouth in the world smiled sadly. "I see. Well, I'm sorry, but I won't be able to stay long. I must run out again very quickly."

"You can't. I won't let you. If you do, I'll live a life of terrible misery."

She took his arm. "You're very sweet. A sweet, silly stranger who does not mind walking on the beach."

The moon had managed to nudge itself out from behind the clouds. Its light outlined the jagged edges of Esterel Heights, above the bay. He stopped and looked at her. The wind blew her hair away from her face. She was something out of a dream, impervious to the intrusion of reality.

"I don't even know your name," Tom said.

"Aha," she said with a smile. "I know yours. At least I know your first name. The bartender called you Tom."

"That's right. Tom Coward."

"Tom Coward from America."

"Tom Coward from Canada," he said.

"Well, Tom Coward from Canada, I'm very much indebted to you. The world was not so pleasant until tonight. Now that you have rescued me and taken me for a walk on the beach in the moonlight, it's a much better place." She reached up. Her fingers lightly caressed the back of his neck. She kissed his mouth. "*Merci*," she said. "*Merci beaucoup*, Tom"

"I still don't know your name."

She didn't say anything, but wrapped her arms around him. The most beautiful mouth in the world opened for him, and this time the kiss had passion. He felt her strain against him. He heard a low groan and it was, he realized, his groan, the signal that he was gone, swept away deep into her soul. This moment could only last forever.

Forever ended abruptly when someone slugged him across the back of the head. Passion exploded into bright lights and swooped up into the night sky. Then everything plunged toward blackness.

2

He came up from a deep, dark place, wrenched out of a beautiful woman's arms, confronting a monster with a grotesque head, a green-and-pink topknot and scar tissue around his ugly, twisting mouth. He jerked awake. There was no woman and there was no monster. Only a throbbing in his head. And dampness. He sat up on the sand at the edge of the Mediterranean. An elderly beach cleaner dressed in worn corduroys carefully raked the beach around him.

"You are early, *monsieur*," the beach cleaner said.

"I beg your pardon," Tom said.

The beach cleaner did not stop raking. "The festival does not officially begin until tomorrow. I usually do not find bodies on the beach until after tomorrow."

"Yeah, well, I thought I'd get a jump on the competition this year." He staggered to his feet. His clothes were wet; sand clung to them. He held his head and said, "Jesus."

"Does *monsieur* by any chance still have his wallet?"

Tom reached into his back pocket. No billfold. "Oh, shit," he groaned. "Oh, shit, shit, shit."

The beach cleaner sighed. "Every year it is the same. In exchange for your wallet, you get an aching head and a night on the beach."

It was just past dawn. It was to be a perfect, cloudless day on the Côte d'Azur. Up the beach, the pallets and umbrellas for the day's sunbathing were being set out. He could hear the gulls cry as they swept low, reconnoitering the shoreline. There was no sign of a mystery woman with the most beautiful mouth in the world. She had disappeared with the darkness and the rain. He wondered if she was all right, if perhaps he should go to the police. Oh, sure. *Monsieur,* they would say, faces drawn into approximations of sympathy, you were lured to the beach by a woman whom you thought was in trouble. There, her partner hit you over the head and removed your wallet. Unfortunate, but not, alas, particularly unusual at this time of the year. Count yourself lucky that you did not come away from the experience with anything worse than a lump on your thick head.

Had he been set up? Had the whole thing been merely an elaborate ruse orchestrated to steal his wallet? The possibility certainly existed. But why go to such elaborate lengths just for a wallet? Besides, there was the woman. And that kiss. He refused to believe she had been merely after his wallet. Nobody who kissed like that could be after his wallet. Could she? Oh, shit. She could.

He staggered back to his car and drove back to the Hotel du Cap, his head pounding in time with the gear changes. He pulled up in front of the hotel and one of the attendants dashed forward to open the door for him. When he caught sight of Tom, his eyes widened.

"Are you a guest here, *monsieur*?"

"I most certainly am," Tom said.

"Forgive me, *monsieur*."

"Just park the car and keep quiet."

"*Oui, monsieur*."

Tom started up the steps. A voice called out behind him.

"Tom! Tom Coward!"

He turned and there, hurrying across the courtyard, was Lacy Bergen. She wore tiny pink jogging shorts and a tiny pink halter top with a matching pink headband that went well with her pink sneakers. The pink set off nicely the duskiness of her tan. She apparently had been out jogging. Jogging kept her perfectly slim body perfectly slim. However, she showed no sign of exertion. The Lacy Bergens of the world do not sweat.

"Oh, yuck, Tom. What happened to you?"

"I was mugged on a beach last night."

"What were you doing on a beach at night?"

"Don't ask."

She touched his scalp.

"Ouch!" he yelped.

"Oh, yuck." She made a face that marred perfection and showed concern. "You've got a small cut, a little bleeding, that's all. Come up to my room. I've got an ice pack and some disinfectant. Did I ever tell you? My ambition in life is to play Florence Nightingale."

"It would be typecasting, " Tom said.

"Smarty." She slapped him on the arm. "Mommy says I shouldn't even be talking to you. Mommy doesn't trust you."

"Mommy's absolutely right."

"Mommy's never been right about anything in her entire born life. The only thing is that now she takes it all so much more seriously. When I was younger and she was drinking a lot, she had fun with my fame. I guess she figured I was too young to have it. Now she's not drinking, and she's has decided neither one of us should enjoy my fame. I've got this grumpy, sober old battle-ax on my hands. It's a real bore."

As she talked, she steered him into the hotel toward the elevator. "Anyway, you must do exactly as I tell you, Tom, or I won't talk to you, and you'll miss out on one of the most interesting experiences of your entire born life."

"What kind of experience is that?"

"I have absolutely fascinating things to say. About world famine. And nuclear disarmament."

"I can hardly wait."

"Are you staying at the hotel?"

"No. I just dropped by for a quick game of tennis."

Louis, the concierge, came into view. His long, sad face became even longer and sadder when he caught sight of Tom.

"Is *Monsieur* Coward all right?" The imperiousness of his tone suggested *Monsieur* Coward most certainly was not all right.

"*Monsieur* Coward is just peachy," Tom said.

"A package arrived for monsieur a few moments ago." He handed Tom a large white envelope.

Tom tore it open. His wallet fell out into his hands. "Jesus Christ," he exclaimed.

"What's going on?" Lacy asked.

"A good question," Tom replied.

Her room was small and littered with clothes. They spilled out of trunks, they were thrown across her bed, the sofa, the chairs, on a bureau. There were clothes everywhere. Expensive clothes. Clothes the young ladies of the Western world would kill for. More to the point, clothes young ladies of the Western world would buy after seeing them on Lacy Bergen's back. He sat on the bed among the clothes and went through his wallet. She emerged from the bathroom bearing a bag of ice. She had removed the headband and loosened the ponytail so that her hair flowed down across her shoulders in the thick, silky waves that caused shampoo manufacturers to tremble and to pay her untold thousands of dollars to hold their product in front of a television camera.

"Is anything missing?" She climbed around him and gently placed the ice against his head.

"God," Tom winced. "That feels cold."

"It's supposed to feel cold. Answer me. Is anything missing?"

"A couple of hundred francs."

"A very polite thief," Lacy said. "He steals your money, but he sends the wallet back to your hotel."

How did they know which hotel? Tom wondered. Had he told the woman he was staying at the du Cap? He couldn't remember.

"Now listen, Tom," Lacy said, trying to make her high, undisciplined voice sound no-nonsense. "I'm going to be very busy at the festival. You have to tell me when you want to talk."

Lacy Bergen's first adult movie, which was terrible and which was not supposed to be a big hit in America, had in fact been a huge hit, much to everyone's surprise. Lacy, at the age of twenty-one, was now a very hot young star. Her movie was to have its European premiere at the festival, and she was present to promote it.

"Perhaps we could do mankind a great service," Tom said.

"What's that?"

"We could save the world from another celebrity interview."

She maneuvered herself so that her pretty round face was very close to his. There was not a mark on it. There are a few things God does not choose to flaw. Lacy Bergen was one of them. Flawlessness was, however, looking petulant.

"You know what I think? I think you don't want to talk to me."

"I didn't say that."

"You avoid me all the time. You avoided me in New York."

"You said you didn't like to give interviews because everyone asked you about your mother."

She ignored this. "And you avoided me in Paris."

"I had to write a book." Water from the ice was beginning to drip down the back of his neck.

"There's something I have to know, Tom. I have to know whether you like me."

"Lacy, the entire world is nuts about you. Even Palestinian terrorists sworn to destroy Western civilization pin your posters up on the wall. Why do you need me to like you?"

"I knew it." She flounced off the bed. "I knew you didn't like me."

"I didn't say I didn't like you."

He was saved from any more of this by a knock on the door. Tom watched the latch go down and, a moment later, Maddi Bergen, Lacy's mother, business manager, chief warder, and all-round old battle-ax, stepped inside. She was in possession of features as frosted as her hair. There were hints of Lacy's beauty around her eyes and mouth, and she often dressed to kill, showing off a figure that was full and not at all unappealing in a *zaftig* way that ran totally counter to her daughter's resolute slimness. Maddi Bergen might have materialized Rubenesque from another age, her cheeks flushed rosy red, ready to entertain the troops in her boudoir. Except that blind ambition and steely determination had got in the way, and given her features a harsh, pinched quality. You got into Maddi's boudoir only to change the sheets.

She was not, it was evident, happy to see Tom Coward in her daughter's room. She was particularly unhappy to see Tom Coward wet, caked with sand and holding an ice bag against a battered, bloodied head. Lacy, as she usually did when Mommy was around, managed to look both truculent and nervous at the same time.

"What's going on here?" Maddi demanded.

"Thank God you're here, Mommy," Lacy said. "I was just about to give Tom a blow job."

Maddi blinked a couple of times. "I'm not going to be drawn out by your coarse language, young lady. You realize, though, that Mr. Coward here is a journalist. Anything you say in front of him could be taken down and used against you. I don't have to remind you what the press is like."

Lacy was all innocence. "That's why I wanted to give him the blow job, Mommy. That way he would keep his mouth shut, you see."

He thought for a moment that mother might hit daughter. Except nobody slaps a face conservatively valued at two million dollars. Maddi held herself in check. Or, more accurately, she turned her laserlike green eyes on Tom.

"Is this your idea of an interview, Mr. Coward? This is how you dress for an interview?"

"Hell, Mrs. Bergen, I always dress like this when I'm doing an interview," Tom said.

"Oh, Mommy, for heaven's sake," Lacy said. "Tom was hurt. Someone mugged him last night in Cannes. I wanted to help him. That's all. He didn't even want to come up here in the first place."

"One can only speculate about what Mr. Coward was up to when he got mugged," Maddi said grimly.

"I can't stand any more of this witty conversation," Tom said. "I'm leaving." He rose to his feet. "Can I take your ice bag with me?"

"You don't have to go," Lacy said.

"It's okay. We can talk later," Tom said. He stepped past Maddi Bergen's glare. "Thanks for your help, Lacy. I appreciate it."

"I'll see you later?"

"Of course," he said.

Outside, he heard Maddi Bergen yell, "Young lady, if you ever speak that sort of language again I'll –"

And he heard Lacy Bergen say, "Oh, Mother. Blow it out your ear!"

He was exhausted when he got to his room. He wanted a shower and sleep. And an end to this headache. He also wanted the girl. He could still feel her body against his, taste that deeply passionate kiss.

His publisher had called again. So had Alvin Jarvis. There was also a message from Renee Furst, the New York publicist without whom it was practically impossible for any North American journalist to do interviews at the festival. Stephen M. Silverman of the New York *Post* wanted to have drinks at the Majestic. Sid Adilman of the Toronto *Star* was anxious for lunch at La Mère Besson. Oh, yes. And Dieter Voss had dropped off a note. It was scrawled across a sheet of the hotel's writing paper. He did not, he wrote, wish to disturb Tom's sleep. However, he was having late-morning coffee and croissants on the lower terrace at the Eden Roc. Perhaps Tom would like to join him? He had a proposition of the utmost importance to discuss.

Hmm. A proposition of the utmost importance. Which was more pressing? Resting his throbbing head? Or a proposition of the utmost importance? He decided reluctantly in favor of the proposition of the utmost importance. He showered, shaved, found some fresh if somewhat wrinkled clothes and discovered that he had left his hair drier in New York. Or was it Los Angeles? Maybe Los Angeles. In any event that was the fifth portable hair drier he had left somewhere this year. He considered this as he slicked back his wet hair and regarded his pale, drawn, sleepless face in the mirror. He decided he looked hellish enough to scare the rich and famous, and headed down to the lobby.

Louis once again eyed him as he made his way through the lobby. "Is everything all right, *monsieur*?" he inquired with a courtesy that was dipped in ice. Tom gave him his most disarming smile, the one calibrated to reassure suspicious hotel help.

Outside, guests in tennis whites as brilliant as the sunshine passed by, delighted enough with the weather and their high rank in life to give him a smile and ignore the way he looked.

A small army, uniformed in open shirts, recently sunburned faces and knit brows, scurried frantically around on the lower deck of the pavilion, as though war had been declared and no one was quite sure what to do about it. A sweet-faced young man who pumped a lot of iron and spent a great deal of time in the sun stopped him as he came down the stairs.

"*Pardon, monsieur. Est-ce que je peux vous aider.*"

"I'm here to see *Monsieur* Voss," Tom said.

A smart-looking Yuppie who dressed to tell the world that he was college-educated dashed over and pumped Tom's hand. He wore a pearl-gray summer suit and horn-rimmed glasses. Sun-bleached brown hair leapt up in amazement, as though trying to escape his forehead.

"Tom!" he said as though he had not seen Tom for years and regretted every moment, "Tom Coward! Damn good to see you, fella. Read your stuff all the time. Excellent. Just excellent. I'm Rudy John Karras. I used to be with Crossringer and Muskin. The public relations firm. You've dealt with our people out of

New York. Now I'm working exclusively with Dieter. Things are pretty nuts around here this morning, what with the final preparations for the *Saudi* launch."

"The *Saudi* launch?" Tom managed to interject. "Is Dieter Voss involved with *Saudi*?"

"Is Dieter Voss involved with *Saudi*? Dieter Voss *is Saudi*. He conceived the movie, arranged the financing, produced it on location. He's a hands-on kind of fella, Dieter is. Have you seen the movie yet?" Rudy was not a man to wait around for answers. "It's fabulous. Everyone at the festival is talking about it. It's kind of a combination of *Lawrence of Arabia, Raiders of the Lost Ark, Terms of Endearment* and *Rocky*. It's gonna knock this town on its ear. The festival people are so excited, they're letting us use the Palais for the world premiere, even though the movie isn't in the official competition. Dieter pulled the strings there. Quite a coup. Have you met Dieter? Of course not. That's what you're here for, isn't it? Well, he's kind of tied up at the moment. I mean everyone in town wants a piece of his time. Poor guy. Dick Zanuck was on the blower to him first thing this morning. They're talking deals. Everyone wants to talk deals with Dieter. He's quite a fella, yessir. A throwback to the old-time movie moguls. Sam Spiegel, fellas like that. Seat-of-the-pants fellas, the sort of people willing to fly the mail plane through the mountains when there's a lotta fog and low visibility and none of the other pilots are willing to go up. I guess you could say he's kind of a hero to the German people. You know he escaped across the Berlin wall when he was just a kid?"

"No," Tom said, "I didn't know he did that. I've got to be honest with you, Rudy. Until yesterday I had never even heard of Dieter Voss."

"There's been a low PR profile on this guy," Rudy conceded with a sad shake of his head. "But that's all gonna change now that we're onside with this. We got Robin Leach of *Lifestyles of the Rich and Famous* coming over later this morning. He's gonna profile Dieter. It's a rags-to-riches story for sure. He dodged bullets and searchlights, risked his life, in order to reach the West and pursue the capitalism he believed in so fervently."

"It brings tears to my eyes," Tom said.

The crowd around Dieter broke open and Tom caught a glimpse of a man in white grinning out at the Mediterranean as though he owned it.

"I think Dieter finally has a free moment," Rudy John Karras said triumphantly, as though he had personally engineered it. "Come on, Tom, I'll introduce you to him."

Rudy John Karras led Tom over to a table littered with scripts, schedules, coffee cups and wineglasses. There was an open bottle of champagne nearby.

"Dieter," Rudy said, "I managed to snag Tom Coward for you."

Dieter tore tiny tadpole-shaped eyes away from the sea, lurched clumsily to his feet, and knocked against the breakfast table, shaking the coffee cups. The smile was half apology, half suggestion of a common conspiracy. That smile was held against an impish cherub's face, framed with blondish-brown hair that fell in a fringe across a wide, sunburned forehead. Dieter Voss was short and rotund and dressed in white from head to foot.

"Mr. Coward," he announced in English with the trace of a German accent. "Such a pleasure to meet you. Won't you sit down? I am such a devil, I have ordered us some champagne. Bollinger. Although I understand you like Mumm's."

"Bollinger is just fine, thanks," Tom said. By the time he had seated himself, Dieter Voss had poured him a glass of champagne. Tom sipped it, then added orange juice to what was left.

A secretary rushed forward and dropped a sheaf of papers in front of Dieter. He flipped through them, signed something, nodded. The secretary grabbed the papers and rushed away as though she now had the donor heart and had to get to the transplant operation.

Rudy John Karras leaned forward. His voice was down to a conspiratorial whisper. "Peter Noble from *Screen International* wants to have a word with you late this afternoon, Dieter. As you know, everyone reads his column here at the festival. He wants to do a major piece. Front-page stuff. He told me confidentially that *Saudi* will be the most important film at the festival."

"That's fine," Dieter said distractedly. He turned and focused the tadpole eyes on Tom. "I'm so decadent when I come here, it really is sinful," Dieter said with a glee that suggested it was not sinful at all. "I drink far too much champagne, eat too much bouillabaisse at Tetou, and in previous years I always made love to far too many young ladies. The only way afterwards I was able to live with myself when I got back to Paris was knowing I also had made many movie deals."

"I see," Tom said. "You don't plan to make love to a lot of young ladies this year? Is that good news or bad?"

He laughed heartily. "This year, Mr. Coward – or do you mind if I call you Tom?"

"Please. If I'm drinking someone's champagne, I insist they call me Tom."

This time he threw back his head to set free the delighted laugh. The tadpole eyes were dancing. Dieter Voss seemed to be having the time of his life. "That really is amusing, Tom, I must say. I am told you are very amusing. Yes, very amusing indeed."

"Oh? Now who would have told you I was amusing?"

The smile became paternal. "Let us say, I have my sources." He turned his head so that it was at an angle, then he pointed to his nose, as if to indicate that it was the source of his information.

Rudy John Karras was huddled down close to Dieter again. "Rex Reed," he hissed excitedly.

Dieter looked startled. "What about him?"

"Jesus, Dieter, Rex Reed. I just talked to him on the blower. This guy is so enthusiastic about *Saudi* he's about ready to pee his pants. I think he wants to do a story about you. Major piece for the *Post* in New York. Great exposure."

"That's fine," Dieter said. "But have you heard anything from the *Times*?"

Rudy John Karras looked uncharacteristically confused. "*Times*? What *Times* you talking about?"

"The *New York Times*. Are they not interested in doing a story on us? I think we should be in the *Times*."

Rudy offered a reassuring smile. "Dieter you want the *Times*? I'll do my damnedest to get you the *Times*. I think Aljean Harmetz is coming in for the festival. Aljean and I go back a long way together. I'll get on the blower to her."

"Wonderful," Dieter said. "I think the *Times* is very important to us. "

"You got it, fella." Rudy, once more triumphant, bounced away.

"You were saying about the ladies," Tom said, in an effort to get him back on the track.

"Ah, yes. No young ladies this year, I'm afraid. Not that it's such a loss. I am married, you understand. I am crazily in love."

"A newlywed," Tom said. "Congratulations."

"You will meet my wife, Tom. She is so incredible, let me tell you. A beautiful woman. Here. Have some more champagne."

Tom gratefully accepted the glass. The champagne, for the moment, caused his head to throb less. Dieter Voss was pleasant, if somewhat volatile company.

"You said in your note that you have a business proposition."

Dieter jerked forward. His eyebrows knit into a position of intense concentration, and the tadpole eyes gleamed darkly. "I am most interested in your book, Tom. I must be honest with you. I don't want to beat up the bush with you. Is that what you say in America? Beat up the bush?"

"Around the bush."

"Ah. Around the bush."

"So, you're not going to beat around the bush."

"I love that book. The drama, the tragedy of Lex Madison. A man destroyed by his own past. Incredible. Wonderful story. You know who I see for it?"

Tom tried to look interested.

"Stallone. Only Stallone could play this role. He is number one in all the world at the box office. He'd make this movie a tremendous success. It would be a huge hit with Stallone."

"It's a movie already? A moment ago, it was only a book."

Dieter Voss once again threw back his head and gave off an utterly delighted laugh. "You are right, you are so right, my friend." He wagged a finger at Tom. "I am getting ahead of myself. Alas, it is one of my great failings. Ever since I was a child, I always get too excited. I am still a child. But then you must be a child to be in the movies. Am I not right, Tom?"

"Certainly, a child," Tom said.

Rudy John Karras bounced back into view. He looked very worried. "Sorry to break this up, fellas. I was just on the blower, Dieter. The Americans want to talk to you, *tout de suite*, as they say in this part of the world."

Dieter issued a resigned groan. "I would like nothing better, Tom, than to sit here in the sunshine, drinking champagne and discussing your wonderful book. But you must understand, this is the busiest year of my life. *Saudi* was budgeted at forty million dollars. To have made it is a dream come true. I am in a daze here at Cannes. I cannot believe my good fortune. When I see the movie, it brings tears to my eyes. It's the greatest movie ever made, I swear to you."

"Isn't that wonderful?" Tom said. "I've always wanted to see the greatest movie ever made."

Dieter failed to note the sarcasm. "We go to meet this afternoon with some American studio people. They are anxious to snap up the movie. Very anxious. They are tremendously excited. We have secured, through the Imperial Holland Trust of Amsterdam, one hundred and fifty million dollars' worth of financing. In the next year, I will produce ten movies. Not bad for a poor boy who came out of East Germany with fifteen marks in his pocket. I escaped in the old, dangerous days, Tom. You paid the right people and you dodged the right searchlights and you came out across the Wall. That's impossible now. But not then. It was harrowing. The most frightening night of my life. The guards spotted us. They opened fire. My companion, a boyhood friend, was hit. It was terrible. He died bleeding in my arms. Do you know what his last words to me were?"

"I have no idea," Tom said.

"He said to me, 'Go, Dieter. Go for freedom.'"

There was a respectful silence as Dieter, Rudy and Tom remembered for a moment the boy who had ordered Dieter off to freedom.

"But worth it," Dieter continued cheerfully. "I am at heart a shameless capitalist. I got a start distributing art films in Frankfurt. I moved to Paris and set up my own production company. Now there is *Saudi* and a very impressive future. There is nothing this company cannot do. We will make great movies."

"Dieter, it's not a good idea to keep the Yanks waiting," interrupted Rudy.

"You must come to dinner with us this evening," Dieter said, standing. "I have a big table at Tetou. I want you to meet my wife, get to know me, so that when you sell me the rights to your book, you'll know that I'm one hell of a nice guy."

"As long as you've got money, Dieter, you don't have to be a nice guy."

Dieter Voss roared with laughter. "You make me laugh, Tom. That is good. Everyone in this business is far too serious. It is, after all, entertainment. We should all be laughing much more than we do. Tonight then? We meet in the lobby here at seven."

"All right," Tom said. "Bring your checkbook."

Rudy John Karras glared. But Dieter just laughed again. "Bring your checkbook. Right. I understand that. Bring your checkbook." He was on his feet. The army gathered protectively around him, everyone waiting expectantly. Rudy John Karras put his hand on Dieter's shoulder and whispered into his ear. "I'm on the blower to the E.T. people, Dieter. They are crazy to hear more about *Saudi*. They already got the word that it's the hottest movie at the festival."

Dieter was mystified. "What is this E.T.?"

Rudy John Karras looked shocked. "Jesus, Dieter. E.T. *Entertainment Tonight*. You've never seen *Enter-*

tainment Tonight? Boy oh boy, fella, we got a long way to go here PR-wise. We got a lot of work to do in the next couple of weeks."

Dieter and his troops disappeared up the stairs. Suddenly, the deck was an empty, silent place. Rudy John Karras came over, shaking his head. "He's a great guy, Tom. Isn't he a great guy? But, boy, these Europeans, they really are out of it. I guess they've got their own culture and everything here. But can you imagine anyone who's never heard of *Entertainment Tonight?* Makes the mind boggle, doesn't it?"

Yes, it did, Tom agreed. It really did.

Tom returned to his room and slept the afternoon away. His sleep was restless and unsettling, full of death's-head villains named Rakko and damsels in distress on lonely beaches. His mystery woman floated deep into his subconscious and lodged there, the focus for his longings and his loneliness. If he could only be with her, he would reach a level place, tranquil, green-pastured, and there would be happiness ever after. He began the tortuous journey down toward her. Damn! Something was pulling him away. She reached out to him, face imploring. He strained toward her. But he was sucked the other way, brought up into an air clogged with the smell of roses. He was sitting up in his bed at the Hotel du Cap, the purple light of dusk seeping in through the open shutters.

He dressed and made himself look presentable for the evening, then boarded the elevator and headed down toward the lobby. As it descended, the small pack Dieter had assembled for the evening came into view. There was Lacy Bergen and her mother, Maddi. And there was Dieter with a slim, dark-skinned woman in a tight miniskirt riding high on the sort of incredible long legs showgirls go to bed each night praying for. She clung to him tightly. Tom blinked a couple of times. No. It couldn't be.

He stepped out of the elevator and approached the group. Dieter turned to him expectantly. The woman with him looked at Tom without interest.

"Ah, there you are, Tom," Dieter said. "I was just about to give you a call. I would like you to meet my wife, Corinne."

She extended a brown hand. He took it and looked deep into the eyes of the woman he had met at the Carlton Bar the evening before. His woman of mystery.

3

The yacht was called, with a sense of irony, *The Hedge*. It was a Hatteras, seventy feet long. At sunset it purred out of the harbor at St. Tropez. On board was a crew of three and the yacht's owner, Sir Cecil House, the distinguished and distinguished-looking senior vice-president of the branch of the Imperial Holland Trust established five years before in the Netherland Antilles. This archipelago of five Caribbean Islands had in the past few years become the destination of choice for international moneylenders and tax dodgers. Sir Cecil had a wife and three children in Willemstad, the yacht at St. Tropez, a winter home in Gstaad and an international reputation as a risk-taker who nevertheless was always careful to hedge his bets, hence the name of his yacht and the source of his considerable success in world banking.

Big movies are mostly an American art form, and the big American banks – among them the Bank of America, Chemical Bank, First National of Boston – finance the big studios. But Sir Cecil always had been a movie nut. A decade before, at Cannes, he had been introduced to the independent German producer Dieter Voss. Voss had no reputation in the movie business. None of the German banks, and certainly none of the Americans, would have anything to do with him. But Dieter did have a certain flair and savvy that Sir Cecil found attractive. Dieter needed five hundred thousand dollars to make a low-budget horror movie in Germany. He had presold the movie to markets in Japan, Germany, England, Italy and France for more than one million dollars. He needed only the movie in order to collect the money. How could the bank lose on such a deal? Sir Cecil wondered. The answer was simple: it couldn't. He let Dieter have the five hundred thousand dollars. The horror movie was made. Everyone made a profit. Since then the Imperial Holland Trust, under Sir Cecil's direction, had become one of the major financiers of independent film production. Always the hedge was the same. The producers came to Sir Cecil only with projects that were largely presold. In turn, he ensured that stars were bankable and would not cause delays, and that the directors could be relied upon to deliver the goods. If Sir Cecil did not like the combination of elements in a given movie, he did not hesitate to say so. Money talks in the movie business. The banker, much to his delight, had acquired a great deal of creative clout.

In the process, he had acquired a second imposing reputation, also international. He was well-known as an accomplished stick man, an inveterate and inexhaustible lover of the opposite sex. In pursuit of this reputation, the banker had on board as his guest this evening the British actress Sybil January. She was a woman of quite astonishing proportions. Now, on the aft deck, she exhibited them to good effect, spilling strategically out of a startlingly short white Louis Feraud dress. Ordinarily, the dramatic curves were on display in a series of low-budget exploitation movies. Sir Cecil, who had met Sybil a few nights before at a dinner party at a villa on the edge of St. Tropez, had confessed he never had seen her movies. She had laughed throatily and said that was probably just as well. *Prison Cell Massacre* and *Rough House Cell-*

mates had been huge hits in America "because teenaged boys like to see my tits."

"Well," Sir Cecil had said, putting into his sharp blue eyes the glint of mischievousness that never failed him in boardrooms or bedrooms, "I can't say as I blame them."

"They also like to see me shooting people."

"I would be content with the breasts," Sir Cecil had said. "Save the shooting for the eighteen-year-old boys."

They had laughed together, and that had led to tonight's dinner invitation. They laughed together again on the yacht, moored about a mile and a half off shore, as Sir Cecil poured champagne for her into a long-stemmed glass. The shoreline of St. Tropez was a glittering necklace in the distance. Night was descending, the wind was dying, the sense of the expensive, exquisitely choreographed romance that Sir Cecil dearly loved was in the air.

There was another reason to celebrate. Sir Cecil, in the past month, had made himself a millionaire a couple of times over simply by orchestrating the embezzlement of five million dollars from Dieter Voss's budget for the film production of *Saudi*. Dieter, of course, had been most cooperative in the enterprise, since he had pocketed three million of those dollars. The money belonged to an Arab gangster named Mehdi Abbas, a client of Sir Cecil's, who laundered his drug money through the Netherlands Antilles branch of the Holland Trust and who would not miss the mere drop in the bucket the five million dollars represented. When one was spending forty million dollars on a movie, what was a few million dollars siphoned off into a dummy corporation that then reinvested the money in American real estate?

Behind them a waiter played his part in the *mis-en-scène,* discreetly setting out the white linen and the silver and the candles for dinner. Sybil leaned against the transom and sipped her champagne. Sir Cecil duly noted the swell of her breasts, the neverending smoothness of her skin, then poured himself a glass of champagne.

"I want to be taken more seriously," she said. Her wheat-colored hair was a wildly scattered burst flaring around a finely chiseled face that boasted cheekbones a high-fashion model would envy.

"As a banker, I'm very much against taking anything too seriously," Sir Cecil said.

"That's why I played the role in *Saudi*. It was a small part, not the sort of thing I'm used to at all. But I want to get away from doing prison pictures."

Sir Cecil raised his eyebrows in surprise. "I had no idea you were in the movie. I spent a great deal of time financing that particular project. It's the biggest thing we've ever undertaken. There is a great deal riding on it."

"I know," she said. "I'm very impressed."

"What part do you play?"

"I'm a CIA agent."

"Typecasting," Sir Cecil said promptly.

She giggled and drank more champagne. "Well, I am required to sleep with the hero."

"In the line of duty," Sir Cecil said. Darkness had descended on the stage. He could no longer hear the background clatter of the waiter. The music rose in his soul. Something by Max Steiner would be appropriate to herald the quickly approaching moment of seduction. He moved closer to her.

"I do it for my country," she murmured.

"Do you enjoy doing it for your country?"

"I always enjoy it. Whether or not it's for my country."

"I'm so glad to hear it," Sir Cecil said. He bent forward and kissed her on the mouth. Her lips were soft and very moist. She smelled of perfume and champagne. She was the kind of woman he loved to love; the kind of woman only the movies could provide a banker. His wife made a momentary appearance in his mind, as she always did at such moments. Nice woman. She ate a lot of chocolates.

"Does the hero kiss you like this?" he inquired.

"Not quite," she said huskily.

"How did he kiss you then?"

"Harder."

He kissed her harder.

"That's better," she said.

She was leaning back against the transom, placing the weight of her generous behind against it. He slid his hand between her legs, up under her skirt.

"Oh," she said. "That's different."

He stopped momentarily and regarded her with amused surprise. "What's different?"

"Most men usually go for my tits first."

"I'm not like most men," he said.

"I'm so glad," she said.

Above them on the bridge, the captain of *The Hedge*, a rugged, flush-faced Englishman named Bennington, watched as Sir Cecil finally weakened and acted like most men, extracting one extraordinary breast from inside Sybil January's dress. God. He was no voyeur, at least that's what he liked to tell himself on these occasions. But this was making him damned horny. He turned to the young crewman he had hired a couple of weeks before.

"Better go below and see how dinner is coming along, Peters. Looks like the boss could be busy for a while."

Peters shook his head in amazement. "Does this go on a lot?"

"Constantly. Bloody porno show. He likes to perform in front of us. Turns him on, I think."

"Well," said the crewman, "it sure as hell turns me on. I wonder if he'd like us to join him? Help him out a bit."

"Somehow I doubt it. Better see to dinner."

Peters, a tall, lanky fellow with bad acne and unruly sun-bleached hair, turned reluctantly away, went down the stairway and along the portside deck toward the front of the craft. He was just about to go down into the cabin when he heard a noise. Just a rustle in the night. He opened the hatchway.

The waiter lay directly below in a pool of light that glinted off the blood. He was headless.

Peters gasped and turned away from the sight. Then he heard the quick, sharp swish, caught the gleam of something flying toward him. The next moment the blade slashed into his neck and the young crewman knew no more.

Sybil January's Louis Féraud dress slipped down her legs to the deck, soon followed by the Lejaby panties. Her belly was surprisingly protuberant, adding to the sense of earthy sensuality she exuded so casually. She stretched her arms along the railing and moaned as Sir Cecil knelt and kissed the inviting roundness of that stomach and used the fingers of his left hand to softly inspect the moistening insides of her vagina. The champagne and the kisses, and his fingers working so expertly, blurred everything into sweet sensation.

"Too much," she murmured as she unzipped his pants. She was not going to do this. Or she was not going to do this so fast, not out here on a deck washed in moonlight with a waiter somewhere in the recesses of the yacht, waiting to serve dinner. But then his throbbing cock was in her hand, and she was no longer thinking about what she would not do, but what she would do next.

"Let's go below," he managed to say hoarsely.

"No," Sybil murmured. "I want you right here."

On the bridge, Bennington thought, God, she's going to go down on him right there on the deck. Sir Cecil was an exhibitionist, but usually he had the good sense to take his guests below to his cabin for the nitty-gritty of passion. Now Bennington felt himself stiffen as he watched Sybil January kneel before one of international banking's brightest lights and take his penis into her mouth.

Then he heard the sound of the crewman behind him and turned agitatedly. "Peters, for Christ's sake, go below and...." At that moment, he saw it wasn't Peters. But it was too late; the blade was already cutting into his neck.

Sir Cecil House leaned forward, grasping the transom with both hands. There was just a slight breeze. The ocean stretched out endlessly. Sybil January had pulled his slacks down around his knees and her fingers caressed his buttocks. Her lips moved with agonizing slowness. He reached down and cupped her breasts in his hands, the ones eighteen-year-old boys paid to see but would never touch. A lifetime of work and commitment, and he got to touch breasts like these. Thank you, God. He thought dimly of the crew, wondered what they were up to. Stewing about serving the meal, he supposed. She worked one of her fingers into his anus. "Oh, God," he exclaimed to the night.

He heard her say, "Come for me, darling, come in my mouth." And that was the last thing he ever heard anyone say.

She was concentrating on him, anxious that he reach climax, because although she was enjoying this, or rather enjoying his reaction to it, her legs were cramping and she was becoming uncomfortable. So she did not see the blow, but rather felt it: a tremendous jolting force. For an instant, she thought he was beginning a particularly dramatic climax. But then she glanced up in time to see the spherical object pop almost comically up into the night air, as though a cork had unexpectedly lifted off from the top of a champagne bottle. Except that it was not a cork. It was the head of international banker Sir Cecil House.

Sybil January fell frantically back across the deck, trying to work her mouth into a scream. She had screamed many times in the movies; she was in fact known as something of a screamer. But now the noise refused to come. It was as though her throat, in the face of such horror, had been sealed off. The headless corpse, which a moment before had been a lover, tumbled down nearby, the blood splashing everywhere.

Then she saw the killer, holding a long, curving bloodstained knife. He was naked except for some sort of bandolier hung from his shoulders. His thin, sinewy body was smeared with blood. He was hairless except for a wildly fluorescent topknot. She whimpered and used her feet to propel herself back so that she was huddled protectively into a corner of the deck.

The killer watched her without emotion. He was in control. She would do nothing. He went over to the table laid out for the romantic dinner that would never be. Sir Cecil's head lay bleeding on the white linen, at a jaunty angle, like a gruesomely amateurish horror-movie prop.

Sybil January, numb and shivering, watched as he started toward her.

4

It was her. Or was it? Tom Coward sat across the table from Corinne Voss at the rear of Tetou, the unintimidating frame cabin overlooking the sea, where, it is said, you get the best bouillabaisse along the coast. There are, of course, any number of restaurateurs who would hotly deny this. And in fact, not far along the road at Le Bacon, Tom had consumed bouillabaisse the match of anything to be had at Tetou. Nonetheless, the reputation stuck, particularly at festival time. If you were anyone, then dinner at Tetou was a necessity. Therefore, everyone who was anyone made sure to make reservations months in advance of their arrival at Cannes. If you did not woo your guests at Tetou, then how important could you be?

Tom tried not to stare at Corinne Voss. But his eyes kept darting back to her. He kept trying to compare this woman with the short, dark hair and the round brown face against the flickering, ever-changing countenance of the woman on the beach. She glanced at him a couple of times; but her glance was uninterested. It held nothing that hinted at recognition or a secret shared. After all, she was a woman used to being stared at appreciatively, a woman who almost demanded the stares.

Corinne acted not at all like the woman on the beach. But then how did the woman on the beach act? Romantic. Wonderful. Passionate. A little scared. Apprehensive. Nothing like this poised bauble of the very rich. Corinne was all expensive flash, dressed to drop 'em dead in their tracks. She wore a sexy see-through sequined halter, and black mini-skirt, slinky and shiny, just like the body it barely covered. The showgirl's legs were sheathed in Christian Dior stockings, a black-lace pattern threaded with gold lurex. The perfume was by Paco Rabanne. The gold necklaces and bracelets were from Baume and Mercier, the eighteen-karat gold wristwatch by Cyma.

She said little, preferring, apparently, to concentrate on snuggling even closer to Dieter. Every so often she would give him a smoldering look and kiss his neck in a delicate, open-mouthed way that was very sensual. Her hands roamed constantly over his body, as though to reassure herself that it was hers. For his part, Dieter seemed to love the attention. He beamed and wrinkled his tadpole eyes and shrugged as though to say, "What can I do?" What indeed.

Maddi Bergen was seated in a kind of exile down the table, across from Rudy John Karras. She kept throwing hot glares at Corinne, as though her disapproval might make Corinne sit up and behave herself, as any polite young woman out for the evening should. Corinne, fueled by passion for Dieter, was not interested in behaving.

Lacy was seated beside Tom. After the first glass of wine, she put her hand softly on his knee. He shot her a warning glance. She replied with an outrageous wink. He carefully removed her hand. She had a second glass of wine. This time her hand was on his thigh.

Maddi's antennae were up. "I think you've had enough wine, young lady," she pronounced.

"Oh, yuck, Mother, I've had two glasses. Big deal."

"Wine makes your face break out, you know that."

"*Mother,*" Lacy said, appalled that there should be any suggestion that her face might break out.

Dieter Voss leaned forward. Corinne clung to him like a sequined vine. "Corinne and I, we were married only a year ago. We are what you would call newlyweds. What do you think of her, eh, Thomas?" Corinne tucked her mouth into the semblance of a smile. "What do you think of my sexy little foreign object?"

"She's very beautiful." Tom spoke directly to her for the first time. "Forgive me, but I get the impression we have met before."

"You have *seen* her before, I am sure," Dieter said. "She was Corinne Verneuil, a very famous model in Paris. On the cover of all the magazines. Very hot stuff. I had to chase her everywhere. Every bachelor in Paris wanted to get into her pants. That is not a word of a lie. But for some unfathomable reason, Tom, she chose me over all others."

"Don't be ridiculous, *chéri,*" she said, brushing her lips against his neck. "You are the most wonderful and sexy man I have ever met."

Dieter beamed. But then, Tom thought, who could fail to beam? Yet there was something about Corinne's voice. It somehow refused to carry the weight of her tender words.

"I can't shake this feeling that we've met before." He looked straight at her. She glanced at him with wide, unemotional eyes and shook her head.

"I don't think so," she said. "I'm sure I would have remembered. You are such a famous journalist."

"We are going to make a wonderful movie out of your book, Tom," Dieter assured him. "The greatest movie ever made."

"I thought *Saudi* was the greatest movie ever made."

"It is the greatest until we film your book."

Lacy's hand became more proprietary, moving higher on Tom's thigh.

"Tom's here to do a story on me," she said. "I'm talking to him about writing my autobiography."

Tom couldn't hide his surprise. "You are?"

"I want to talk to you about it." She looked at him, and he realized suddenly that her lovely, wine-flushed face was full of something he had never before seen in it: adoration. "You don't want to help me write my autobiography?"

"It may be a little early to write your autobiography," Tom tactfully suggested.

"Do you think so? How old do you have to be before you write your autobiography?"

"It's usually something that comes at the end of life, not at the beginning."

"But so much has happened to me, Tom. I want to get it all down before I forget it."

"I've had enough of this," Maddi announced, raising her scowling face from its study of the silverware. "I think we'd better be going."

"Mother," Lacy said quietly, "I'm having a good time."

"Come, come, Mrs. Bergen," Dieter Voss said jovially, "it's so early yet. We've hardly digested this wonderful bouillabaisse."

Maddi flared. "I don't want any arguments, Lacy. You have to be up first thing in the morning. I won't let you ruin your career by staying out all night. I'm not having any of it."

Dieter sighed and said, "Permit me to allow my chauffeur to drive you back to the hotel."

"That would be very kind," said Maddi Bergen formally. "And if you'll tell me how much the bill is I...."

Dieter Voss looked profoundly pained as he raised an objecting hand. "My dear lady, that is not necessary. It is my honor to host such a beautiful and talented mother and daughter."

Lacy gave Tom a fleeting – longing? – glance as she rose from the table with her mother.

"Goodbye, Tom," she said. "I'll talk to you tomorrow." Then, impetuously, she leaned forward and kissed him quickly on the mouth.

Lacy had had her moment of rebellion. Maddi spotted the kiss, and reacted to it by opening and closing her mouth very fast. Lacy was across the restaurant like a shot, so that a reprimand was impossible. Good for her, Tom thought. Dieter Voss and Corinne stared at him with a new interest.

"I had better make sure they get to the car all right," Dieter said.

"I'll tag along," said Rudy John Karras, getting to his feet. "I need a breath of air."

Dieter turned to Tom. "Would you object to entertaining Corinne for a few moments?"

Tom smiled fleetingly. "Not at all."

As Dieter and Rudy went out the door after Lacy and her mother, Tom lifted the wine bottle out of the silver ice bucket. "Would you like some more wine?"

"I'd love some." Corinne gave him a smile that undoubtedly kept the young men of Paris dazzled and hard at the chase. "I adore wine," she added as he filled her glass.

"You know," Tom said, "I was hoping we would have a moment alone."

"Oh?" Her eyes were amused.

"I wanted to make sure you were all right."

She looked at him for a moment, as though she was not sure exactly what he meant. "Of course I am all right. I am very happy."

"I mean, after last night. On the beach."

Now Corinne looked perplexed. "Last night? What beach? I'm afraid I have no idea what you are talking about."

Tom saw Dieter coming back across the restaurant and decided to give up. "I'm sorry," he said with a smile. "I thought we'd met before. Apparently, I was mistaken."

What is bad? Nietzsche had asked. His answer: All that proceeds from weakness. Rakko was not a weak man; therefore he reasoned, he was not a bad man. The logic, to him, was inescapable. When he was finished with her, he threw Sybil January's body into a corner of the deck. He had an ability, one he valued above all others, to focus on the task at hand, to expunge from his mind anything that might get in the way of accomplishing what he set out to do. Therefore, he did not think about the murders; that would come later. There would be some remorse. This minor irritant was of some concern. To him it was an indication of weakness. But he insisted to himself that he was not a weak man. He looked at his profession rationally; his business was to kill, and he was very good at it. There should be no guilt. It was something he did, something that, at the time, he actually enjoyed. So later, when the small shards of remorse cut into him, he was vaguely alarmed. He reminded himself of Nietzsche. The revolt against the whole civilized environment in which he existed, that was the key to Nietzsche's thinking. It was the key to Rakko's actions. Nietzsche talked. Rakko acted. That was the difference.

Now, however, remorse was the last thing on his mind. He went down into the engine room and stood between the two GM diesels. On the tool bench at one end of the room, he found the half-inch wrench he needed, then he expertly disconnected the fuel lines from the Racor filter. Seven hundred gallons of fuel began to fill the bilge. The smell was vile. Standing at the hatchway, he lit a match, set an oily rag aflame, then dropped it down into the engine room.

By the time he was a thousand yards away, the yacht was engulfed in yellow flames and was burning quickly. The shore, he estimated, was about a mile away. An easy swim. He concentrated on his arms and legs and on his body, cutting smoothly through the sea. What is happiness? Nietzsche asked. The feeling that power increases, the feeling that resistance is being overcome. As he swam, Rakko was a happy man. Only once before he reached the shore was his concentration broken. He thought of a name. Dieter Voss.

When they returned to the hotel, Dieter Voss invited Tom into the lounge for a drink. But Tom, who had had enough confusion for one night, declined, saying he was tired. That certainly was not a lie. Corinne Voss continued to hug Dieter. Tom took one last look at her before he turned to the elevators. She smiled. Dieter waved.

"I will see you soon, Tom," Dieter said. "We must talk. About many things. "

Tom went up to his room, switched on the light and threw open the shutters to the night. Offshore, the running lights of a luxury yacht glittered. A couple in evening clothes strolled up the path from the pavilion.The woman, blond and quite lovely, giggled at something her escort said. Tom sighed. There were no beautiful blonds to giggle at the things he said. Perhaps he really was cracking up, mistaking Corinne Voss for his woman of mystery. It occurred to him that he once again was playing the romantic fool, chasing after images. As usual, when his dreams evaporated, he was left drained and depressed, wandering aimlessly and alone. The telephone rang. When he picked up the receiver, a woman's voice said, "Hello, Tom."

"Who is this?"

"I was worried about you." She sounded hurried and her voice was a whisper but he knew who it was. "I hated to leave you on the beach like that. But there wasn't much choice. "

"Who hit me on the head?"

There was silence for a moment. "Rakko," the voice said. "He followed us to the beach. I'm so sorry, Tom. Are you all right?"

"I woke up with a headache and a lot of sand in my clothes. Listen, clear up some confusion for me, will you? Was that you at dinner tonight, or wasn't it?"

"I have no idea what you are talking about. I didn't have dinner with you tonight."

"Then I really am confused."

"Don't be confused, Tom, please. Don't be anything. Forget that you ever met me. That's the best. Please, please do as I say. Otherwise, it would be very dangerous for you. *Bonsoir,* Tom. And *merci.* You will always be my gallant knight in shining armor."

The line went dead.

5

The sky was overcast and threatened rain. Nonetheless, at eleven hundred hours precisely, a twenty-year-old French model who wanted to be in the movies took her top off on the Lido beach below la Croisette. A freelance photographer who drove his beaten-up old Porsche down from a dingy Paris suburb each year to cover the festival for several North American publications snapped her picture. The annual film festival at Cannes was more or less officially under way. The marquees were up along la Croisette. An American producer from New York suggested to a Filipino distributor that *Death Hunt Massacre* would become the hit of the marketplace and that it would be best if the distributor got his bid in now. The press office at the Palais had no record of at least a dozen prominent North American journalists. It was neither a good beginning nor a bad beginning to the festival. It was merely the usual beginning.

The whole idea of film festivals originated, interestingly enough, with the Fascists. In 1930, Giuseppe Volpi, then the Italian finance minister, whispered into the ear of his movie-mad boss, Benito Mussolini that it might be a good idea to host an international event devoted to the cinema. Thus the Venice Festival was born in 1933 in the gardens of the Hotel Excelsior. In 1936, the French arrived with Jean Renoir's pacifist masterpiece, *La Grand Illusion*. The Italians had as a guest that year Joseph Goebbels, and were in no mood for pacifist masterpieces. Therefore, the grand prize, the Golden Lion, was awarded to a German film titled *Kaiser of California.* The French, in a snit, decided their only recourse was to create their own festival at Cannes, a fishing village whose presence in history had gone unnoticed until an Englishman named Lord Brougham was unexpectedly delayed there in 1834 on his way to Nice. Lord Brougham loved the place, its azure skies and temperate climate, and decided it was the perfect place to spend the winter. Before long, Brougham's aristocratic friends were also wintering there. When Prosper Mérimée, who wrote the original book upon which the opera *Carmen* is based, discovered Cannes, the French got a little of their own back, and sent all sorts of writers and artists to inhabit the place. Wherever money and art are to be found, film and young women in bikinis are certain to follow. Alas, the timing of the French was bad. The festival was to open in September of 1939, on the same day World War II was declared. Faced with the prospect of war or a film festival, the world chose the war. The film festival at Cannes was delayed until 1946, at which time the soprano and film star Michelle Morgan and director Erich von Stroheim were among the guests. Such a good time was had by all that the party has continued annually ever since.

It is often said that the old-time glamor of Cannes, which rose to an apogee of sorts in the 1950s when the Americans and the Europeans fought to see who could be more lavish and wasteful, has largely disappeared. That may be so. Nonetheless, Cannes remains an annual spectacle unlike anything else in the movie world, a combination orgy, business conference and fair-to-middling party. Oh, yes. Films are also shown. Anyone who is not a film producer, a distributor, a movie star, a journalist, a pretty boy or a beautiful girl, need not attend. They are, to be blunt about it, not welcome. The festival is a private affair, closed to outsiders, although God knows they swarm up and down la Croisette seeking a glimpse of Pia Zadora. People come basically to do business. Either to be acclaimed a genius – and some of the unlikeliest people are acclaimed geniuses – or to sell their piece of cheaply produced schlock to distributors around the world, who appear to be prepared to buy tits-and-slasher movies in quantities that are quite unbelievable. To spend much time in the marketplace at Cannes is to wonder at the future of Western civilization. There are, of course, complaints that there is too much hucksterism at what is supposed to be basically an art festival. There is not too much hucksterism – there is nothing *but* hucksterism. Even the art movies are hyped hysterically, for if you can gain a reputation at Cannes, then you have some hope of selling your masterpiece around the world. The actual competition itself is very political, and the French, who can turn the baking of bread into politics, have a field day. The Yugoslavian masterpiece is not to be acknowledged? Off with their heads! Boycott the festival. Tears are shed. Nerves are frayed. It is only a film? What a ridiculous comment! There is nothing *but* film. Nothing else exists. Certainly not the outside world. The news of the Falklands war never did make it to the festival. It was drowned out by the hot rumor that the festival jury might give Jerry Lewis a best-actor award.

Cannes itself sprawls out over nine kilometers between the La Bocca quarter and the rocks of La Fourcade. But you can attend the festival for years and never be aware of the fact that there is an entire city rising above the main thoroughfare, the Rue d'Antibes. The life of the festival pulsates along la Croisette, the promenade that winds around the bay.

It is a tightly knit, self-obsessed little world. After a few days it is possible to know everyone; and everyone knows you. The demarcation lines are drawn to the east by the Hotel Carlton, and to the west by the Hotel Majestic and the new Palais des Festivals. The action to the south is on the beaches, and it wanders as far north as the Rue d'Antibes. This is because there is shopping along the street and because the theaters there are turned over to the festival for screenings. The Petit Carlton is also located along the Rue d'Antibes. The Petit Carlton is the informal headquarters of the serious film buffs who attend the festival with no more interest in cutting a movie deal than they have in saying a nasty word about Rainer Werner Fassbinder. Here, young men, the black leather providing a nice contrast for the pale countenances, can drink beer, eat steak *au poivre* and argue into the small hours about cinema's merits or lack thereof.

Despite the new Palais, whose presence, it was initially thought, would shift the focus of the festival to the west, the terrace of the Carlton Hotel remains the center of activity. People grumble about the prices, the overcrowding, the surliness of the waiters. But year after year it is packed, as it was at noon, when the clouds finally gave up and permitted the sun to make an appearance. Tom Coward threaded his way through the tables, nodding to familiar faces, shaking a few hands, noting the interesting cleavages. He spotted his friend, independent movie producer Alvin Jarvis. Alvin looked surly under the emerging sun. The day was half over and he had neither made a deal nor met a starlet. For a producer at Cannes, that is known as a waste of time.

"Where the hell you been?" Alvin demanded when Tom sat down. "I've been calling you for two days now."

He was already on his second Pimms. Alvin had lost weight. Or more to the point, his new wife, Lea Madison, had made him lose weight. She had also replaced his uniform windbreaker and jeans with lightweight Polo slacks and Italian jackets. To Alvin's relief, Lea approved of the LaCoste shirts. He had not had to give up those. But he no longer wore glasses. Now it was contact lenses. "They keep falling out," he grumbled. "I spend my entire fucking life looking for contact lenses. It's a conspiracy. They make 'em so they fall out. Then you have to buy new ones." Lea thought the clothes befitted a man of Alvin's new status. True, his latest hit was a teen-exploitation flick titled *Buns* that no one with an IQ higher than seventy would be found dead at. But that was all changing. Alvin, Lea had announced, would now produce pictures of quality and prestige. Tom had asked Alvin to explain what those words meant. Alvin merely shot him a dirty look and said he was only too happy to be up and away from the exploitation gutter. His father had sold books and had made millions at it, an entirely decent way of becoming a rich man. His son made bad movies, a source of family shame. Who could be proud of a son who had provided the world with *Death Elevator* and *Buns*? His father was surely turning over in his book-lined grave. So Alvin was anxious to improve his image. Or so he thought. Now, however, as the hustle and bustle of Cannes commenced, he was having second thoughts. In the marketplace a movie like *Buns* made you a king. Quality gave everybody heartburn and cases of nerves. *Buns* you could sell in Paraguay. Quality got you long interviews with boring journalists with bad breath from little cinema magazines. Quality got you glazed looks from distributors who had more important things to do with their lives than sit through the masterpiece of cinema you had thrown away good money on.

"Sorry, kiddo," Tom said. He motioned to one of the waiters, who hurried over. He ordered a Kronenberg beer, while Alvin looked on in amazement.

"How the fuck did you manage that? It took me an hour sitting here to get one goddamn Pimms."

"I told you a thousand times, Alvin. When you get here, the first thing you do, you go to the head bartender and you slip him a five-hundred-franc note. Then you never have to wait for a drink."

"Bullshit. You mean you gave some son of a bitch five hundred francs?"

"Well, no, not exactly," Tom conceded. "But then I don't have any trouble getting drinks. It's the only talent I have, Alvin. People see me, and they immediately want me to order a drink. I don't know what it is."

"What have you been up to?"

"I came into town a couple of nights ago to have a drink in the bar. The lights went out, and the most beautiful woman I've ever met in my life walked in. A guy with a Mohawk haircut attacked her. I kicked the guy in the balls. The woman and I kissed on the beach. Then someone knocked me out and stole my wallet."

Alvin was so shocked he actually put his drink down. "Are you serious?"

"Just another day in the hectic life of a journalist at the Cannes Film Festival."

"Jesus Christ, the festival hasn't even started yet."

"I have to find this woman, Alvin. I've never experienced anything like it. This electrical charge shot through my body the moment I saw her. I haven't been able to think of anything else since. I think I'm in love. At the very least I'm in obsession, which is worse than being in love."

"Oh, Jesus," Alvin moaned. "Here we go again. Tom Coward seeks true love. Remember the last time you were here? Remember that French distributor's daughter you made such a fool of yourself over? The old man was ready to kill you. You almost got yourself thrown out of the du Cap."

"It's different this time, Alvin."

"It's always different. But it's always the same. Christ. I thought you were going to settle down with Stormy."

"Stormy won't even talk to me."

"No wonder, after that fucking book of yours. Why don't you quit chasing these goddamn women who give you nothing but trouble? Settle down with Stormy. She'll take you back."

"I can't take time out from my search for the meaning of life."

"The meaning of life, my friend, is not hidden between some starlet's legs."

Tom looked amazed. "It isn't? That isn't what you used to tell me, Alvin."

"That was before I met Lea. That was before I started to spend all my time looking for contact lenses."

"Some of us search for the meaning of life, Alvin. Some of us search for contact lenses."

"Believe me, you'd be much happier looking for the contact lenses."

"And where is the new Mrs. Jarvis? Out buying you more Gucci loafers?"

"Go fuck yourself," Alvin said good-naturedly." She is shopping, though. Thank God. She won't give me a moment's peace. She's afraid I'm here to cut a deal for *Buns II*."

"Are you going to make a deal?"

Alvin's features took on a benign innocence. At that moment he could have sung in a church choir. "It never crossed my mind."

"So you are going to make a deal."

Alvin avoided the question by suddenly discovering someone he knew. "There's Jerry Alt. He said he'd meet me here for a drink. I like him, but he's an acquired taste. Be prepared for boredom."

"I wanted to talk to you about Dieter Voss," Tom said.

Jerry Alt sat down in a seat beside Tom. Raymond Chandler once wrote of old men "with faces like lost battles." Jerry's face had lost the battle. It was tanned a deep brown, which helped to obscure the defeat. And amid the ruins, there was the suggestion of a sly, street-smart guy. The suggestion was heightened by his clothing. Jerry Alt, at a festival where dressing casually was a given, was turned out with impeccable formality: a suit of lightweight, beautifully cut English fabric from Austin Reed of London's Regent Street, a classic striped Woodhouse shirt, complete with gold tie clip, cuff links and a glittering gold Rolex watch. He reminded Tom of a slick gambler who longed for tea at Buckingham Palace.

He shook Tom's hand and said, "Hey, Tom, I was just talking to Menahem Golan. He's an old buddy of mine. We're talking a few deals. You know he's just so damned hot right now. I was telling him, I said, 'Hey, Menahem, everybody out here on the terrace has got fifty percent of the budget for their next project. Now if we can just put all those fifty percents together, Menahem, just think of all the deals we can make.' Hey, he got a real kick out of that."

"It never seems to work out that way, though," Alvin said glumly. "That's the fucking problem. You can never get 'em together."

"Hey, you know what I hear? I hear the marketplace is shit again this year. All the same old stuff no one sold last year."

Jerry was the kind of guy who was always hearing something. He always knew the marketplace was no good. Or that it was very good. Or that it was only so-so. He knew everything, talked to everyone. But no one really seemed to know him. Or, more to the point, they did not know what he did. Whenever anyone asked, Jerry always replied he was "in production," and let it go at that. But the production of what? He handed out expensively embossed cards that announced "Jerry Alt Productions," accompanied by an address and telephone number on New York's lower East Side. There were rumors he had made a fortune in real estate. But they were only rumors. No one who ordered a drink within a hundred feet of him ever paid for it. At Cannes, good cheer and an open wallet go a long way toward making anyone popular.

"Hey, I was just talking to my old buddy Touch Lathrop," Jerry reported, laying a half-finished pack of Marlboros on the table and placing a Bic lighter beside it. "We're talking about doing a couple of things together. The guy's hot, let me tell you. He makes a lot of action pictures, and they sell like crazy at the festival. That guy, he can't walk down the street in Manila."

"Yeah," Alvin said sarcastically, "but he can't get arrested in Beverly Hills."

"Okay, maybe he's lacking that American breakthrough picture. But he's gonna get it this year with a little number called *The Adventurer*. Listen, the guy's better than Stallone, Schwarzenegger, any of those guys. He's the real thing. Fought in Nam, then spent a couple of years as a mercenary in Africa. Tough guy. But gentle. Real nice fella. I like him a lot. Stick around, Tom. You can see him in action."

"What's he going to do? Spray the terrace with machine-gun fire?"

"In a few minutes," Jerry said, "he and a buddy are going to climb down the front of the Carlton. It's to promote his new movie. And it really is Touch coming down off the roof. No stunt guys. I'm telling you, he's the real thing. There's nothing like him in the movies."

"Tom wants to know about Dieter Voss," Alvin said. He looked at Tom. "Why do you want to know about Dieter Voss?"

"He says he's crazy about my book. Wants to buy the movie rights."

"Stormy will be delighted to hear that," Alvin said.

"Dieter, yeah, well, everyone wants to know about Dieter." Jerry Alt made the statement in a hushed voice, as though it was part of a conspiracy. " He's a good friend of mine. We've talked a number of projects together. Dieter is a hot number at Cannes this year. Very hot indeed. Everyone's talking about *Saudi*. Everybody's wondering where he got the forty million to make it."

"Where did he get the money to make *Saudi*?" Tom asked.

"That's the forty-million-dollar question, isn't it?" Jerry touched delicately at the gold wristband of his Rolex, as though to reassure himself it was still there.

"According to Dieter he was financed by a Dutch bank," Tom said. "The Imperial Trust of Holland, I think. He claims he has a $150 million line of credit with them."

Jerry snorted. "Well, he may have the line of credit all right, but he needs collateral to back it up. Nobody just gives Dieter that kind of money because he's a cute little fellow oozing a lot of charm – although that certainly helps."

"What else helps?" Tom asked.

"Egyptian gangsters could be a great deal of help," Jerry said.

"Are there such things as Egyptian gangsters?"

"It's my experience," Jerry Alt offered sagely, "that there are gangsters everywhere."

"But why would Egyptian gangsters be interested in movies?"

"Same reason as the Italian gangsters are interested. Investing in movies is a great way to launder money. And movie producers, unlike a lot of other people, are notorious for not asking questions like, 'Where does the money come from?' "

"So you're saying Dieter is laundering money? That's how he was able to make *Saudi*?"

The ruin of Jerry Alt's face crumpled a little more. "Hey, hey. Hold on there just one moment. Jesus, Tom, I didn't say that at all. I just said those are the rumors. You put your ear to a railroad track, you hear a hum. Doesn't mean a train is coming. I'm just giving you the hum, that's all."

"What I wish," Alvin Jarvis said, "is that some Arab hood would come along and launder forty million dollars through me."

Jerry Alt pointed toward the roof of the Carlton. "There's Touch," he announced. "There's my boy."

Tom watched as a couple of black-clad figures began to bounce down the wedding-cake facade of the hotel at the ends of ropes. It only took them a couple of moments. No one except Tom, Alvin and Jerry paid the slightest attention.

"Hey," Jerry Alt said as the figures reached the floor of the terrace and began to unhook their ropes. "Did I tell you? Touch and I are getting a couple of projects together. He's very hot here this year, Tom, very hot indeed." He leaned closer to Tom and his voice dropped to a conspiratorial whisper, carried along on the breath of too many Marlboros. "Look, I'd just as soon not be associated with anything that is said about Dieter. Like I told you, he's a pal. But, listen, you got more questions, talk to the Director. He has a line on everything that goes on at this festival."

"The Director?"

"That's what everyone calls him. Hey, you don't know the Director? How long have you been coming here anyway?"

"I know," Tom said. "He's an old buddy."

"Hey, it so happens that he is," Jerry Alt said. "Not that I know a hell of a lot more about him than anyone else. There are all sorts of rumors around about him. Some say he once really was a director. Others dismiss him: a producer whose luck just ran out. Anyhow, he's always here, always watching. Talk to the Director, Tom. He can tell you anything you want to know. That is, if he likes you. If he doesn't like you, he just tells you to go fuck yourself. He's a little moody."

"Where can I find this guy?"

"Where can you find him? Jesus." Jerry rolled his eyes. "I tell you, Tom, you surprise the hell out of me. I thought you were a bit more plugged into things. You find him where you always find him." He pointed to the corner at the rear of the terrace. "Right over there, Tom. You can get your answers right over there."

6

The Director sat in a corner, against the hotel wall, so that he had an unobstructed view of the entire terrace. From this vantage point, the world was a huddled mass of supremely comfortable people. There was no ugliness or poverty. The poorest peasant in this universe was watered by Perrier delivered on overcrowded silver trays by hustling waiters. It was one way to view the world, Tom thought; perhaps the only way. The Director sat alone, close to an ice bucket into which had been tilted an open bottle of Dom Perignon. He wore a navy fisherman's cap, the peak pulled down over his eyes. A thick gray beard and dark glasses effectively hid most of a pink, jowly complexion without taking away from the air of superiority that hung around him like an expensive scent. This was the face of a snob, and there were not many such faces. The Director took great pleasure in his aloofness. He did not run with the pack, and his face showed off his pride in the fact. The snobbishness and the sense of superiority were perhaps necessary when his obesity was taken into account. He was terribly fat, a bloated thing spreading out alarmingly below that proud patrician head. Surely, no one could be that fat. But the Director tipped the scales at more than three hundred pounds. Superiority, not to mention the good life, required a price. The Director looked as though he paid it cheerfully.

"Ah, Tom Coward," he said in a deep, rich baritone voice. He showed off yellowed teeth as he leaned forward, resting his weight rather precariously on a delicate-looking carved-ivory walking stick. The stick was a necessary affectation. One suspected that without it he would topple over.

"Sit down, have some champagne. It's the first day of the festival. Wouldn't be the first day without champagne. The TV cameras already have been around. How do I remember Cannes in the old days? they ask. I tell them the story about Bobby Mitchum holding that actress's bare tits. The Italian thing. Who was that? Anyway, I tell 'em that story. Caused a scandal around the world at the time. No one holds Italian starlets' tits these days. Too many of 'em, wouldn't know which ones to grab first." His laughter was mirthless, employed as a break in the monologue. "Mind you, some of the TV people heard that one last year when they asked the same question. If they have, I tell them the one about Jean-Pierre Aumont, a good friend of mine, as it happens. He came here in 1955 and announced his engagement to three women in fifteen days: Bella Darvi, Nadia Gray and Grace Kelly. Something of a record, I should think. If all else fails, I tell them about Mike Todd and the time he shipped in a truckload of lions to promote *Around the World in 80 Days*. They all like that one. They don't bring the lions to Cannes anymore, Tom. Those days are over." He opened and closed his hands on the cane. "I read your stuff. Enjoy it. You're better than you let yourself be. 'Course, that's a peculiar disease that affects us all. Orson Welles used to say that he sat in a chair in his house in Hollywood when he was twenty-two, and when he got up again he was sixty-four." He jiggled with more mirthless laughter. "So there you go. Happens to all of us. We undercut and undervalue ourselves – and we come to Cannes to sit around and drink champagne, look at the bare tits and talk about movies that are never going to get made."

There was, finally, the pause for breath. Tom jumped into it. "Actually, it's not funny stories about Cannes I'm after," he said.

"Aha," the Director said with a knowing nod. "You want to know about the state of the movie industry today. I can give you that in one word: deplorable. Spielberg. Lucas. The movie brats. They correctly divined that kids were going to the movies, therefore you should make movies for the children. Because they made millions, Hollywood, as it usually does, jumped on the same bandwagon. The result has been catastrophic, a lowering of standards, a preoccupation with a common denominator delineated by the mind of a fifteen-year-old. It is no longer a business for adults. Which, I guess, is as good a reason as any why I am not a part of it." He drew a long-stemmed glass from the ice bucket and poured champagne into it. He handed the glass to Tom. "You see, I have opinions for all occasions. Others bring their scripts to Cannes. Or their diaphragms. I bring my opinions."

"Believe me, no one appreciates opinions for all occasions more than I," Tom said. "However, at the moment I'm more in the market for information."

"Ah, information, not opinions." He seemed slightly disappointed. He was obviously a man in love with his own view and did not like the idea of hastily dismantling it. "Opinions are the cheapest commodity available at this festival. Information is something else again. That is more valuable. So few of us actually know anything. We do not come easily by our knowledge. Thus we are careful about whom we impart it to."

Tom sipped at his champagne.

"Now, let's take you, Tom. What do I know about you? Well, I know you're a journalist, a bit of an international drifter. You're here. You're there. A hard fellow to pin down. You live on charm, a portable word processor and the next hotel room. There is surface to you, but depth? I don't know about the depth. I do know you've written a best-selling book about Lex Madison. I also know that Dieter Voss is interested in acquiring the rights to that book."

Tom raised his eyebrows. "Good God, I barely know that myself."

The Director looked pleased with himself. He raised his long, almost aquiline nose as if to put it on display. "Deals are part of the air here. I sit, and I sip my champagne, and I sniff the deals. They all have smells. Some of the smells are delicious, like good Canadian bacon frying in the morning. Other smells, well, other smells are like dead dogs lying in the Jamaican sun."

"And Dieter Voss," Tom said. "How does he smell?"

The Director touched the edge of his champagne glass. "The dead dog in the Jamaican sun."

"What about his wife?"

"What about her? It's Dieter who wants to buy your book."

"But it's his wife I'm interested in."

This made the Director pause. He seemed to inspect Tom more closely from behind the sunglasses. "You want to sleep with her? Dieter can probably arrange that, if it means getting his hands on your book. Good wives are easily come by. I should know, I've had several of 'em." He raised and lowered his shoulders. "Good movie deals are not so easy. I should know. I've lost many of 'em."

"I don't want to sleep with his wife," Tom said. "I want to find out more about her, though. I think she was with a man named Rakko the other night. I thought she was in some danger."

The Director's hand hovered near the stem of the champagne glass a moment, then moved away. He leaned heavily forward. Tom wondered if the fragile walking stick would snap. It held. "Rakko. That's a name I haven't heard for some years. You're sure that was the name? Rakko?"

"I'm sure. This guy is not easy to forget. A walking skeleton all dressed up in black leather with a Mohawk haircut."

"Yes, yes," the Director said meditatively. "That's Rakko, all right. However, I doubt very much Corinne Voss would be wandering around Cannes with such a man. Could it have been another woman?"

"It's possible," Tom said. "You know Rakko?"

"He's not exactly a personal friend. But I am in possession, as I said, of a great deal of information. Rakko is part of the information I possess. I don't know him. But I know of him."

"Who is he?"

"A killer. Professional. Some of us make movies. Some of us write stories. Some of us kill people. All necessary occupations, I suppose. Rakko happens to be very good at killing. In the old days, it's said, you could hire him for one hundred francs and he'd slit the throat of your choice. The Moroccans who dealt in heroin in Paris never liked him, though. They cut out his tongue."

"Nice people," Tom said.

The Director took a sip of his drink."Not a man you mess around with." He placed the wineglass back on the table, and looked at Tom. "Have you messed with Rakko, Tom? Is that what this conversation is all about?"

"Let's just say we met on the beach," Tom said. "But what would Rakko be doing at the Cannes Film Festival?"

"There is only one reason a man like Rakko goes anywhere," the Director said. "To kill people."

Across the terrace, a young woman, an actress, naturally, mounted the ledge abutting the street. A moment later she shrugged out of her dress, and stood naked in the early-afternoon sunlight. The photographers, tipped off as to what was transpiring, abruptly swarmed onto the terrace in droves, pushing aside tables and patrons in the rush to get at the actress. She remained amazingly calm amid the pandemonium. Her body was thin, showing the hard, unattractive strain of too much exercise. Such stark public revelation was somehow unappealing. Tom felt embarrassed for her.

The Director sighed. "She's here to promote her line of video porn. It's all the rage this year. Dirty movies on videotape. Twenty years ago, the gendarmes would be here with a blanket. Now, who cares? There are much more attractive women down on the beach at this moment, showing nearly as much flesh. But everyone rushes to snap that woman's picture. It's an outdated ritual. Rather like Cannes." He smiled broadly and once again showed the yellowed teeth. "Rather like movies themselves, come to think of it."

Tom returned to the Hotel du Cap later that afternoon to find the lobby jammed with the very best of Louis Vuitton and Gucci. Their owners, the newly arrived American movie mavens, moved restlessly through the luggage in search of someone else to embrace, to buss on the cheek or to arrange a tennis date with. The people here, the men and the women, already had tans in place; they radiated good health and confidence. They owned Mercedes. Their houses in Beverly Hills were properly decorated. They could get a table at Spago. These were not the Carlton terrace hustlers, the wheelers and dealers who stood anxiously outside screening rooms along the Rue d'Antibes or moved restlessly around the windowless, airless marketplace in the basement of the Palais. These were the young and not-so-young hotshots, studio executives, producers and directors. Their deals and their pictures were already made. They were not under any pressure to sell the product. They had legions of hucksters to do that for them. Their problems would start up again when they got back to L.A., over the next lunch at the Polo Lounge or at Le Dome. For the moment, this was the good, golden time. Everyone smiled and smiled and showed off miles of perfectly capped teeth. The white teeth flashed off the white marble of the lobby. Everything dazzled. It hurt the eyes.

Tom retreated to the terrace where a TV crew was filming an interview with Lacy Bergen. Maddi Bergen sat nearby, watching the proceedings with the same dedicated intensity with which a Secret Service man might keep an eye on the president of the United States. Lacy looked extraordinarily beautiful sitting in the sun-dappled shade, her dark hair loose and lustrous. She wore white shorts. A little pink sweater was thrown over her shoulders.

"My motto is 'Virginity Is Fun.' I mean, I don't see anything wrong with it, do you?" she was saying to a young, intense television interviewer.

The interviewer looked flustered. "Um, no, of course not."

"There you go," Lacy said, satisfied her point was made. "I don't think virginity is something we have to be afraid of. I think it's something us girls should cherish and enjoy. Well, not for our entire born lives, of course, but for as long as we are able."

"But of course," the interviewer said.

Lacy looked over and saw Tom standing there. She gave him a wink. "Anyway, that's the sort of thing I want to talk about in my autobiography."

The interviewer perked up considerably. "You are writing your autobiography?"

"It's just that I've been through so much in twenty years," Lacy said brightly, "and I've got so much to say. About everything. I mean girls are constantly coming up to me and wondering about their hair and their makeup, their diets, that sort of thing. I mean, they don't know where to turn. Often they say to me, 'Lacy, you should write a book about your life,'... "

Tom groaned inwardly and made his way down to the pool. He saw Corinne Voss lying on her back on one of the pallets. She wore a pair of Ray-Ban sunglasses and a narrow white strip of bikini bottom. Everything else about her was gold: golden tan; thin gold chain around her waist; gold ankle bracket; gold at her neck and wrists. He went over to her.

"Good afternoon," he said.

She propped herself up on her elbows and pulled the sunglasses halfway down her nose.

"*Bonjour*, Tom," she said with a smile. "Dieter has gone into Cannes. Meetings. This thing with *Saudi*, it is so crazy. It never seems to stop. Phone calls. More phone calls." She sighed deeply, emphasizing the swell of her quite magnificently upturned breasts.

Tom arranged to look off toward the cabanas hidden amid the pine trees behind the pool.

She said, "I was just thinking of you, as a matter of fact."

"That's good news," he said.

"Come. Take off your jacket. Sit down beside me." She patted the edge of the pallet. He shrugged out of his jacket and plopped himself down uneasily. "I was trying to remember where we might have met before."

"I have some ideas on that subject," Tom said. "How about the bar at the Carlton the other night? I bought you a cognac."

"Was I terribly sweet?"

"You were darling."

She shook her head. "Oh, Tom. *Pardon*. But I'm afraid it was not me. I was nestled in my little bed, beside my little husband."

"I can't be going crazy. It's only the first day of the festival. I don't start to go crazy until well into the second week."

"Incidentally," she said, "I read your book. I was very intrigued with Stormy Willis, the girl you love, but cannot be with."

"She's mad at me for writing the book," Tom said.

"But you still love her?"

She was very close to him. He could smell the heat and the suntan lotion rising off her. She had fathomless dark green eyes, with little specks of gold cast into the pools, and long damp eyelashes.

"I'm not sure," Tom said. "At least I'm not sure I can love her quite the way she wants me to."

"It is so sad," she said. "When I read that part of the book I cried." She shifted her long legs. The thin fabric of her bikini bottom stretched tight across her vulva. The foreman in charge of Tom's body heat threw the switch marked "Desire."

She began to gather up her things. "Dieter says it would make a marvelous movie. I agree with him."

"How long have you known Dieter?"

"About a year. We met in Paris. He makes business deals and he makes love. That's all that interests him."

She was standing now, shoving tiny feet into high-heeled slip-ons. Her body was slick with lotion and perspiration. She put on a terry-cloth robe. "Why don't you walk me back to my room? We can talk."

"About the other night?"

"Tom, you just won't give up, will you?"

"You're sure it wasn't you?"

"I am positive. Absolutely positive." Her manner and her laughter were resolutely good-natured. She carried her sexuality and sex appeal like casual luggage. They were contained in the sway of her hips as she made her way up to the steps of the hotel, in the way she pushed her hair behind her ear, in the way she touched Tom's arm as they approached the elevator. They were in the way she opened her robe once they were inside the suite.

"I am so thirsty," she said huskily. "Would you like a beer?"

"Thanks," he said. He could not take his eyes off her.

She bent down to a small refrigerator and extracted two Heinekens, snapped them open with a bottle opener that lay on top of the refrigerator and handed one of the bottles to Tom. "*Salut*," she said. She took a big swallow and the beer foamed over the top of the bottle, down her chin. She wiped at her chin and chest. "It's so warm in here," she said.

She came over to him. The heat and smell of her were like a musky cloud cover. He once again inspected the gold flecks in her eyes.

"When is Dieter going to be back?" he asked.

"It doesn't matter," she murmured, touching the buttons of his shirt, then raising her hand so that it grazed the skin along his chest. "You should get out into the sun, Tom. You are so pale. Look, look at me. I am so dark." The robe slipped from her shoulders. He was not sure who kissed whom. He would have sworn that it was her, taking his bottom lip between her teeth and biting into it gently. But he wasn't quite sure. He remembered his hands resting on her golden flanks, touching at the edge of the bikini. He remembered the sharpness of her teeth, and the long eyelashes now lowered to cover those amazing gold particles in her eyes. He remembered her tongue running along the edges of his teeth, remembered the kiss suddenly taking on a passion. He remembered the press of her breasts against his shirtfront as he drew her to him. He remembered touching the gold waist chain, then slipping his hand down inside her bikini bottom, between the cheeks of her behind. He remembered all that. He did not remember, though, how they got into the other room, the one with the canopied bed, or how she got his pants open. But then he was running his mouth along the gold ankle chain, feeling it cut gently into his lip, and she was saying something in French he could not understand, and feeding him into her mouth. And Rudy John Karras was standing at the door, casually watching everything from behind the horn-rimmed glasses, and Corinne was raising her head up from Tom's cock and screaming something. Rudy John Karras turned and marched from the room as Tom stumbled off the bed, pulling frantically at his pants.

"Jesus Christ," he said.

Corinne Voss lay back on the bed, raising her flanks and pulling the bikini bottom down. "Don't worry about him, *chéri*. Come back to bed."

"For Christ's sake," Tom said, "he's bound to tell your husband."

Corinne laughed. "Darling, Dieter is an adult. He understands these things. He won't mind. Now come here. I want that beautiful cock of yours inside me."

But his pants were zipped and passion was following Rudy John Karras out of the room. "Wait a minute, wait a minute," he said, trying to catch his breath. "This is all a little too fast and crazy for me. I'm from Canada, for Christ's sake."

She got off the bed and embraced him. "Tom, it was a hot afternoon; we were both horny; we did something about it. Don't take it so seriously. It is not the end of the world. It means nothing."

"There we have the problem," Tom said. "You see, it would mean something to me."

She kissed him on the cheek and her smile was understanding. "You are so...North American, darling. But I understand. You are very sweet. Run along, and don't worry about Dieter. If he says anything, I will confess that his horny little foreign object just got carried away with the sexy journalist."

"Is that all you are, Dieter's little foreign object?"

She looked at him coquettishly. "Maybe I am what he wants me to be," she said. "Maybe this is all he wants from me." She kissed him again. "Goodbye, Tom," she said. "Don't think I am terrible. Please."

"I hardly think you're terrible," Tom said.

"Then if I do not have a lover this afternoon, perhaps I have a friend."

He touched her chin, paused over those green eyes. "You have a friend."

He slipped out the door.

He got back to his room, still shaken, already regretting the sudden attack of puritanism. If Dieter's little foreign object wanted to fuck him on a hot afternoon, who was he to say no? Except he kept wanting her to be more than a quick fuck. He wanted the rain, and the night, and the mysterious woman in the trench coat. But perhaps it was time to get the message through his head: Corinne was not that woman. She was friendly and available, and no more than that. Right?

Then he saw the women's clothing strewn everywhere. The contents of the open suitcases exploded in whites and pinks and reds across the bed. The bathroom door opened and out stepped Lacy Bergen.

"Where have you been?" she demanded as though she had been in the room for years.

"Isn't that silly of me," Tom said. "I've walked into the wrong room."

"What makes you think you're in the wrong room?"

"Because you're here. If I was in my own room, you wouldn't be here. These suitcases wouldn't be here."

"I've decided to move in with you." She regarded him with a clear, eager face.

"Do I have any say in this?"

The expression was truculent. "Tom, please. My mother and I had a terrible fight. "

"Over what? Who gets to use the hair drier first?"

"She doesn't want me to get a scooter, you see. All my born life I've wanted a motor scooter, and what with these narrow roads, and being so far from Cannes, I thought it would be a perfect time to get it. But she had this big fit about it. So I told her I was moving out. The only problem is, I've no place to go."

"She'll be delighted to learn you've moved in with her old friend Tom Coward."

"It's better this way. I mean, you want to interview me, right? Well, now we'll be together. You can get to know me. It'll be very helpful when we do my autobiography."

"Lacy, when you do your autobiography, you'll do it without me."

"You don't want to write my life story?"

"Not particularly."

"But why not?"

"Let's just say your life is still a work in progress."

She looked miffed. "It's because you think I'm a virgin, isn't it? Well, I just want to reassure you, Tom, darling. I am no virgin."

"It has nothing to do with whether or not you're a virgin."

"You don't want to sleep with a virgin, do you?"

"This is not a subject I've given a great deal of thought to, Lacy."

"Look," she said, trying to sound tough and worldy, "I've slept with lots of men."

"I'm sure you have. I'll sell the story to the *National Inquirer*: 'Lacy Bergen Teen Nympho.'"

"I am not a teen."

There was a knock on the door. If Tom had thought twice about it, he would never have opened the door. But at that point, he was not even thinking once, let alone twice. Maddi Bergen steamrolled into the room. Her scowl was a work of art, magnificent to behold. It was aimed directly at Tom.

"I suppose you're proud of yourself, being the sort of animal that thinks nothing of luring an impressionable young star into your room. Well, let me tell you something. I can have you thrown out of this hotel for corrupting the morals of a minor. You'll go to jail for sure."

"Maddi, there are many crimes in France, but I don't think young women in hotel rooms is one of them." He opened the door. "Look, I'm going to leave now. Oh, I know it's my room and everything, and I shouldn't be involved in this. But what the hell, I'm a nice guy. So you two stay here as long as it takes to get your problems ironed out. Except when I get back this evening, I don't want to see either one of you in here. Is that understood?"

Maddi started to snap. Tom slammed the door.

Downstairs in the lobby, he encountered Dieter Voss, looking agitated and flustered. As soon as he saw Tom, however, he started grinning.

"Tom," he said merrily, "I was looking for you earlier. Did you speak with Corinne?"

Did I speak with Corinne? Tom thought. In a manner of speaking, yes. "Yes," Tom said. "I saw her at the pool."

"Then she told you I want you to be our guest at the premiere of *Saudi* at the Palais the day after tomorrow."

"Uh, yeah, she mentioned it."

"Then you'll come along? It will be a tremendous evening, I promise you."

What could he say? No, Dieter I can't come because I feel a trifle guilty about wrestling around on a bed with your naked wife? That somehow did not seem appropriate. Tom said, "I'd be delighted."

"Oh, no, my friend," Dieter Voss said. "It is I who am delighted."

"How are you doing with *Saudi*?"

"Oh," Dieter said, "the Americans are very excited. It is a wonderful picture, Tom. A great picture." But as the producer turned and started up the stairs, it struck Tom that Dieter Voss's voice, for the first time since he met him, sounded hollow and without conviction.

Dieter Voss carried a large Scotch across the room to where his wife lay naked on the bed. She moved her hips suggestively. "Tom Coward was just here."

Dieter allowed a distant smirk. "Was he not satisfactory?"

"I'm afraid we were interrupted. Anyway, baby, I am all horny. Come to bed and fuck me."

Dieter sipped at his Scotch.

"Sir Cecil House is dead," he said quietly. "His yacht burned in the sea last night at St. Tropez. They are searching for survivors. But so far, nothing. I don't expect they'll find anyone alive."

"Look, darling," Corinne purred. "Look at what I am doing to myself with my fingers."

Dieter ignored her. "He was with one of the actresses from *Saudi*. It's all over the papers. The police are investigating. There is as yet no suggestion of foul play. I could tell them a thing or two, I suppose. But of course, I won't."

"Dieter," she interrupted sternly. "Please, come and fuck me. I can't stand it."

Dieter stopped inspecting his glass, and looked over to his wife. "You really are quite remarkable," he said in a quietly admiring voice. "You care only for the pleasures of the flesh. You don't give a shit that Sir Cecil is dead. And there is the small matter of five million dollars that he helped us steal from the *Saudi* budget. Don't you think –"

"Baby, baby, please –"

The ice cubes tinkled against the side of Dieter's glass. He was speaking almost to himself. "I suppose you are right, my darling. When the flesh calls, you must obey the call. I wish, though, our young friend Mr. Coward had taken care of you. Then we could talk, and he would feel terribly guilty and sell me the rights to his book very cheaply. Better yet, he would help me convince Lacy Bergen that it would be in her best interests to make a Dieter Voss film. At the moment, I'm not sure she thinks it's in her best interests."

He finished the Scotch and went over to the bed. He bent over and kissed Corinne's breast. She arched against him. "Come," she demanded. "Do it to me. Do it –"

"And I'm afraid there is more bad news. I have not talked with everyone as yet. But initially there is no interest whatsoever in distributing *Saudi* in North America. The American view is that the whole enterprise is a disaster."

Corinne shook her head and seemed to come out of a trance. "I don't believe it," she said. "All that money, all those production values, surely–"

"It means nothing to them if they do not think *Saudi* is commercial." Dieter shrugged. "And they don't think it's commercial."

"Obviously, Mehdi Abbas must not know about this," she said.

"Obviously." Dieter snorted with laughter. "Wouldn't he be delighted. Hello, Mehdi. Not only have we robbed you of five million dollars, but we also fucked up your movie."

She sat up and stopped his words with her lips. "Shh, my darling," she murmured, pressing herself against him. "Everything will work out. I know it will. You are a genius. My beautiful genius. Now you know what I want you to do? I want you to let me undress you. Then I want to brush my titties all over your face. I want to get you nice and hard. Can I do that, my darling? Will you let me do that?"

"Yes..." he moaned.

"Then I want you to let me ride on top of you, darling. You know how I like that, don't you? With that beautiful big cock very deep inside me. And we will do that, and have this wonderful fuck, and then you will go out and sell the movie to those Americans. You will do that. Won't you, darling? Won't you do that?"

A few moments later, success, failure, everything was forgotten. She rode atop him for a time, then he insisted on working her over. She made all the special sounds and noises that he liked so much, the ones that spurred him on and made him believe he was the greatest of all lovers. He was not. But even if he had been, it would be of no interest to her. She was not here because she loved Dieter Voss. To the contrary. She put up with all this because she wanted revenge. And soon, she thought, oh, God, soon, she would have it. Dieter looked up at her, perplexed, and she realized she had lost her concentration.

"Is everything all right, darling?" His thin hair was tousled across his forehead.

She threw back her head and moaned loudly. "Oh, please, Jesus, darling, don't stop. Eat me. Oh, please, please eat me!"

7

Moulin de Mougins is a Michelin three-star restaurant in the Cannes area. Its reputation, particularly during the festival is as formidable as the prices are high – which is very formidable indeed. The restaurant nestles in the fortified town of Mougins, north of Cannes. The walls are white. The atmosphere is Provençal and informal. The customers bring their own chic. The food more or less lives up to its reputation.

That night, Alvin had organized the menu: Bouquet de homard Breton, legumes et sauce d'Agrumes followed by Le blanc de Daurade Royale de Méditerranée, Belle Mouginoise and then by Les Tendres noisettes d'Agneau de Sisteron. Everything was washed down with Blanc de Blancs Ott.

Alvin had secured a large table at the rear of the restaurant. He presided over the festivities with his wife, Lea, at his side. Tom was among the guests, as was Jerry Alt. Alt had announced loudly that afternoon on the terrace that he would bring his "old pal" Touch Lathrop to dinner. No one paid him the least attention until he actually walked into the restaurant with Touch. With them was a little man in a flowing black caftan. The movie star who could not walk down a street in Manila had chosen denims for the occasion, and a pair of alligator-skin cowboy boots. His newly rinsed blond locks fell softly around a sun-blushed face that had yet to own up to age. The blue eyes sparkled with wonderment.

"Hey, it's real good to meet all of you," he said in a soft drawl. "Any chance of getting a beer around here?"

The little man in the black caftan looked horrified. "Touch, you aren't going to have beer? This is a three-star French restaurant. If Roger Verge were here he probably would throw you out. As it is, I think he went off to Disney World or some awful place like that. He's over there making nouveau-cuisine hot dogs."

"Everyone," Touch announced, "I'd like you to meet the Shree Ramana."

The little man bowed from the waist. "A delight to be with you all at this wondrous restaurant," he said with an English accent, the cultured beauty of which was not lost on anyone. "The last time we were in the south of France, we were the guest of Aly Khan and his beautiful wife of that time, Rita Hayworth."

"Shree here is a guru," Touch said. "I guess you might call him my guru."

Shree Ramana did not looked pleased with that. "Touch, please. We are here to guide you, to be of some help in your long quest through life. But we are not yours. We are of this universe. And if you are of this universe, you do not belong to anyone."

"Of course, you're right," Touch said in a voice that was properly humble. "I tell you, this man has done more to make me see into myself. I can't believe what this man has taught me. The mind, for example. He has that nailed right down. A wondrous power in the Self. That's what he calls the mind. No wonder they call him the Illuminating Light."

"They call him the Illuminating Light?" This from Alvin, who was consuming copious amounts of Blanc de Blancs.

"It is our opinion that Touch here was a great warrior in another time. He has been reincarnated in this time to be once again a great warrior. You can see that in his life. And you can see it in his films."

"That's what I try to bring to my movies," Touch affirmed, "you know, that sense of a mystic warrior, a man who has lived forever. I have come to believe that I will live forever. I will change, God knows, and be many people in many different lives. But I am one with myself."

"A great warrior," Shree affirmed.

Touch looked appropriately sheepish. "Well, I wouldn't know about that."

"That is why we are with you, Touch," Shree Ramana said reassuringly. "To lead you down to the path of inquiry, to determine a course of conduct for life. To discover the eternal Self. The old boys of India, and we certainly are indebted to those sons of the earth, called this *prarabdha*."

"Isn't this fabulous?" Alvin said between mouthfuls of lamb. "Isn't this great? I've been coming here for years. Even when I was hustling slasher flicks along the Croisette, I always used to come up here for a meal. It was always worth it."

"Frankly," Lea said airily, "I prefer the Relais à Mougins."

Alvin eyed her narrowly. "Oh, we do, do we? And which one of our husbands took us there?"

"Not the present one," Lea said. "I can assure you of that."

"That is because your present husband likes the Moulin. Don't give up hope though, sweetheart. Maybe husband number five will prefer the Relais."

"Husband number five won't be sneaking around behind my back trying to make *Buns II*," Lea replied acidly. Tonight she looked very dark and sexy. But there was an air of trouble about her. She had a way of lifting an eyebrow that suggested it might be wise to fasten seat belts; the ride was about to be bumpy.

"Now listen, you two," Tom said. "You're not supposed to fight at the Moulin de Mougins. It's against the house rules. There's a sign posted as you come into the place."

"Besides," said Alvin sulkily, "I'm not going to make *Buns II*."

"Alvin," Lea snapped, "you're a liar."

Touch Lathrop turned to Tom. "I understand you're a journalist, Tom."

"Please. I'm trying to keep my dark past as quiet as possible."

The blue eyes were leaden with seriousness. "I hope you won't be quoting anything I say here tonight, Tom. I mean this being a sort of private thing and all. You know, everything sort of off the record."

"Trust me, Touch. I won't write a thing."

Shree said, "It's our experience that journalists are particularly unpleasant people, and certainly not to be trusted. They lack realization of the Self. They live their lives through others, and, of course, they are no one themselves." Shree had a hard, lined face dominated by the sort of hooded eyes that are necessary before one can get work as a guru. Those eyes now gleamed suspiciously as they inspected Tom. "We see a dangerousness in you that we do not like," he said. "You bring nothing good with you. You are to be watched. We think you will make Touch very unhappy."

"Don't be silly," Tom said. "I'm going to dedicate myself to making Touch's life as happy as possible."

Touch gave the kind of all-American smile that reminded you of football and kids who stand up for "America the Beautiful." He slapped Tom on the back.

"Hey, Shree, lighten up, will you? Tom looks like a good guy. You're a good guy, aren't you, Tom?"

"One of the best," Tom affirmed. He picked up the Blanc de Blancs. "Let me pour you some wine."

"Be careful, Touch." There was a warning note in Shree's cultured English voice. "You know alcohol doesn't sit well with you."

"What's a glass of wine, Shree? Come on. We're among friends."

"Yeah, Shree," Tom said. "Turn off your illuminating light for the evening and enjoy yourself."

The hooded eyes were now hostile. "We are watching you, Mr. Coward. We know what you're up to."

Alvin and Lea continued to bicker throughout the meal, forcing Tom to listen to Touch Lathrop, who had decided the Blanc de Blancs, while it wasn't a glass of beer, went down just fine. He consumed large amounts of it. His boyish face became even redder. The gentle drawl became a little slurry, and a moist haze fell over the blue eyes.

"You see, Tom, what sets me apart from those other guys, you know, Sly and Clint and Chuck, is that I am the real thing."

"That's what I told him," Jerry Alt interjected excitedly. "You're the real thing. That's why I'm so enthusiastic about our involvement together, Touch. You bring authenticity to the roles you play."

"I want you to shut up for a moment, Jerry. Those other guys, they don't understand the first thing about automatic weapons, Tom. Not the first thing. But me, I've handled automatic weapons in Southeast Asia, in Nam and on the African continent. I know how those mothers feel. I know how to break 'em down and put 'em back together again."

"Touch was a mercenary in Africa," Jerry interjected.

"I'm going to have to ask you again, Jerry. Shut up. Anyway, Tom, I hate to say it pisses me off, because with the Illuminating Light here, I've learned to control my angers and hostilities, to channel them into useful purposes, like my acting and that sort of thing. So I don't get pissed off. But if I did get pissed off, it would be at those guys. I mean they get all those big budgets and everything, and they are just not authentic. Let me ask you this, Tom. Do you think Clint Eastwood has killed anyone? Actually shot a man down?"

"I hope I'm not implying any disrespect toward Clint by saying no."

"There you go," Touch said.

"Is this to suggest, Touch, that you have killed people?"

Touch unsteadily picked up his wineglass. "Only in the line of duty, Tom. Only in the line of duty."

"See what I mean by authenticity?" Jerry Alt said. "When this guy mows down a bunch of Commies on the screen, you know he's been there. Now you sure as hell can't say that about Stallone. Tell him about the headband, Touch."

"It isn't a big thing," Touch said. "But I was wearing that headband when I was in Nam. Then when I came to make *Mercenary Hunters* five years ago, I wore it then. Next thing I know, Sly is wearing the same thing in *Rambo*, making it like his own. Well, I wore it first. I didn't copyright it or anything like that, but it's like I said before, if I got pissed off at these things, well, I'd be pissed off."

Then Tom heard Alvin announce loudly, "I want it to last, goddamn it. I want this marriage to mean something."

"Then don't make *Buns II*," Lea snarled.

Jerry Alt looked surprised. "No *Buns II*? After the first one grossed thirty million dollars? Domestic?"

"But Jerry," Lea said. "Alvin can do better than that."

"How can you do better than $30 million domestic for an independent picture?"

"Oh, Jesus," Lea said in exasperation.

"Marriage," Touch Lathrop said. "I'm afraid I could never marry."

"What is it, bad for your image?" said Lea.

Touch swallowed more wine. "You don't understand. She was the girl of my dreams. She was my obsession."

Lea Jarvis looked confused. "Did I miss something here? Did someone drop the first reel from Touch's latest movie?"

"Hush now," Shree Ramana hissed angrily. "This is very traumatic for Touch. It is at the core of his search for the Self."

"I always think about her," Touch was saying. "I never forget her. It's sort of messed me up for anyone else."

"She must have been some woman," Jerry Alt said.

"Her name was Ginger Shane," Touch said morosely. "She was beautiful. Beautiful and damned. It was tragic, actually."

"What happened to her?" Tom inquired.

Touch didn't say anything. For a moment Tom thought that either he didn't hear the question or was not going to answer it. Finally he said, "She's dead."

"Alvin," Lea said, "I'm not having any fun. I really am not having any fun."

"Oh, for Christ's sake," Alvin said. "I give up. Let's get the check and get the hell out of here."

"I loved that woman, loved her more than I ever loved anyone or anything."

"We told you not to have so much wine, Touch," Shree Ramana said gently.

"I wanted a beer," Touch said. "A place like this, they should have some beer around."

On the way back to Cannes they had to pull the limo over to the side of the road so that Touch Lathrop could throw up his three-star dinner. After that, he collapsed against the hood, and Alvin and Tom had to help him back into the car.

"He's just not used to wine," Shree Ramana observed.

"No kidding," Tom said.

They started up again, and Lea and Alvin got into a fight. When they arrived at the Carlton, Lea bolted from the car in tears. Alvin swore and climbed out after her. Touch had regained consciousness.

"Where did they go?" he demanded. "I want everyone to come back to my suite at the Majestic for a nightcap."

"We think you've had enough for the night, Touch," Shree Ramana said.

Touch did not like that one bit. "Look, I don't want to be nasty here or anything, Shree, but the Self craves a beer." He turned to Tom. "Come on, I want to show you guys something."

Tom was just drunk enough. "Sure," he said. "My Self could use another drink."

Shree Ramana launched the sort of dirty look that could stop reincarnation.

Touch's suite at the Majestic overlooked la Croisette and the Palais des Festivals. Tom stood watching the stream of cars turning up the drive and coming to a stop at the front entrance. Shree Ramana placed the earphones of a Sony Walkman over his head, adjusted the volume and curled up in the fetal position on the floor. Jerry Alt busied himself pouring drinks. Touch fiddled with a video-cassette player. He had sobered considerably.

"Shree, what's the matter?" Touch demanded when he noticed the guru on the floor. "What are you listening to?"

"We are listening to our Huey Lewis and the News tape," Shree said.

"Well, get up off the floor."

"This is our nonviolent form of protest against this nonsense. We will lie here like this until you exorcise that woman from your soul."

"I like you better when you're telling stories about the Aly Khan."

"The Aly Khan at least listened to me."

Touch sighed and shoved a tape into the cavity of the video recorder. "Just ignore Shree," he said. "I want you guys to see this."

Tom sat down on a sofa and Jerry handed him a glass of wine. On the screen a title announced, "Ginger Plays Alone." Touch slumped down on the floor very close to the television screen. A woman stood before a mirror. She was very young with white-blond hair that curled thickly around a pouty, delicate face. It was the kind of face that got girls on cheerleading squads and drove college quarterbacks to throw touchdowns. Parents who recalled Grace Kelly on the cover of *Life* magazine wanted their little girls to grow up and have faces like that. It was not the face of a young woman who took her clothes off in front of a video camera. But Grace Kelly was dead, and the world was full of surprises. The cheerleader wore a striped top and white shorts. A moment later she removed the top and began to inspect her breasts.

It was at this point that Tom began to understand what Touch was making all the fuss about – and so did Jerry.

"God," Jerry said in some amazement, "look at her, will you?"

"That's Ginger," Touch said in a tone that suggested the view here was very special and privileged. "That's Ginger Shane."

Tom had to concede that she did possess one of the most incredible bodies he had ever seen: the high, upturned breasts topping a torso that fell sharply away at an angle to a great swell of a derriere. The camera had caught Ginger at the precise moment in her life when everything was set into a rosy-pink perfection, nothing too big or too small, everything perfectly proportioned. The Impressionists would have painted her avidly, and it would have been a celebration of color and form. But this was the twentieth century, and the pornographers had her. Nonetheless, there was a certain kind of raw art here; her body was too fabulous for there not to be. As she meticulously preened and stroked herself she seemed to understand that she was special. There was a star quality about her. She was on the bed now, sinking her fingers into her vagina and groaning loudly, her feet curling inward. It was cheap and obvious and exploitive, but the young woman gave it a certain class, and that allowed for the most unexpected of bonuses: eroticism.

Tom shifted on the sofa and took a long drink from his wine to help break the spell Ginger Shane cast so effortlessly. So Touch's dream girl, his obsession, was a porn actress. The all-American cutie pie who got off for a video camera. The screen had gone blank now, and Touch reached forward and shut off the television set. His face was set with a kind of smug defiance.

"There," he pronounced, "I told you she was something special. I told you that, didn't I?"

"Whew!" said Jerry Alt. "I thought I was beyond being turned on by that sort of stuff."

"Who is Ginger Shane?" Tom asked.

"She was an actress," Touch mumbled. "A beautiful actress."

"I guessed that much," Tom said. "But did you know her personally?"

"I never met her."

"But you say she's dead."

"Years ago," Touch said.

"How did she die?" Tom asked.

"She was killed," Touch said.

Jerry and Tom looked at one another. "Who killed her?" Jerry asked.

Touch paused over this for a time. "She did," he said finally. "She murdered herself."

Tom didn't understand. "What do you mean 'murdered herself'? You mean she committed suicide?"

Shree came to life at that moment. He whipped off the earphones and bounced to his feet. "There is no life and no death," he announced. "This is what you fail to understand, Touch. Ginger Shane is not dead. She is living."

"I don't think so," Touch said.

Shree was suddenly in a rage. "Then all our teachings are for nothing! All our time is wasted! If you do not believe in the reincarnation of the Self, then there is nothing to believe in. All life is senseless, unless it continues. Believe me. Ginger Shane is alive. Not in a flesh-and-blood way perhaps. But she is with us. Her spirit. The Self."

"I don't like hearing this shit," Touch said darkly.

Jerry Alt was on his feet. "I'm bushed. Think I'll turn in. It's been a long day. A lot of guys sitting around on the Carlton terrace announcing they got fifty percent of the budget. Hey, Touch, can you imagine what would happen if you put all those fifty percents together?"

Touch Lathrop said nothing. Maybe he couldn't imagine what would happen.

At two thirty in the morning, la Croisette was all but empty. The wind was damp with expectant rain and hints of old ghosts. Tom shivered slightly and pulled his jacket around him. On the sidewalk, against a fashionable jewelry store, dark forms huddled. These were guests of the festival who would never have to worry about the development deal or about how to get a good suite at the Carlton. In a town where the next meal was taken for granted and discussed endlessly, they were unique. They did not know if there would be another meal. The poor of the world, Tom thought, were so inconsiderate. They kept muddying the view for the rich.

He reached the Carlton and went into the tiny jewel box off the lobby that was the Petit Bar. It remained open all night. If you wanted the party never to end, then it could continue here. This evening a woman sat alone drinking out of a bottle of champagne. She was very drunk, barely able to sit up in her corner seat. Across the way, Clint Eastwood drank beer with his friend and producer, Fritz Manes. What was he doing here? Did he not understand that Touch Lathrop lusted after his stardom? Did Clint know Touch was more authentic, because Touch had actually killed people, while Clint was content merely to pretend? Probably not.

Tom wandered across the lobby and into the bar in search of his mystery woman. They could walk along the beach, and he could feel her lips and be reassured she was not Corinne Voss. But it was not a night for women of mystery. Jacques was on the verge of closing. Two beautiful French women sat deep in conversation at one of the tables. One was red-haired and wore a sequined floor-length evening gown. The other had light-brown hair pushed back into a ponytail. She wore a wool sweater and jeans shoved into leather boots. They were an interesting contrast. The redhead smiled, and said in English that if he wanted company, he might join them. He sat down. She said her name was Colette. She sat close to him, and he could see the spray of light freckles bouncing across her button nose. The other one was Catherine, who could not speak English but who nevertheless jabbered away constantly in a lilting, excited French. They were impressed when he ordered champagne. Colette's eyes grew very excited. She suggested he could only be a movie producer. Tom said he was not a producer, but he knew lots of them. Colette sat closer still and put her hand on his thigh and said that for five thousand francs he could have the both of them for the rest of the evening. For a moment, he was almost tempted. They were both alluring and, for a price, infinitely available. It would be fun to lose himself inside the two of them for a few hours. But then, no matter how long he staved it off, there would be the inevitable climaxes and he would be left drained and empty, the world coming in on him more relentlessly than before. He smiled sadly and said no. The sensual atmosphere disappeared in a flash. Capitalism took over. The two women were up and out of the bar like a shot. Tom watched them go, amazed by their speed and efficiency. Then he sat back and laughed.

He took the champagne bottle out onto the almost-deserted terrace. The Director still clung to his corner. The hands remained folded atop the ivory-handled cane. Even the sunglasses were still in place below the peeked fisherman's cap. However, the champagne bottle beside him was empty. Tom set his down on the table.

"Ah, reinforcements," the Director said. "Reinforcements are always welcome."

He reached forward and poured himself some of the champagne.

Tom said, "I didn't expect to find you here."

"I'm open for business twenty-four hours a day, Tom. What brings you out this late on a rainy night?"

"The endless search for true love."

"In the movie business, true love is simple enough. It's someone who will actually give you the money to make a film. That sort of commitment requires all the love in the world. There is, alas, little true love. My old friend Orson Welles used to come to the festival all the time. And the French loved him. Oh, how they loved him. But it was not *true* love. They would never give him money to make movies. Orson was loved for his legend, and that's no love at all. Too bad. If the great Orson could not find true love, could not make films, where does that leave the rest of us hacks?"

"It leaves you sitting on the Carlton terrace at three o'clock on a rainy morning, sipping champagne." Tom said. "And solving mysteries."

"Are we solving mysteries?"

"I think so."

"Very interesting. It doesn't beat getting drunk on champagne. But it will do. And just what sort of mystery is it?"

"I am trying to establish the identity of a beautiful woman at the Cannes Film Festival."

"There are many beautiful women at Cannes; very few of them are difficult to identify. Just the opposite, in fact. They are here to be identified. It is usually the only reason they are here."

"This one is different. This one makes a cameo appearance in the Carlton bar, disappears on a beach with a killer named Rakko after her. Then she turns up later, only this time she may be playing a new role, the part of Corinne Voss. The question is this: the mystery woman and Corinne Voss, are they one and the same? Or are they two different women? If they are different women, then there is not so much of a mystery. But if they are the same woman, then what is she up to?"

"And that is a concern of yours?"

"Let's say I'm curious."

The Director peered at him more closely in the darkness. "I can't quite figure you, Coward. Is this infatuation I'm witnessing? Or merely a pushy reporter after a story?"

"I'm not sure myself," Tom conceded. "Maybe I'm bored with the movies and life in general. Maybe it's just more interesting to play detective."

The Director's hands moved restlessly atop the cane. "Well, then, Coward, you'd better cut back on the champagne and the late nights. If you're a detective, you'd better get on the trail, stop hanging around old men who don't know much of anything."

"I'm not so sure about that. I'm not so sure you don't know more than you're telling me."

"I'm flattered, I must say, but I don't know where you get your ideas, Coward."

"At the moment it's mostly intuition."

The Director's face withered with contempt. "I don't think it's a mystery you're trying to solve. I think you're snooping in the dark corners looking for yourself. Why not stay out of the dark corners? There's nothing that needs to be shaken up at this late date. Not at this festival."

Tom rose from the table. "I'll leave you the champagne. We'll talk again."

"I don't want your champagne," the Director said but he made no move to hand the bottle to Tom. It sat there on the table, like a barrier between them. After a pause he said, "And we will not talk later. I am tired of talking to the press. I have told all my Cannes stories. Go away. Leave me alone."

"*Bonsoir,*" Tom said. He turned and started to move away.

The Director called after him. "Coward."

Tom looked back at the old man in the fisherman's cap, looming ominously out of one of the dark corners he had advised Tom to stay out of.

"Yes?"

"If I were you, I would be very careful."

It was almost dawn by the time he arrived back at the du Cap. The first gray light was seeping in through the shutters, revealing Lacy Bergen curled up on the sofa, a blanket thrown over her. She stirred as he pulled the blanket around her shoulders. She moved her lips, made some funny noises and rubbed her nose with her hand. He bent down and kissed her softly on the cheek. The lips turned upwards into the hint of a smile. Very inviting. He kissed the lips gently, thought of himself as a prince kissing a sleeping beauty then shook off the thought. He was a reporter with a movie star on his sofa, and he was getting horny. Time for bed. There had been a time, he mused as he pulled the covers over him, when he had been much more superficial about these things. Everything was beginning to take on too much importance. In the overall frivolousness of his life, that could only be a mistake. But then, he was a veteran of big mistakes. He would probably make a number of them before this festival was over. He thought of Lacy Bergen for a time and wondered how she had come to believe in the midst of the great adolescent flush that never takes reason into consideration, that he was the man for her. He could shake her up considerably if she chose to pursue that notion. Then he thought of Ginger Shane. It was funny how images became someone's true life. On film and on videotape you lived forever. On film you watched the dead live. Ginger Shane still excited and titillated, even though she had not existed for a decade. Curious. Even scary. Her sweet, pink face flashed before him as he drifted off into a restless, dream-clogged sleep. It suddenly occurred to him that Ginger Shane reminded him of Corinne Voss.

8

The press occupied the third level of the Palais des Festivals. Tom followed the smell of Gauloise smoke up the escalators. A blue-coated security guard ensured that he was indeed one of the three thousand journalists accredited to the festival. Once the guard was satisfied that the face on the laminated press pass bore at least a passing resemblance to his, he was allowed to pass into the broad foyer that, in another time and another place might have been called the press room. To the right were the rows of *casiers* that each morning were stuffed full of the press kits, releases, invitations, and announcements that are the lifeblood of reporters covering the festival. One could attend the 8:30 a.m. screening of a film in competition, then slip up to the press area, clean out the *casier*, sip a café au lait, disagree over the relative merits of the new film by Godard or Marco Ferrari or Jean-Jacques Beineix, or whoever else was fashionably controversial at that particular moment during the festival. Then, having aired one's views, finished one's coffee and inhaled the omnipresent Gauloise smoke, one could stroll a few paces to the morning press conference.

The press conferences at Cannes are a savage rite of passage for any filmmaker foolish enough to place his film into the official competition. The members of the French press in particular are political, dogmatic, committed to a point of view and just plain rude.

Therefore, the press conferences can be extravagantly vicious theater pieces. In fact, the conference room is set up like a theater, with a raised stage in front where the cast performs a daily version of the Spanish inquisition, the inquisitors cross-examining furiously from seats below the stage. At the rear of the room, television cameras meticulously record the productions. Questions are yelled, allegations made, threats voiced. Pandemonium reigns at these conferences, nothing is settled and absolutely no information is revealed. They are, for the most part, senseless sideshows, yet attending them is rather like watching a man being publicly beaten. You know it's disagreeable and that you should do something about it. But you don't move and you can't keep your eyes off the spectacle.

That morning as Tom Coward walked into the conference room looking for Paul Wheeler, an American journalist who lived in Paris and covered the French film world, the atmosphere was particularly volatile; the anticipation for the kill was running even higher than usual. The morning's film was French, which always helped to raise the temperature among the natives. What's more, it had been greeted with hoots of derision and walkouts at the morning screening. "It's about a man who starts walking down this rain-slicked street, and ninety minutes later he is still walking down this rain-slicked street," a journalist observed.

"Yes, I know," his companion said. "Wasn't it brilliant?"

Tom took a seat at the back of the room, facing the stage where Henri Behar, who would act as the festival's official interpreter for the press conference was ushering in the morning's victim. He was a small, intense-looking man, with long black hair shoved carelessly behind extraordinarily large ears. Henri introduced him as Jacques Noiret, the *auteur* of the disaster in question. As Noiret took his seat and adjusted the microphone on the table in front of him, the photographers, young toughs dripping with leather and cameras, elbowed each other out of the way to get a shot. Noiret, a veteran of various feedings to the lions of French film criticism, took it very much in stride. Eventually, the photographers were ordered away so that the journalists, now straining and frowning in their seats, could commence the throwing of questions. The photographers, as was their habit, ignored the orders and continued shooting. Finally, Henri lost patience, stood up and began to scream. Reluctantly, the photographers either moved away to the sides or squatted in front of the stage.

Tom saw Paul Wheeler sitting ahead of him. A chubby, walnut-colored man, Wheeler was taking great pains to look bored with the proceedings. His body was slumped low in the chair, one leg tossed over the other, his chin nodding into his chest. Wheeler had shaved his head and carefully clipped his mustache. He hid a pessimist's eyes behind dark, wire-rimmed glasses.

Jacques Noiret was explaining in somnolent French that his film was the story of a man obsessed, going toward madness, but trying to find another way. He was not, he said, trying to make a funny film.

"You could have fooled us," someone yelled. Noiret ignored the remark and lit another cigarette, using the end of the one he had just smoked.

Another questioner noted that no one liked the film. Lots of people had walked out of the morning screening.

Noiret shrugged. "The people who interest me are those who stayed."

The journalist sitting beside Paul Wheeler gathered his tote bag and notebook and got up and left. Tom hurried forward, crowded along the row and plunked himself down in the empty seat.

"For me," Jacques Noiret was saying, "the image is the message. I am not interested so much in story, plot, character. This is not a literary film because it is no longer a literary world. It is a world of the image. The image is what counts. That is what interests me. The rest is so much window dressing."

There was a hostile stir at this. Paul Wheeler grimaced and shook his brown head. "*Vendeur de merde,*" he murmured.

Tom tapped Wheeler on the shoulder. The critic's eyebrows shot up above the rims of his glasses in a show of abject horror.

"Oh, good God," he said, betraying the slight midwestern twang that still clung to his voice after ten years in Paris. "Tom Coward the pop journalist."

"Yes, indeed, the pop journalist. How are you, Paul? Long time no see."

"A very long time."

"I'm wondering if we could have a talk."

"Ah. Now, I don't mean to be rude," said Paul Wheeler jocularly. "But I have no interest whatsoever in talking to pop journalists. Pop journalists write shit. It is my mission in life to resist shit."

"It's just that some of us resist it less well than others," Tom said. "But let's have a talk anyway."

Someone in the audience of journalists yelled at Jacques Noiret in French. He again shrugged and lit another cigarette. "Daily reality does not really interest me," he allowed. "For me, film has to move toward a new reality. I have situated myself outside reality. Film is like opening the window to the beyond."

Immediately, Wheeler was on his feet, waving his hand. "That may be so," he yelled at the stage, "but that still does not explain why Monsieur Noiret made such a piece of *merde* as was shown at the Palais this morning. Can he tell us how that happened? Can he tell us how he became such a shit merchant in such an inordinately short time?"

Henri scowled and leaned into the microphone. "Paul, I don't think that question is at all appropriate."

Noiret's pale face flushed with anger. He threw down his cigarette and grabbed the microphone away from Henri. "You call me *merde*? You dare to call me *merde*?"

"I don't call you *merde* at all," Wheeler retorted calmly. "I call you shit. That is much worse than *merde*, believe me."

"You are *merde* – shit – yourself, Wheeler," he yelled back. "You are not even human. You are a critic. You are worse than that. You are a *lousy* critic. You have never liked my films."

"A man who does not like your films could not possibly be a lousy critic," Wheeler said reasonably.

"You are an asshole and a fag, and I do not know which is worse," Noiret shouted.

"*Asseyez-vous*," someone shouted from behind. "*Asseyez-vous*!"

"Does this mean," Wheeler went on, "that Monsieur Noiret is only going to insult a member of the press? He is not going to explain to us how he is able so constantly to make such unmitigated pieces of shit?"

A journalist sitting in front of Wheeler stood up screaming that Noiret was a great *auteur*, and that Wheeler had no right to insult him.

"You're the type who likes Steven Spielberg," Wheeler snarled.

The journalist threw a punch at him. Wheeler casually ducked the blow. Someone else was grabbing at his elbow. Tom got to his feet and knocked the second attacker away.

"It might be just as well to get the hell out of here," he said.

"Not until that shit merchant sitting up there wasting our time answers my question," Wheeler cried. "I am an important critic. He has an obligation to answer me."

"If you are an important critic, pigs can fly," Noiret shouted. Next thing, he was on his feet, howling abuse in French at everyone present. All pretense of calm was now lost. The audience began to boil over. In France, no one fails to take a side. Some members of the press, therefore, were urging Noiret to end Wheeler's life once and for all. Others were loudly suggesting that Paul Wheeler at this moment might very well be saving French cinema. The photographers, the pragmatic capitalists, understood only that conflict meant money. So they clawed and shoved at each other trying to get the shot that would capture conflict and ensure the money. Henri, the failed referee, was on his feet, calling for order. He might as well have cried for peace in Beirut.

"Fassbinder faggot!" Noiret called out.

"Imitator of Sydney Pollack movies!" Wheeler shouted back. "When do you sell out to Universal Pictures?"

At that, Noiret started to come down off the stage. Henri valiantly tried to restrain him.

"Will you get out of here?" Henri called out to the critic. "Will you please leave?"

Eventually, Tom managed to get Wheeler out of the press conference, down to the ground floor of the

Palais. Wheeler straightened his clothes and adjusted his glasses on the bridge of his nose.

"A fine morning's work," he said in a satisfied voice. "Another blow struck for art. Once more the shit merchants have been driven from the marketplace." He seemed to notice Tom for the first time since they left the Palais. "Thanks for your help back there, Coward. You know how to block a punch pretty good. But being with the popular press, I suppose that's the sort of thing one must know."

"One must also know where to find lunch. After beating hell out of the shit merchants, you look as though you could use a drink."

"Being as you are one of those pop writers, I will permit you to buy me lunch. Trash brings cash. Does it not?"

"Not fast enough for my taste," Tom said.

They had lunch at the Lido Plage, where they both ordered salade Niçoise, and Tom got a bottle of rosé. The Canadian contingent at the festival, which gathers each day for lunch at the Lido, was at a table adjacent to theirs. Tom waved to Helga Stephenson, Canada's gift to the Cannes festival. She smiled and raised a wineglass in salute.

"Oh, dear," Wheeler said unhappily, "I see you still like women."

"It's one of my many failings," Tom said.

"You understand, of course, that you don't *really* like them," Wheeler maintained. "You're just hiding behind the sham of heterosexuality because in a bourgeois society that's what's expected of you."

"I know," Tom said. "If only I could show the world the real me."

Wheeler wasn't listening. He was distracted by the action along the beach. He appreciatively noted a young blond Adonis strolling past, sighed over a dark-haired Greek god in a bikini that showed off the over-sized magnificence of his genitalia.

"That is beauty," he said adoringly. "True beauty. There is so little of it at this festival. It's all such shit. It gets worse every year. The Chabrol film is passable. But only just. The Antonioni, a disaster. Three hours of dripping taps. My God. The Japanese are boring, as usual. The Americans, commercial shit, of course. The only brilliant films are coming out of the Philippines. I was in Manila last year, fabulous stuff, all of it made by these darling handsome men with sensuous lips and long dark eyelashes. They're all mixed up with blood and murder, sex and art. Fascinating stuff." He took a long sip on his glass of rosé, smacked his lips together and again ran his eye along the beach .

"As you by now well know, Tom," he continued, "I abhor the commercial cinema, although I must confess I maintain a certain long-standing lust for the French heartthrob, Alain Delon. He is one of the most beautiful men God ever put on this earth. He used to come down here in the early days, did you know? A beautiful young beachboy. Perfection itself. Everyone lusted after him.

"But then, of course, in those days, one was not after sex. One was after art. Cahiers du Cinema was just coming into flower. André Bazin was writing about cinema. He was bringing along the young Truffaut, and Godard. By then, all that Left Bank intellectual crap was in decline. You know, all those shitty French writers who sat around in the thirties pontificating over Pernod at some café along the Seine. By 1950, who was listening to them? They weren't listening to themselves. They were all running around yelling and screaming about Algeria or something. And, anyway, they didn't turn out to be such hotshots after all. Even André Malraux finally admitted *Le Temps du Mépris* just didn't make it. And have you read *Man's Fate* lately?" He made a face. "Makes you gag."

He finished off his rosé, and Tom quickly poured him more. "That asshole Jacques Noiret was right about one thing this morning. It is no longer a world of literature. It is a world of the image. Therefore, the real writing no longer has to do with literature or ideas, it has to do with images. That's why the film critic has emerged as the preeminent figure in modern-day letters. It's as Malraux said. We draw images powerful enough to define our nothingness. Well, these days, the images come from the cinema. I must say, Tom, this rosé goes down very well indeed. Ah, take a look at that one, will you? Italian and hairy. But with a waist you could put your hands around. Good wine. Hot sun. Cute boys. It makes you understand that the pleasures of the flesh must sometimes take precedence over the demands of the mind. Malraux again: 'The essentials are the external, the realm of sex, the realm of blood.' On a day like this, who could disagree? At this festival we go to the movies. But we seek after the sex and blood. Don't you think?"

"In pop journalism, Paul, we want only the sex and the blood. They are the staples. Without them we perish."

Wheeler removed his glasses. His eyes gave him the air of a man who could rouse himself to care about nothing. For a critic, the eyes were perfect. "And what are we looking for this noontime, Tom? Sex or blood?"

"Today, it's the sex," Tom said. "Corinne Verneuil. She is now known as Corinne Voss."

Wheeler attempted to hide his surprise by replacing the dark glasses. "She's Dieter Voss's – well, I suppose the loose term for it would be wife. "

"You know her, then."

"I know everyone in Paris. Or, more to the point, I know *of* everyone in Paris. I would not say so much that I know Corinne as I would say I know of Corinne. What can I say? She is new. She spills to great effect out of very expensive clothes. I'm sure she would cheerfully suck Dieter's cock on the Champs Elysées, and I'm sure that's exactly what she did in order to capture him in marriage. Certainly she was a nobody before Dieter married her. Some sort of model. Maybe a coke whore. Who knows? She was hardly setting the town on its ear."

"Dieter says she was a very famous model. Everyone in town was lusting after her."

"Dieter would say that. The man lies about everything. But it's simply not true. She just appeared out of nowhere. I remember asking around about her when I first saw her on Dieter's arm. Nobody knew a thing." He held up a finger. "Ah. Wait a moment. That's not quite true. I heard somewhere that her mother was American. Now I heard that only because Americans are such a big thing in France at the moment. My God, American garbage culture is polluting the world. That's why Dieter is so popular at the moment, I suppose. He is making American garbage such as *Saudi*, which, incidentally, I hear is a piece of shit. Even the Americans won't touch it."

"You hear that reliably?"

"My sources, while not impeccable, are very good on these things," Wheeler said. "There was a screening yesterday afternoon. Apparently several American distributors emerged throwing up the foie gras they had consumed at lunch. When a film is so bad that not even the Americans can stomach it, it is very bad indeed."

Tom took all this in while Wheeler busied himself ordering a second bottle of rosé. By now the sun was hard and bright in the flawlessly blue sky. The beaches were full of half-naked men and women neglecting world cinema in favor of a suntan. Packs of photographers cruised the shoreline, shirts open, cameras slung around their necks. There was a certain unspoken etiquette at work here. One did not indiscriminately shoot photos of naked breasts, although certainly there were hundreds from which to choose. One waited until a young woman signaled her desire to have herself exploited. One of the young women on the beach began now to play through the ritual. She was brown and slim, with a tangled mop of blond hair, a tiny white bikini and pounds of gold chains and bracelets. She stood, casually stretched and began to apply suntan lotion to an unbelievably flat tummy. There was one photographer, and then there were five. The young woman, almost certainly a model who wished to become an actress, smeared suntan lotion across the golden expanse of her arms. Shutters clicked furiously to record the moment.

Tom took his eyes off her and said to Paul Wheeler, "Do you know Dieter Voss well?"

Wheeler reacted with horror. "How could a man like me possibly know a man like him? He is a *vendeur de merde* of the first order. I am not seen with such merchants of shit, not if I can help it, that is."

"But when you are, do you see Dieter?"

"Of course. I must say he is rather legendary around Paris. The story is interesting even if his movies are not. "

"And what is the story?"

"Dieter was born in Leipzig three years after the war ended. Apparently he showed some promise, although I can't imagine what kind of promise. Anyway, he ended up at the Lodz Film School in Poland. This was after the heyday of Wadja, Polanski and Skolimowski, but it was still a very special place to learn about film. Dieter must have skipped the classes. Anyway, he no sooner graduated than he decided Communism was not for him. He slipped across the Polish border and headed for Paris, where he got involved with the rough trade around Les Halles. Some say he was a pimp for a time, though he vehemently denies this. There is little doubt, though, that he got involved in the porn trade, mostly I think as a distributor, selling films to the theaters in the area."

Tom interrupted. "Dieter has a slightly different version of events."

"I'm sure he does. What does he say?"

"He says he escaped across the Berlin wall, dodging spotlights and bullets so that he could pursue the glories of capitalism. He claims to have gotten started by distributing art films."

Paul Wheeler screamed with laughter. "Oh, dear, dear," he said, with tears in his eyes. "He really has no shame. The Berlin wall. *Art* films. Gawd! Well, don't listen to any of it. Everyone in Paris knows the real story. At the time Dieter was peddling art to the porno houses of Les Halles, he met an Israeli named Ygal Ben-Josef. He apparently had a very successful hashish business around the tourist haunts of Eilat. But he was having trouble getting rid of the money. Now the story goes that Ygal Ben-Josef was very impressed with the German Dieter Voss. Dieter could stay up all night in the Les Halles bars, fix Ygal up with the best girls and still come across as quite the little capitalist. Just what Ygal Ben-Josef was looking for. Dieter wanted to make movies. Ygal Ben-Josef wanted to launder his hashish money. It is said Ben-Josef set up Dieter Voss in the movie business; Israeli gangster money financing a German pimp living in Paris. And we wonder why the cinema is such shit."

Now the golden-haired girl removed her bikini top, slowly drawing it down the length of her breasts, until her large brown nipples were revealed. This threw the photographers into a frenzy. They were like sharks around the sewage drain from a morgue. The ceremonial breast-baring swelled their ranks. There must have been fifty of them now. The herd of paparazzi in turn drew mobs who pressed against the railing above the beach, hundreds of blank-faced tourists straining to witness the moment of tawdry glamour. Through it all, the actress, the object of the attention, pretended that absolutely nothing was happening. Her face remained in sullen repose as she poured more suntan lotion into her palms then applied it to one round breast and then the other. It was an amazing performance. There must have been two thousand people watching her. But she was all alone, caught deep within the mystery of herself. Or at least that was the part she was required to play this afternoon on the beach.

"Now, however, times have changed," Paul Wheeler was saying, "and so have Dieter's partners. At least that's the scuttlebutt around Paris. A certain Egyptian gentleman named Mehdi Abbas is said to be financing *Saudi*. Apparently this Abbas is a truly nasty individual, into heroin and other deadly substances throughout the Middle East. Apparently he sells the stuff to the Iranians and the Iraqis, who go through it by the kilo on the battlefield. It's a multimillion-dollar business. Abbas masquerades as an international financier, headquartered in the Netherlands Antilles, where he can get his money laundered with absolutely no hassle. He supposedly acts as a middleman for Arab capital in the West. It's a very good cover. But it's mostly his capital he is investing. He also happens to be a movie fan. Or at least he is attracted to what I suppose he sees as the glamor of movies. Make a film. It's a great way to mix commerce, shit and laundered money. It is from such recipes that movies like *Saudi* get cooked up.

"With a setup like that, Dieter must be sitting pretty."

"Not necessarily. Only rumors again. But I've heard talk around that Abbas and Dieter had a falling out. Don't ask me for details. I don't know any. And there may be nothing to it. Except that if *Saudi* is as bad as I hear it is, Abbas could be miffed. Not even wealthy Egyptian gangsters are very happy about losing forty million dollars." Wheeler finished off his rosé, looked regretfully at the second empty bottle and pushed his chair away from the table.

"Anyway, there is a sense of impending disaster in the air. It's mixed in with the salt and the Paco Rabanne and the suntan lotion. Nothing stinks at Cannes worse than the corpse of a dead movie. But enough of this. I must be going, Coward. There is a Thai film I hear is absolutely wonderful. It begins in a few moments. Enough sex and blood. Back to art. Besides, I hear the director is a young kid in his twenties, awfully cute and willing to do just about anything in order to get his film on the festival circuit. Sounds promising. Thanks for lunch. Oh, my God, look at that pale thing. English probably. Run away from Eton, no doubt. A boy wanting to play with the men. I should live so long."

"One more thing," Tom said as Paul Wheeler stood up. "What do you know about the old guy they call the Director?"

"That old blowhard who sits around the terrace drinking champagne and carrying on about the days when he knew Robert Mitchum? A phony. The terrace is full of them."

"Know anything about where he comes from?"

"He lives in Paris, I know that much. From the looks of him he gets up every morning and starts eating éclairs."

"Somebody said he once was a director. Or a producer."

"I heard director," Paul Wheeler said. "An American director. Of what, though? Maybe he directed traffic."

"But you don't know who he is?"

"Well, he ain't Orson Welles, that's for sure. Who knows? Maybe he did television. Nobody remembers television directors. Nobody cares. I don't think he's been coming to the festival as long as he makes out. Maybe five or six years. No more than that. I've been here for the past fifteen, and I certainly don't remember him."

Paul Wheeler started off, then paused and turned. "Oh. You know what I forgot to mention?"

"What?"

"Curious rumor. Never thought too much about it until now. Dieter Voss. Someone once told me he was arrested. For murder. A long time ago. Not convicted, mind you, just arrested."

On the beach, the golden girl abruptly pulled on her bikini top and flipped back down on her pallet, leaving the photographers shooting away at thin air. For a moment, the paparazzi swirled around in confusion. A few called out entreaties, urging her to pose again. But she shook her mane, inspected her fingernails and would have nothing further to do with them. Eventually, the photographers began to break up, drifting away in clumps along the beachfront in search of more acquiescent prey.

A few moments later, the girl on the beach sat up again. Tom caught sight of her face, oval-shaped, puffy and somehow brutalized. Tom finished his rosé, and got up from the table, vaguely wondering why she had done it. Why anyone did it.

Ostensibly, Corinne was shopping in Nice for the afternoon. Dieter understood beautiful women who wished to shop. Besides, Dieter was much too preoccupied with the problems of desperately trying to find an American distributor for *Saudi* to worry about his wife for an afternoon. She drove the red Fiat Croma that Dieter had leased for her along the wide boulevard of the Promenade des Anglais and saw the magnificent dome of the Hotel Négresco ahead. She left the car with an appreciative doorman, hurried inside and across the Salon Royal, where a ton of Baccarat crystal dangled above the world's largest Aubusson carpet. The Négresco sheltered one of the world's great restaurants, the Chantecler. But this afternoon as she reached the elevators she had no time for the visual wonders of one France's most estimable hotels. She stepped off the elevator at the fourth floor and hurried along the corridor. At the end of the hall she found suite 455 and knocked on the double doors. A moment later, the door opened a crack. An eye blinked at her.

"*Il m'attend,*" she said.

"*Bien sûr.*" The door opened, and she stepped past the slim, muscular guard, dressed in a superbly cut Italian suit. He carried an Uzi submachine gun.

The decor inside was muted gold. The ceilings were coffered. The fireplace was seventeenth century. Mehdi Abbas, wearing a white floor-length terrycloth caftan, stood in the center of the suite, sipping at herbal tea from a china cup. Seated on a nearby Louis XVI sofa was a guard who could have been the brother of the man who opened the door. He was similarly impeccably dressed in a dark Italian suit. On his lap lay an Uzi submachine gun. Over by the windows that looked across the promenade out onto the Baie des Anges stood a third guard, also with an Uzi.

Mehdi Abbas was a tall, florid man with large shiny black eyes and thickening jowls that threatened to double an otherwise strong chin. The overall impression was of a soft, almost delicate, olive-skinned man, a Sybarite, in restless search of the very good life. He took great pride in the gracefulness of his movements. He loved to watch his small, pudgy hands carefully pick the china cup off its saucer and deliver it to his mouth. He desired that everything in his life match the grace he brought to his movements. He had admired his countryman Sadat for his grace. It was the sort of grace Westerners also appreciated. He had admired Sadat even as he quietly put up some of the money that financed his assassination.

She stood a few paces from him, removing her sunglasses but otherwise not moving. She wore high-heeled red pumps and a short, white skirt that set off the darkness of her legs and excited him.

"I had a long night at the gaming tables," Abbas said with a sigh. "I lost all sorts of illicitly earned money. I only hope the French can appreciate how I am fueling their economy."

"I didn't expect you quite so soon," she said. "I thought we agreed we weren't to see each other, that we would use the go-between. I would get messages to you through him."

Abbas shrugged elaborately. "Forgive me, my dear, I was impatient to see you. I am on my way to St. Tropez. The yacht's there. We are going to bring it around to Cannes for a few days. It would be difficult to talk to you then. This way, who will suspect anything?"

She came up to him and kissed his mouth.

"What are you wearing underneath the dress?"

"What do you think I am wearing?"

"Nothing," he said.

"Then –" she smiled, "– that is what I am wearing."

"Let me see."

"Later."

"I want to make love."

She danced away from him. "Not in front of the guards."

"In my particular business, the guards are a necessity. They are used to it."

"I want to do dirty things to you, darling. I don't want witnesses." She smiled. "Do you have more tea?"

He motioned to one of the guards who promptly poured from an elaborate silver service.

"You are a terrible tease," he said. "All the beautiful women in the western world are willing to sleep with me. A little coke, champagne. A ride on the yacht. A nice dress. And they can't wait to open their legs for this poor Egyptian son of the desert. But you? You give me a bad time. Why do you do that?"

"Perhaps I want you to suffer a bit for passion, darling. Perhaps I want you to know that I cannot be bought for a little coke or a nice dress or a ride on your yacht." She paused for a moment, then said, "Dieter thinks you know all about him. He is convinced you killed Sir Cecil House because he stole your money."

"And what do you think, my love? Do you think good-natured Mehdi Abbas would stoop to such a thing?"

"I thought we were agreed that Dieter would be destroyed. We never said anything about killing him."

"No, we didn't." Abbas shrugged elaborately. "However, Cecil House was another matter altogether. Dieter, well, Dieter is a fool, put on this earth to be manipulated by people stronger than he. Dieter merely was a pawn for Sir Cecil's embezzlement scheme. It's only fair that perhaps Sir Cecil would pay a little more heavily for his miscalculation."

"And Dieter?"

"You are worried about your poor Dieter now, are you? A little blood is spilled. It makes you a little less anxious for revenge, does it?"

"Not at all. I want him finished. Not dead. Just finished."

"Then we will finish him for you, my love."

"That's part of the reason I'm here," she said. "He may have done the job for us already. *Saudi* is a terrible disaster. The Americans won't touch it. He has some idea that he can save himself by signing the American actress Lacy Bergen. But I don't think she's very enthusiastic."

He gazed at her, his face losing some of its good-natured ambiance. "Rakko is concerned about you," he said softly. There were smudges of suspicion around his eyes. She knew she must be careful with him.

"Why should Rakko be concerned?" She accepted the tea from the guard and made a production of sipping at it.

"It is Rakko's business to be concerned, I suppose. It is his business to kill and to be concerned. He thinks you need protection."

"I need protection? Perhaps I need protection from Rakko."

Abbas laughed heartily. "Nobody, my love, could protect you from Rakko."

She put the tea aside and ran her hands up and down her bare arms. "I tell you, Mehdi, I just want to get this over with."

"Do you love me?" He came over so that he was standing close to her.

She nodded, kissed his mouth again. "You know I do."

"But it surely is more than passionate love for your Mehdi that drives you to see your husband humiliated and destroyed. Your own husband?"

"I told you, I have my reasons. You have yours. What does it matter beyond that?"

"That is what makes my friend Rakko so uneasy. This woman who wants her husband ruined but doesn't say why. Rakko finds this very curious indeed." Then Abbas sighed, smiled and seemed to relax. "But you see what a fool I am? The prospect of your love, my dear, that is what keeps me going. "

She came into his arms, her face pleading. "Then let's get away now, Mehdi. The two of us. Without the guards. Without Rakko. Dieter is finished. He cannot possibly recover from *Saudi*. It's over and you have won."

"But it's hardly a victory. I win but I don't even play the game, and meantime Dieter gets away with five million of my hard-earned dollars. No, he must do some more paying first. We will await the premiere of *Saudi*. If it truly is a disaster, then it will be time to have a little chat with Dieter about certain matters, including what he has done with my money. Until that time, my love, you must be patient."

She looked disappointed. "All right," she said. "I will try to be patient."

"And do me a favor, will you, my truest love? Try not to fuck your husband too much. Save some for your Mehdi."

She went down to the Négresco's side entrance and waited while they brought the Fiat around. When she slipped into the driver's seat, she laid her forehead against the steering wheel. For the first time she began to realize what it was she had gotten herself into. She had been confident of her ability to control both men but now she realized that Mehdi was using her. This was not what she had planned, she told herself. Could she possibly play cat and mouse with a man like Mehdi Abbas and still be that naive? As she drove away from the hotel, she tried to push the question out of her mind.

The adjoining door opened, and Rakko stepped in. Mehdi Abbas watched him accept a cup of tea from one of the guards. Rakko's mouth was a straight, noncommital line, the dark glasses in place. He was like a machine at rest. Pump a franc into him, Mehdi thought, and he would go out and kill someone for you.

"You heard?" Abbas asked. "Certainly you heard. You cannot speak, my good friend, but you can understand. Yes, yes, I share your suspicions of her. But she is so beautiful, and in bed, my friend, it is like trying to put out a fire. So one takes the chance. But naturally we kill the Kraut fucker. Nobody steals five cents from me, let alone five million dollars. Otherwise, I would never stay in business. Besides, I like the idea of violence. You and I, we play in a rough world, my friend. Why not use the roughest of methods when appropriate? Otherwise, we might just as well go out and play the stock market." He shoved his hands deeply into the pockets of his robe. "So, we will have some fun. We will scare the shit out of our duplicitous Kraut friend and his little wife who would have him ruined but not dead. Tomorrow night is the premiere of *Saudi,* is it not?"

Rakko nodded.

"Good," Mehdi Abbas said with satisfaction. "We will prepare an amusing surprise."

9

"This will be the greatest evening in the history of cinema," Dieter Voss announced into a radio reporter's microphone. "I want to dedicate this evening to Wilhelm, my boyhood friend who died helping me escape over the Berlin wall so many years ago. Soviet border guards gunned him down. He died in my arms. And do you know what his last words were to me? He said, 'Go for freedom, Dieter.' Tonight, with the premiere of *Saudi*, we salute Wilhelm and his sacrifice, and we celebrate freedom!"

The radio reporter hurried off and Rudy John Karras, hanging off the end of Dieter's elbow, nodded eagerly. "Those are beautiful words, Dieter. I think everyone will be inspired by those words. It's really incredible what's happening here. I've never seen anything quite like it. We got press flying in from all over the world for this. I spent the whole day on the blower just saying no to people. There just aren't enough invitations to go around. This is the hottest ticket in town."

A couple of people standing too close to ignore the statement smiled dutifully. But something was very wrong. Considering Dieter was hosting the greatest evening in the history of cinema, everyone was amazingly subdued. The guests shuffled on the lime-green carpet of the Eden Roc pavilion, studied the trompe l'oeil paintings and downed cocktails. They crowded along the buffet tables and nibbled at the salad, the smoked daurade, the lobster ravioli, the carpaccio, and the crayfish in grape leaves. But their chatter lacked excitement; there was no sense of anticipation in the air. There was rather a feeling of dread, as though a bad accident was about to be witnessed.

Tom felt the tension as soon as he entered the pavilion and started looking around for Dieter. He found him surrounded by a wall of tuxedo-clad security guards.

"Tom, I was beginning to think you were never going to come," Dieter called out cheerfully.

"I just got back from town," Tom said when he had waded through the guards. "There are five hundred demonstrators raising hell in front of the Palais. They're threatening to close down the festival."

Rudy John Karras frowned, as though trying to figure out whether this news constituted bad publicity for *Saudi*. Dieter kept the rictus grin, which he had adopted for the evening, propped open.

"Nonsense, Tom," he said with the merry, reassuring voice he seemed incapable of losing. "The authorities have assured me they can contain any trouble. Now, relax, my friend. Enjoy yourself. This will be a magnificent evening, you will see." He spotted Jerry Alt, squeezing his way through the crowd. "Jerry. How are you? So good to see you!" He threw his arm around Alt, who blushed at the unexpected attention. He wore a luxuriant white dinner jacket that did not go with his battered countenance. Jerry's head was out of place on his own body.

"Hey, Dieter, I was on the Carlton terrace this afternoon. You know those guys; everyone's got fifty percent of the budget. Can you imagine what would happen if we put all those fifty percents together?"

Dieter smiled wanly. "I'm afraid I don't quite understand, Jerry."

"Hey, it's just a little joke there, Dieter. Actually, everyone's talking about one thing and one thing only. They're talking *Saudi*, Dieter. It's the hot number at this festival. You know what they're talking, Dieter? They're talking hit. That's what they're talking. You hear that kind of talk and you hear the cash registers start to ring. Hot, hot, hot, Dieter. I feel the heat."

"It will be a wonderful evening, Jerry. A great evening."

Dieter drifted off through the crowd to greet three of the American stars of *Saudi*.

Someone close to Tom said, "Where's John Philip Law?"

Someone else said, "John Philip Law? That guy from the sixties? Why would you want to see John Philip Law?"

"He's the star of *Saudi*."

"How do you make a forty-million-dollar movie when your star is John Philip Law?"

"I hear John Gielgud has a cameo."

"Yeah. In this movie he plays a cameo herder."

Corinne slipped by wearing a quite astonishing black-silk jaquard gown. It had no back and plunged to the waist in front. The form-fitting skirt was slit to the thigh. She kissed Tom.

"You look –"

Her smile was a tease. "How do I look for you, Tom? Dazzling? Stunning? Alluring?"

"All of the above."

"You cannot keep your hands off me?"

"I think I had better try. Dieter might not be pleased."

She raised an eyebrow. "On the other hand, Dieter might be very pleased."

"I'm not so sure. Has he hired all these security guards for his protection, or yours?"

"I guess everyone is concerned about terrorists. Do you think there is a great deal of security?"

"Well, this is a movie premiere, not a meeting of OPEC oil ministers."

"Darling, he doesn't want people shooting me," she smiled. "Fucking is something else altogether." She pecked him on the cheek. "*Ciao*. I must mingle so that the investors can look down the front of my dress."

She disappeared into the crowd as Lacy Bergen made her entrance. Lacy wore a champagne evening skirt with a white-lace top, mostly obscured by a matching jacket. She was flanked by two young men the size of small houses. They were dressed in white evening jackets. Lacy had brought along her own security guards. When the photographers leapt at her, the boys were only too happy to push them back. Lacy posed dutifully. Tom came over and handed her a glass of the Tattinger the waiters were pouring like water. The bodyguards looked at him as though he might have dumped arsenic into the champagne.

"Who are your friends?" Tom asked.

"One's Tony and one's François." Both men beamed down at her. "But I don't know which one is Tony and which one is François. They don't seem to speak a word of English."

"I feel left out of all this. I gave my security force the night off."

"My mother hired them," Lacy said with a grimace. "She's worried about my safety. At least she says she is worried about my safety."

"Where is the beautiful and charming Mrs. Bergen this evening?"

"We had a fight. She says she has a splitting headache. She's not coming."

"The fight didn't have anything to do with me, by any chance?"

"As a matter of fact, it did. My mother thinks we're sleeping together."

"What did you tell her?"

"I told her we weren't sleeping together – yet."

"Oh, great," Tom said.

She took his arm. "Tell me I look beautiful and desirable."

"You look beautiful and desirable."

"And you look very handsome in that tux, Tom. You really do"

"It was made for another me. The one who lived twenty pounds ago."

"Do you know what I think?"

"I'm afraid to ask."

"I think there is something mystical about us. Something that was destined to be."

"You are destined to give me an interview in which you relate the unbridled joys of virginity. I am destined to sell it to newspapers around the world. This is our fate, Lacy. Our destiny."

"You're afraid of commitment."

"I'm afraid of you."

"Don't worry, Tom," she said, pulling him close. "I'll protect you. I'll protect you with all my heart and soul."

Tony and François, did not look happy about their charge hugging tall strangers in ill-fitting evening clothes. They scowled darkly at Tom. He drank more champagne.

Dieter announced that it was time to depart for the Palais in Cannes. He had hired a fleet of limousines to ferry his guests to the premiere. The cars had begun drawing up outside the front entrance to the hotel.

The queue stretched out the gate and down the highway.

Tom and Lacy rode in the lead limo with Dieter and Corinne. Tony and François somehow folded their enormous bulks into the front beside the chauffeur. Lacy was not happy, particularly when Corinne crossed her legs, exposing them to the thigh, and leaned forward so that her breasts nearly fell out of her dress.

"Careful, my darling," Dieter said with a laugh. "You're about to show Tom everything. And we haven't even made a deal yet for his wonderful book."

Corinne sat up straighter. "There would be nothing he hasn't seen already, *chérie*. Tom saw me at the poolside the other day."

"Tom, you wicked devil," Dieter said, smiling. "As soon as my back is turned."

"It's all right, Dieter. I was topless, too."

Everyone laughed. Except Lacy. She shot Tom a suspicious look.

"You know what I was thinking just this morning, Tom?"

"No, Dieter. I never know what you're thinking at any time of the day, not even in the morning."

"I was thinking about your book, of course. And I was thinking Lacy here would be perfect for the part of Stormy Willis. You know, the girl you loved."

At that, Lacy's eyes lit up. "Oh, Tom, what would you think?"

Tom looked out the window at the traffic. "I think we are going to have trouble getting to the world premiere of *Saudi*, never mind making my book into a movie."

The motorcade had reached la Croisette. The traffic was hopeless, despite the gendarmes' attempts to clear a path. The limos slowed to a crawl as they approached the Palais des Festivals. Tom noticed battle-ship-gray buses lining the side streets off la Croissette. Undoubtedly they were full of *Compagnies Republicaines de Sécurité* – CRS riot police. Lacy noticed them, too. She turned to Tom.

"What are the demonstrators upset about?"

"I think they regret that the United States exists." Dieter sighed. "They pray for a world of chaos and anarchy."

"And what do you pray for, Dieter?" Tom asked.

"I pray for a world that goes to see *Saudi*," Dieter replied.

"I just don't see why everyone can't live in peace," Lacy said.

"And go to Lacy Bergen movies," Tom added.

"If they live in peace, they don't even have to go to my movies."

"And who says Hollywood won't make sacrifices for world peace?"

"Oh, Tom," she said impatiently. "You're such a cynic. Sometimes it really is tiresome."

"I am not a cynic," Tom objected. "I know all the words to 'We Are the World.' "

Ahead, they could hear the sound of chanting and shouting. The crowds were beginning to thicken along the street. Suddenly there were helmeted riot police everywhere and a lot of faceless young men waving placards and screaming. Someone managed to slam his fist against the hood of the car.

"Will we be all right?" Corinne looked worried.

"We will be fine, my darling. The CRS are wonderful at this sort of thing. They enjoy nothing better than to kick the shit out of rioters. The rioters know this. They will behave."

A kid wearing a T-shirt and jeans whacked his placard against the windshield. Everyone jumped.

The demonstrators had been pushed back across the wide Esplanade Georges Pompidou in front of the Palais. They were held back by steel fences and phalanxes of club-carrying riot police. Perhaps two dozen tuxedo-clad photographers and cameramen waited along the red carpet that swept up to the foot of the steep stairs leading to the Grand Auditorium Lumière, where *Saudi* was to be screened.

The limousine crunched to a halt at the curbside as floodlights began revolving into the deepening purple of the evening sky. The chauffeur yanked open the door with a flourish. Corinne was first out, followed by a beaming Dieter Voss. He took Corinne's arm, and the photographers and cameramen went crazy getting photographs.. Dieter was in his element. This was his moment of glory. His face was flushed, and his eyes had a special sparkle. He drew Corinne to him. His smile was as wide as the possibilities for international cinema. He waved jauntily at the crowd.

There were not a great number of movie fans present. Furthermore, they did not know much about Dieter Voss's background.

"Yankee fooker!" they cried. "Capitalist asshole. Pawn of fascists!"

Dieter, in his exuberance, turned the catcalls into songs of praise.

"This will be a wonderful night," he chanted between smiles. "This will be a great night."

Inside the car, Lacy watched the scene and frowned. Then she turned to Tom.

"Okay, kiddo. Hang on real tight." she said. "You ain't seen nothing yet."

Lacy bounced out of the car, Tony and François hurrying after her. If Lacy was not much else at the age of twenty-one, she was at least a star. And the gods tend to make things work at the right moment for stars. Therefore, the lights, as though by some divine prearrangement, swung around and caught her just as she shrugged off her jacket. Beneath it there was a double strand of pearls, and there was the scooped white-lace top, held up by shoestring straps. Beneath the lace there was only Lacy Bergen, star of the silver screen and, in this light, practically naked from the waist up. The French press would later comment that the real riot began when the photographers saw what *La Vierge Americaine* was wearing. The CRS riot police had to wade in to help a frantic Tony and François hold off half-crazed paparazzi. The photographers, frothing and cursing, were finally driven back across the esplanade, but not without a fight, and not without a few bloody noses and torn evening jackets.

The two bodyguards hustled the shaken but still smiling Lacy forward toward the entrance. Dieter, a genius at spur-of-the-moment improvisation, maneuvered himself so that he was between two of the most beautiful and alluringly dressed women at the festival. The light from the flashguns could have lit a small French town for a week.

Eventually, everyone was seated inside the Grand Auditorium Lumiere. There was a welcoming speech by an excited Dieter, whose English at such moments was not entirely appropriate. Therefore, Tom, sitting in the audience beside Lacy, was not sure exactly what he said. Something about *Birth of a Nation* and now *Saudi*. The audience shifted uneasily. The lights went down. The curtain opened. And the disaster began.

Actually, considering what was unfolding on the screen, the people in the audience behaved themselves pretty well. At the press screening the next morning, journalists and critics would be bolting for the doors in disgust. But this audience maintained a certain dignity throughout the first twenty minutes of the movie. It was only then that laughter began to break out in all the wrong places. After forty-five minutes it became apparent to the Middle Eastern members of the audience that fun was being poked at not only them, but at their religion and their customs, by the American adventurers who were supposed to be having such a rollicking good time gunning down Arab bad guys. Someone finally yelled an objection, although Tom, dozing a bit in his supremely comfortable seat, missed it. He leaned over to Lacy.

"What did he say?"

"Something about 'an insult to the Arab peoples of the world.' "

The French have a uniquely nasty form of hissing that they employ at movies they find particularly repugnant. That hissing now started up. There was also old-fashioned Anglo-Saxon booing. An hour or so into the movie and you could hear the thump-thump of seats all over the theater as people vacated them. Tom stuck it out to the very end, listened attentively to the hissing, the booing and even some scattered applause – some people, apparently, would do anything in exchange for Tattinger champagne on the pavilion. A bit dazed by it all, he trailed Lacy up the aisle toward the exit.

"What did you think?" he asked her, as they emerged into the foyer outside the theater.

"God," she said. "It was even worse than one of my movies."

"At least your movies get released. That mess is never going to see the light of day in North America."

Rudy John Karras hurried past. He did not look well. Dieter approached, mopping the sweat off his forehead with a large white handkerchief.

"Well, what do you think, eh, you two?" he said. "We have a very controversial picture on our hands. No doubt about it. You either love it or hate it. No one is ambivalent about *Saudi*. It is quite an evening. A great evening."

Jerry Alt walked by and Dieter grabbed his arm. "What do you think, Jerry? A great audience picture, is it not? Lots of action, lots of spectacle. Something for everyone."

Even with the deep tan, Jerry's face looked ashen. "Something for everyone," he mumbled.

Dieter took him by the arm and led him toward the door. Tom glanced at Lacy, rolled his eyes, and the two of them followed. Lacy's bodyguards crowded around.

Outside, at the bottom of the steep grade of the stairs, the demonstrators continued to mill about, pushed back and forth by the police. As the guests began to emerge from the screening, a cry went up. The pushing became more intense. The riot police, lulled by the lazy ebb and flow of the demonstration, were caught off guard. Unexpectedly a flying wedge of students broke through the line, bolting for the stairs and the beautifully dressed people emerging from the theater. Then more students got through, and abruptly the police were losing control of the situation. Tom watched as the demonstators leapt up the stairs.

Dieter and Jerry, who were directly below Tom, had come to a stop. There were all sorts of security people around, but they were at a distance. Tom saw Dieter take his arm off Jerry's shoulder. A moment later he saw the gunman. He was small and curly-haired, eyes bulging with a combination of excitement and fear. He was among the students. Or he was among them until he raised the pistol and fired it. The gunshot stopped the oncoming students, froze them to the spot, as though they were already posing for the statue commemorating their escapade. The freeze lasted only a moment. Then they were tumbling away in alarm, trying to escape the gunfire.

Now the gunman was exposed and alone, his armed raised. He fired again. There were screams of fear and panic. Security guards reached frantically in-side tuxedos, fumbling for guns. For a moment Tom thought the gunman was shooting at Dieter. And Dieter stood motionless, his arms outstretched as though to receive the bullets. Except he never got them. It was Jerry Alt who stumbled back, the front of his white dinner jacket splashed red with blood. He fell against Tom.

"Oh, Jesus Christ," he said.

Tom cradled him in his arms and lowered him to the steps. In the distance he could hear the harsh blare of police and ambulance klaxons. Jerry Alt tried to say something, but his mouth only moved a couple of times.

"It's okay, Jerry," Tom said. "It's all right."

But it was not all right. Jerry Alt looked up at Tom. His eyes were glazed. He struggled a bit on the steps, as though trying to hold the life inside his body. It was then that Tom saw the key. It must have fallen from Jerry's pocket. Without thinking, he reached down and picked it up. Then Jerry's mouth went slack and he died, right there on the steps of the Palais des Festivals after having just seen the last – and worst – movie of his life.

On the esplanade, the students had broken through the steel barricades and were fighting with the riot police who hacked furiously at them with their clubs. A teargas shell was fired. And then another. The stinging, nauseating odor of the gas began to drift across the esplanade. It was caught in the shafts of white light from the floodlights. Soon everyone was a ghost running in and out of the smoky swirls of some operatic netherworld. The sound of the sirens increased. Tom saw Dieter Voss. He was surrounded by security guards, their guns drawn. He stood like some Wagnerian monster above it all, his eyes glued to the surreal spectacle below, ignoring the dead man a few feet away. There was no business like show business.

Tom opened his clenched fist and stared at the key.

10

The consensus on the Carlton terrace the next day was that poor Jerry Alt had been killed by the only guy at the festival who was not a friend of his and with whom he was not involved in a project. The consensus also was that the bullets were intended not for Jerry, but for Dieter Voss. There was speculation that a critic had pulled the trigger, someone whose appreciation of cinema drove him to kill the man responsible for *Saudi.* Except for the fact that the wrong man had died, most of the sympathy was for the gunman.

Otherwise, there was not a lot of reliable information about the shooting. The gunman could have been one of the demonstrators. Or he could have been a terrorist, anxious to let the West know what he thought of the way his people were portrayed in *Saudi.* There were all sorts of possibilities. In the pandemonium that followed the shooting, the killer had managed to escape and there was only a sketchy description of him.

Tom spent most of the afternoon listening to the chatter and the speculation, sipping Pimms and fingering the key in his pocket. It was a large, old-fashioned iron door key. But for what door? And why would Jerry have had it in his pocket? Tom had not said anything about the key to the police. He wasn't sure why.

Alvin Jarvis sat down. He looked tired and drawn. Jerry had been a friend of his. He was taking the death hard.

"Jesus, I need a drink," he said. "I just talked to Jerry's widow in New York. She's naturally pretty shaken up. Can't imagine why anyone would want to kill her husband. Frankly, neither can I. He was a bit of a bullshit artist, God knows. And if he told that joke one more time about everyone on the terrace having fifty percent of the budget, I might have killed him myself. But he was harmless. I don't think he had any real enemies."

"Everyone thinks the killer was trying to shoot Dieter."

"That would seem to be the only explanation."

"Except Jerry was hit twice in the chest," Tom said. "If the killer had been trying to shoot Dieter, it would have been easy enough. Dieter was standing right there, not moving."

"Maybe he got confused and mistook Jerry for Dieter Voss."

"Or maybe this guy wanted to shoot Jerry Alt."

"Or maybe it was just another goddamn indiscriminate terrorist shooting. The guy wanted to kill an American, and Jerry happened to be standing in the way of the bullets." Alvin sighed and shook his head. "Anyway, Muriel, that's Jerry's wife, wants me to go to his suite and pack up his stuff. The police say it's okay, and I got a key from the hotel. Do you want to give me a hand?"

"Sure," Tom said.

Jerry had had the same suite on the second floor of the Carlton for the past ten years. It was done in shades of pale blue, and the French windows opened onto a terrific view of the crowds along la Croisette. Jerry had managed to turn the room into a reflection of his own long-standing failure in the movie business. There were scripts everywhere with titles like *Teen Holiday Massacre, Dutch Treat Terror* and *Deadly Valentines.* There were beautiful clothes hanging in the closet and letters from Empire Pictures and Crown International rejecting Jerry's efforts to make a picture called *Blood Sunrise.* A writing desk was piled high with copies of *Screen International.* One of the copies was opened at Peter Noble's column announcing that everyone was having a great time at the festival. Beside the pile of papers was a letter from American Express informing Jerry that his gold-card privileges were being canceled forthwith.

Alvin came in from the bedroom. "The police didn't find any money on Jerry, and there's only a couple of hundred dollars in traveler's checks here. Jerry was just about broke."

Ton handed him the American Express letter. "I think Cannes was Jerry's last stand in more ways than one."

"Christ, you would never have known it. He was always beautifully dressed. He was always talking projects and more projects."

"The idea is to look like you're having the time of your life, even when you're drowning."

"Let's get this stuff packed up and get the hell out of here. I don't know what we're going to do about the hotel bill. There isn't enough money to pay for a round of drinks on the terrace."

Alvin lugged a couple of Samsonite suitcases back into the bedroom. It was then that Tom found the daybook on the desk. It had lain beneath the American Express letter. It had an imitation-leather cover with Jerry's name stamped in gold lettering. Tom picked up the book and opened it.

In the merry month of May at Cannes, Jerry had made no dates, arranged no business meetings. But there were lots of reminders to phone people. He had planned to phone Samuel Zarkoff and Robert Evans. There was a note to call Roger Corman and Menahem Golan. He reminded himself to once again try Sybil Danning's suite at the Carlton, that Robert Ginty had not called back, and neither had Robert Forster. Tom kept flipping pages. Early in May, about five days before the start of the festival, there was a notation that read: "Call D re apartment." Then, as an afterthought, almost, "de la Castre."

Why would Jerry Alt, sitting in a hotel suite at the Carlton, need an apartment? Tom pulled out the old iron key and looked at it. Was this the key for Jerry's apartment?

Alvin returned to the sitting room carrying one of the suitcases. "The cops don't seem to have touched much of anything," he said.

"Maybe they think what everyone else thinks. That the wrong man got shot."

Alvin put the suitcase by the door. "The wrong man did get shot. Terrorist killing. That's what it has to be."

"De la Castre." Tom pointed to the notation in the daybook. "What would that be?"

"There's a Place de la Castre in the old town, up on the hill, Le Suquet. There's a church and some ramparts. Maybe Jerry did some sightseeing up there."

"Maybe he did," Tom said vaguely. He threw the daybook back down on the desk.

They didn't finish packing Jerry Alt's things until midafternoon. Then there was a fight with the hotel over the matter of the bill. Finally, Alvin slapped down his American Express card, which surprised Tom.

"What the hell," Alvin said. "He was the only guy I ever met who genuinely liked *Buns*."

By the time Tom came to the conclusion that it was a very long shot, but still it might not hurt to go up and take a look around, it was twilight. Below him, the town was spread out around the Golfe de la Napoule, with Ile Ste. Marguerite beyond. The weakening sun glanced off the red-tile roofs that climbed resolutely into the hills. He found the Place de la Castre on top of the hill. Fourteenth-century ramparts and a beautiful Gothic church were set among the pine trees. A quartet of boys in shorts and jersey pullovers were half-heartedly kicking around a soccer ball, sending it spinning off the cobblestones, awaiting the call to dinner. The ball bounced and skittered toward Tom. He took a kick at it and missed. This produced laughter from the kids. He ran and retrieved the ball. Immediately the laughter was shut off, replaced by tiny frowns of worry that in retaliation, the stranger might take their soccer ball. As Tom approached them, they moved into a protective knot and stared at him. He balanced the ball in one hand.

"*Parlez-vous anglais*?" he inquired of the nearest youngster.

"*Un peu*," the boy replied. He was about twelve. He had a mop of curly brown hair and a fine bow of a mouth. In a few years he would be driving the girls crazy at the beach.

"I am looking for a man who came here. Do you understand?"

The boy nodded.

"This man is an American. Very well dressed. But he has a funny, ugly face. Really old and wrinkled-looking. Do you understand?"

Again the boy nodded.

"Have you seen such a man. *Americain*?"

The boy nodded more slowly. He turned to his companions and they traded a fierce stream of French back and forth. Then the boy turned back to Tom.

"*Oui, monsieur*. There is such a man. Maybe."

"Maybe?"

"Yves sees him. That is what Yves says. But Yves is not always correct."

"Where does Yves see him?"

"He sees him in his apartment building. Not often. And maybe it is not the same man. But he is American. That is what Yves says. With ugly face, and nice clothes."

"Where is Yves' apartment?"

The boy pointed a dirty finger across the square to number fourteen. "But I tell you, *monsieur*. This Yves. He is not always correct." Tom threw him the ball. The quartet looked very relieved.

Number fourteen was down the street from the church. A heavy door opened reluctantly onto a dark, dank stone courtyard. A staircase at one side disappeared up into the darkness. There were eight apartments, two to each of the four floors, all of them looking out onto the courtyard. He tried the key in each of the doors. Although it fit snugly into the locks, it turned in only one of them. The fifth door he tried, on the third floor.

He hesitated for a moment before opening the door. Perhaps he should knock. But who would he be alerting? Jerry's killer, perhaps. Hello there. Tom Coward's the name. Just thought I'd drop by and see if you wouldn't like to give yourself up. He turned the knob and pushed the door open. Its hinges complained loudly.

The apartment was empty. Well, not quite empty. A big marmalade-colored cat blinked at him from a sagging old sofa. The cat rose up from its resting place, stretched luxuriously then hopped down to the floor as Tom closed and relocked the apartment door. The cat paced in front of a row of closets with louvered doors. To the left there was a sink. The sofa the cat had vacated stood adjacent to a curtained doorway that led into a tiny bedroom. There was an iron bed with a patched quilt thrown across it. The bed left barely enough room for a dressing table with a cracked mirror. Beyond the dressing table – and one had to squeeze past the bed to get to it – was a shower stall with a plastic curtain drawn across it. There was a toilet beside the shower.

Tom opened the louvered doors. The marmalade cat rubbed itself along his legs. "Hello there, kitty," Tom said. "Seen any killers today?" In answer the cat purred loudly. The closets were full of women's clothes. No sign of anything that might belong to Jerry Alt. It occurred to Tom that Jerry might have kept nothing more dangerous than a mistress here. Perhaps he used this place for the occasional rendezvous. "Well there, kitty," Tom said to the marmalade cat. "Is your mistress one of the great lays in the south of France? Is that what brought Jerry up here?" The cat merely cocked its head and watched as Tom went back into the bedroom.

The drawers of the bureau were full of women's cosmetics. Expensive stuff, too. A bottle of Gucci perfume. Eau de Toilette from Christian Dior. A selection of Crabtree and Evelyn bath products. Tortoiseshell and ivory hairbrushes and hand mirrors. A gold-plated manicure set. A black cosmetic case stamped "Harrod's."

He yanked open another drawer. The cat leapt up on the bed and curled up, blinking lovely yellow eyes as it watched Tom. There was a copy of *Paris Match* and beneath it a manila folder full of newspaper cuttings and a glossy magazine piece whose pages had been carefully torn out, then stapled together. The article was titled "Memoires de Ginger." He found himself staring at a photograph of Ginger Shane, the porn actress of Touch Lathrop's dreams. The article was in French. But Ginger was an international language of her own. She looked out from the page in a kind of golden ecstasy, her lips parted, her eyes smoldering. Inviting. But an invitation to what? He flipped quickly through the rest of the clippings. They all dealt in one way or another with the death of Ginger Shane. At the bottom of the pile was a passport. It was Canadian. Made out to a woman named Catherine Bujold. Catherine Bujold had been born in Montreal, Quebec, on December 9, 1958. She was five feet eight inches tall, and she had green eyes. There was the usual passport photo. The young woman who looked up at him had no expression on her face. There was no past in the face, no present, no future. Just a countenance in need of photographing in order to fulfill the dictates of identification. But that was fine with Tom. He could identify the photograph. Catherine Bujold was the mystery woman at the Carlton Bar. And she was Corinne Voss.

Then, from outside, he heard the sound of a key turning in the lock. The cat leapt off the bed and padded quickly into the living room.

11

Tom closed the manila file and pushed in the drawer. He barely made it to the closet and got the louvered door closed behind him when he heard the apartment door open and someone step inside. He squinted between the slats in the door and watched the intruder come into the room. It was Rakko.

He stood in the semidarkness of the apartment for a moment, his head lifted high, seeming to smell the air around him. He carried with him two empty duffel bags. He went into the other room. Tom could see the cat glide past. It glanced toward the closets, meowed. From the other room he could hear the sounds of drawers and doors opening and closing. It sounded as though Rakko was packing up the apartment. If that was the case, would he discover that the manila folder was missing? And if he was packing up, would he not also pack the clothes hanging in the closet? He would. Oh, shit, Tom thought.

Rakko emerged from the bedroom a moment later carrying the duffel bags. He stopped and glanced around the room, as though something was wrong.

At that moment, the cat scratched at the louvered door.

It meowed loudly.

Rakko had been about to open the apartment door. Now he stopped and turned toward the cat.

Once again, the scratching noise. More insistent this time. Tom dared not move. Sweat popped out on his forehead. Oh, shit, he thought. He was going to die because a marmalade cat was lonely.

Rakko moved across the room. Tom watched him. Rakko removed the dark glasses. There was only a sharp indentation and a lot of deathly white scar tissue where his right eye had once been. Tom drew in his breath. Rakko stood very still. Not moving.

The cat scratched at the door again.

Rakko looked down at the cat. Then he reached out toward the door. Tom shut his eyes. Christ. This was it. What to do? Bolt past him and hope for the best?

Then, abruptly, there was a shriek of pain as Rakko kicked the cat away. Tom jerked back into the far corner of the closet. There were pipes going from floor to ceiling. Tom wedged himself behind them. He thought for sure Rakko would hear him. But Rakko merely opened his mouth in a show of soundless laughter, yanked open the louvered door and began to pull armfuls of clothes off hangers. Tom tried to disappear into the corner. Rakko worked quickly, shoving dresses unceremoniously into the duffel bags. In a moment, the closet was empty. He slammed the louvered door shut. Tom watched him through the slats, pushing the clothes into the duffel bags, then carrying both bags toward the door. Rakko closed and locked the door behind him, and Tom heard his footsteps receding down the stairs. The cat was lying dazed in the corner, but it seemed all right.

It was dark now. Tom looked out the window at the Place de la Castre and caught a glimpse of Rakko's mane as he sauntered past the fountain toward the ramparts. He stuffed the manila envelope into the waistband of his pants, then hurried downstairs and out into the courtyard. Beyond the ramparts, a long flight of steps led down to the Rue Georges Clemenceau. From the top of the steps, Tom watched as Rakko turned left, then followed him as he made his way to the Rue du Port, turned right, moving nonchalantly down past the stucco edifice of the Sofitel.

At the Quai St. Pierre, Rakko veered to the left. The port was outlined in light, choked with yachts and sailing craft. Rakko headed for the largest of the yachts. It was a superbly sleek 130-foot corten-steel motor yacht with an aluminum superstructure. The yacht was called *Furyo*. There was a helipad at the stern. Three guards in naval whites watched but said nothing as Rakko went up the gangplank and disappeared into the interior of the ship.

Tom hung around on the jetty pretending to inspect a rebuilt 1938 Fife yawl that was moored a hundred yards or so away from the *Furyo*. He stood there for perhaps fifteen minutes, uncertain what to do. Then a Rolls Royce pulled along the jetty and came to a stop in front of the *Furyo*. Almost immediately, a handsome but rather plump Arabic gentleman in a crisp white linen suit bounded down the gangplank and threw open the door of the Rolls. A moment later a slightly nervous-looking woman emerged. It was Maddi Bergen. The Arab in the white linen made an extravagant ritual of kissing her hand. He ushered her on board. Maddi, as she disappeared onto the yacht, looked very impressed by it all. What the hell was Maddi Bergen doing on a yacht owned by a linen-suited Arab who kissed hands and gave shelter to a renowned killer like Rakko?

Tom waited perhaps five more minutes then strolled along the jetty past the *Furyo*. No one was in sight. The guards had gone below. It would be madness, of course, to go up onto the yacht. Mind you, it was a big yacht, and one could probably elude detection. Nonetheless, it was madness. Rakko was on that boat. And so were armed guards. But what was

Maddi Bergen doing there? There was only one way to find out. He hopped on the gangplank before he had a chance to talk himself out of it. Suppose he was stopped? Give them the "aw, shucks" tourist grin. So sorry, old chap. No idea it was off limits. Thought it might be one of those tour things. Oh, hi, Maddi. So it was you. Thought it was. Lacy isn't with you? Okay, just checking. Beautiful night, eh? Great boat. Just great. See you back at the hotel.

Tom stood on the enclosed aft deck. He could hear Rod Stewart singing "Do You Think I'm Sexy" somewhere below. He followed the singing. A stairway led down to a narrow, teak-paneled corridor. There were staterooms on either side. Tom tried one of the doors. Locked. Then he heard voices at the hatchway. Someone was coming. He went to the next door and turned the latch. It was locked as well. He raced along the corridor. There was one last door. He turned the latch. The door sprung open and Tom fell into the darkened interior.

He turned and leaned against the door, breathing hard. Jesus. That was close. Then he saw the bed. A naked young man was rising from it. Then Tom saw Rakko. He, too, was rising slowly, as though from the deep pool of a long, dark dream. He was also naked. His cyclops face was working itself into a rage. There was a gleaming curved knife close by the bed. Rakko grabbed it.

Tom clawed at the door handle. Found it, got it open and charged into the corridor past two startled crew members.

In a flash he was on the deck, rushing down the gangplank to the quay. He glanced back. Rakko was on the deck, still naked, the curved knife in his hand. He'll stop at the deck, Tom thought. He can't go any farther than the deck. He was safe, thank Christ.

But then Rakko was bounding down the gangplank and running pell-mell along the quay after him. Tourists stopped, gap-mouthed, as he flew past them. A naked crazy man at the Cannes Film Festival. They had heard of such carryings on among the film folk. Miss Rona was absolutely right.

Tom raced up the quay and turned right on La Pantiero. The crowds, thicker here, were full of tourists with red faces and white pants who had come to see all the fancy boats before dining at one of the nearby seafood restaurants. The tourists would stop Rakko. He couldn't go chasing Tom naked along a street crowded with tourists. Definitely not.

He looked behind him. People were screaming and leaping aside. Rakko came crashing through. He was gaining on Tom. Gaining very fast.

His lungs were beginning to ache. He was not a runner, for God's sake. He was a creature of the Carlton terrace and the Hotel du Cap. He could not beat some inhuman killing machine that ran naked through the town. His mind whirled toward the large pocket where panic was stored. Once it broke in there, he would be finished. Somehow, he picked up speed. He had to think. La Croisette. That was it. If he could reach la Croisette with the traffic and the police and the glare of lights, then he would be safe.

But as Tom came abreast of the Palais des Festivals, Rakko still was after him. Maybe twenty feet behind. And gaining. He appeared to have ditched the knife so that, for the onlookers, he was now just a colorful addition to the street scene. For Tom, he remained the killer.

The traffic on la Croisette was stalled bumper to bumper. He looked frantically around for a cop. Last night the area had been thick with them. Now there was not one in sight. Oh, damn! Oh, hell. He wanted to stop and cry. But he doubted that would do much good. Rakko was now just a couple of feet behind him. He could hear his hunter exhaling sharply as he came toward him. Tom was close to collapse.

He veered into the traffic, hopped across the hood of a car. Rakko was right behind him, a silent, deadly shadow. He was past the Palais now. Approaching the Majestic. Maybe he could get in there. He jumped on the rear of another car, scampered up over its roof, then down on the hood. He leapt on the auto in front of it. He could hear motorists loudly cursing him. He kept going. Something bounced down hard beside him. Tom could smell Rakko's pungent body odor. He glimpsed Rakko's lean sweating body just as he rolled off the hood and down onto the pavement. Instantly, Rakko was on top of him. Tom was on his back, trying to roll away. Rakko reached down and chopped him in the mouth with the edge of his hand. That produced searing pain. And blood.

Rakko was reaching down to pick Tom off the pavement when the motor scooter hit him. It knocked him forward, sending him sprawling against one of the cars parked along the street. He struck his head against the chrome edging around the roof, and for a moment was dazed.

Tom looked up and saw Lacy Bergen sitting astride a red Honda scooter wearing a matching red helmet.

"Hurry," she said grimly. "Get on the back."

Tom staggered to his feet. He looked over at Rakko, who was now wheeling around trying to clear his head. His body was scraped, and there was a bloody gash on his forehead. He started for Tom.

"Hurry, Tom," Lacy cried.

A moment later he was behind her, wrapping his arms around her waist. Rakko was very close, reaching out to grab the scooter. Lacy gunned the motor, threw it into gear and the scooter lurched forward, sideswiping Rakko. He spilled back on the pavement. For a moment, Tom thought the force of hitting Rakko would knock the scooter out of control. They were about to crash into one of the autos caught in the traffic jam along la Croisette. But Lacy somehow managed to bring the scooter around, and a moment later they were shooting through the narrow gap between the cars parked along the side of the street and those stalled in the middle.

"Are you all right?" Lacy called out.

"I'm not sure," Tom said.

"Should we go to the hospital?"

"No, no. I'm not hurt. I just don't know whether I'm all right."

"What do you mean?"

"I mean you just saved my life, Lacy. What the hell am I going to do now that you've saved my life?"

"I am a princess on a red scooter," she announced triumphantly. "And I just saved a guy in distress. What a night!"

12

Princesses who also double as movie queens do not ordinarily careen around on red motor scooters, Tom observed as they headed toward the Hotel du Cap. That was true, Lacy Bergen agreed. But she had always wanted a motorbike. Naturally, when her mother said she could not possibly risk her very valuable neck on a motorbike, she went out and bought one that afternoon.

"So what were you doing in Cannes?" Tom shouted, clinging to her for dear life as they whizzed around a particularly sharp curve just outside Juan-les-Pins.

"I was road testing my new scooter," she said proudly. "Incidentally, who was that horrible guy chasing you?"

"An irate actor who doesn't like the press."

She gave him a look. "Tom."

"It's very complicated," Tom said. "I'll tell you later. I promise. That is, if I survive this ride."

"Don't worry," she said. "You'll survive. But honestly, Tom. You get yourself into the weirdest situations."

She was right on both counts. He did get himself into the weirdest situations. And they did survive the ride. The scooter swept into the courtyard in front of the hotel entrance just as Dieter Voss came down the steps. Lacy didn't see him until she was in the process of turning the scooter over to a parking attendant and removing her helmet. Her face darkened as he approached.

Dieter was, as usual, playing the merry cherub. "Ah, there you are, Lacy. I just telephoned your room. We're leaving in about twenty minutes."

"Uh, all right, that's fine," Lacy said. "But I want Tom to come along with us."

Dieter's smile slipped a bit. "Good God, Tom. What happened to you? Wrestling on the streets of Cannes, were you?"

"I was just out for my evening jog," Tom said. "It's not easy staying in shape."

Dieter turned to Lacy. "As much as I'd like to have Tom along, it is a private party, Lacy. I thought you understood that."

"I don't think they'll mind," Lacy said. She could add a haughty movie-star quality to her voice when necessary. "I want Tom to come along as my date." She looked at him imploringly. "You will come with me? Won't you, Tom?"

He smiled at her. "How could I say no?"

"I suppose it will be all right," Dieter said dully. "Why don't we meet you in the lobby, say, in a half hour?"

"In a half hour," Lacy said.

As they walked into the hotel, Tom said, "What's this all about?"

"Dieter and his wife want me to go to some big, splashy private party. Yuck. I don't want to go. I don't like either one of them. They give me the creeps. The guy is crazy, if you ask me. And his wife is the worst tramp imaginable."

"What does your mother think about all this?"

"She likes Dieter. At least she says she likes Dieter. But then she wants me to sign the movie deal he's offering. But why should I? I don't need him. Anyway,

Mom's putting me under a lot of pressure about this. She thought it was a great idea if I went to this stupid party."

"Where is your mother?"

"She's having dinner with a friend. She said she needed a night off."

Louis, the ever-vigilant concierge, was coming around the desk when he caught sight of Tom. He was not pleased with what he saw.

"*Monsieur* Coward," he called out, "could I have a word with you for just a moment?"

"I'll see you in the room," Tom said to Lacy.

Lacy nodded. "Is everything all right?"

"In my life, nothing is ever all right."

The concierge cleared his throat as Tom came over and leaned against the desk. "*Monsieur*, are you quite all right?"

"Everyone seems very concerned about me this evening. I can't tell you how reassuring that is. But, yes, I'm just fine."

"If I may say so, *monsieur*, you do not look just fine. Now this is an establishment that takes great pride in the informality of its formality. But really, *monsieur*, you take informality too far. We like casual elegance here. But we do not like bums. If I may be so bold as to say so."

"I've run into a little bad luck since I arrived here in the Cannes area, Louis, there is no doubt about that. But I opened an account at the local Giorgio Armani store just this afternoon. I'll be looking better from now on, I promise. You know, knitted sweaters, linen pants, those cute white-leather Nikes everyone bounces around in. I love those Nikes. Except I can't for the life of me figure out how everyone keeps them so clean."

Louis the concierge once more cleared his throat.

"Now, *monsieur*. One thing further. We have also received complaints about the sleeping arrangements in your room."

"Oh?" Tom said, putting on the expression he liked to call Innocent Schoolboy. "What sleeping arrangements are those?"

"*Madame* Bergen objects to her daughter staying in your room. She has asked us to step in and handle the matter. Naturally, this is not a situation in which we are comfortable. But madame is a valued guest of this establishment."

"*Madame*'s daughter, I would think, is the valued guest at this establishment," Tom said. "And it is *madame*'s daughter who will not get her ass out of my room. You had best speak to *madame*'s daughter about that."

The concierge's eyes lost their warmth and took on a gunmetal hue. "*Monsieur*, given your deportment the last time you stayed with us, I knew you would be trouble as soon as you arrived." He paused for effect. "You have, I must say, in no way disappointed me. I will tell you this, and this is all I will tell you. I will give you one more of what you say in English is an opportunity. But if there is any more trouble, I will regretfully have to ask you to leave. Almost never in the history of this hotel has it been necessary to ask a guest to leave. Even F. Scott Fitzgerald, *monsieur*. Even he behaved himself here."

What could one possibly say? A specially appointed guardian of wealth and elegance had found Tom wanting. He could only hang his head in abject shame. He retreated to the safety of his room for a shower and a change of clothes. He tried to find something clean with a designer label. It was not easy.

Three quarters of an hour later, Tom was sitting beside Dieter Voss on the jump seat in the rear of a white stretch limo. He watched Corinne Voss as she poured champagne for everyone. She sat next to Lacy, and, as usual, she was dressed for the sensual kill. She wore nothing but a sequined silk-chiffon vest, open to show off the swell of her breasts, a very short black leather miniskirt, diamond-patterned black stockings and high-heeled leather tie shoes. She was, she reported breathlessly, a little giddy from the champagne. She leaned suggestively against Lacy.

"You got some marvelous sun today, my darling," Dieter purred. "I have never seen you quite so dark."

"I'm brown everywhere," she said and opened the vest to demonstrate the truth of her statement. She turned to Lacy. "You see, Lacy. I'm so brown."

Lacy gulped champagne and giggled nervously. Then Dieter produced cocaine and the de rigueur silver coke spoon.

"Very fine stuff," he announced. "Corinne and I did some of it before we left the room."

"But don't tell them how we did it, *chéri*," said Corinne, taking the spoon from her husband.

Dieter laughed. His eyes were bright and dancing. "No, my darling. We will not tell them how we did it. But it was very interesting."

Lacy giggled and spilled some of her champagne.

"Maybe you'd better go easy," Tom said to her.

"Oh, Tom, don't be such a spoilsport," Dieter said. "Lacy is here to have fun, like the rest of us."

Tom looked at Dieter. "Are you having a good time at Cannes, Dieter?"

"Of course, my friend. I am having a marvelous time. Why shouldn't I? I am surrounded by beautiful women, fine drugs, good food."

"To say nothing of murderers and a lot of people who don't like *Saudi*," Tom added.

There was a tick in the corner of Dieter's left eye. "Come, come, Tom, there is no reason to be nasty with me. You know there are problems with *Saudi*, and I know there are problems with *Saudi*. But we will overcome those problems, believe me." He shrugged. "Besides, it is, as the great Hitchcock said, only a movie. You must keep that in mind. "

"You're not worried about your investors?"

Dieter laughed jovially. "Of course I am worried about my investors. But not tonight. I cannot worry tonight."

Lacy was in the process of moving a spoonful of the cocaine toward her nose. Tom reached out and gently held her arm. "Do you really want to do that shit?"

Lacy gave him a hostile frown. "Fuck off, Tom. You're not my mother. Or are you?"

"Don't worry," Tom said grimly. "I'm not your mother."

"You don't have to do that stuff, Lacy. The champagne's just as much fun," Corinne interjected. Tom looked at her in some surprise. So did Dieter.

"Don't be ridiculous, darling." Dieter's voice had a brittle edge to it. "A little recreational cocaine is not going to hurt anyone. We are going to a party. It loosens things up, that's all. We are not, as you might say, a bunch of John Belushis here."

"I want to try it," Lacy said petulantly.

Corinne turned away and stared out the window as Lacy did the cocaine. Tom looked over at Dieter, who shifted uneasily in his seat. He wondered what the hell was going on.

The villa where the party was being held was on the sea just outside Antibes. A pastel-pink edifice built originally in the 1920s, it was set among pines and palms, overlooking a sumptuous garden that rolled off toward a huge swimming pool and the Mediterranean beyond.

The vast neoclassical living room, adorned with hanging tapestries, was bursting with all the beautiful people who come to Cannes looking for the next party. In this crowd, getting to the right parties is much more important than seeing movies. The actresses want to meet producers; the producers want to get laid. You cannot accomplish those things sitting in a screening room. Therefore, the parties are a necessity. Everyone drinks a lot, snorts a lot and tells vast lies. You are who you manage to convince someone you are. As a consequence, you can be anyone.

This evening, as Tom made his way through the crowd, he decided he would merely be Tom Coward. Not an easy role to play, sticking this close to reality. But what the hell. He would give it a try. He found Alvin Jarvis out by the pool talking to an incredibly formed brunet.

"Do you speak any Italian?" Alvin asked Tom hopefully.

"I can say *si, prego*, and *antipasto*," Tom replied.

"That's not good enough." Alvin sighed. "I think her name is Gina. And I think she's an Italian starlet."

"Where's Lea?"

Alvin scowled. "I have no idea," he said.

"Uh-oh."

"Now don't give me any of your fucking lectures, Tom. I'm sick and fucking tired of the way she's been carrying on."

"How's she been carrying on?"

"She keeps saying junk like, 'I want you to be better than you are.' Christ fucking almighty. You are what you are. There is very little you can do about it."

"I thought you were going to make *Places in the Heart,* Alvin. I thought you wanted to make bold cinematic statements."

"I want to make *Buns II,*" Alvin said lamely. Beside him, Gina the Italian starlet shifted her large bosom around and started to look bored. "Look, I gotta take care of this or I'm gonna lose it. You know how it is, Tom. I'm the same as you, for God's sake. Settling down. Being responsible. That's for other people. Give me a deal for *Buns II* and an Italian starlet. That's all I want out of life. Lea wants artistic fulfillment, or some fucking thing. I can't give it to her. I'm not even sure what the hell it is."

"Oh, Jesus, Alvin," Tom said. "What's going to happen to us?"

"Now don't start asking questions like that. I started asking questions like that, and look where it got me."

Tom glanced at the Italian starlet. "Yeah," he said. "Look where it got you."

Tom went into the house in search of Lacy. David Lee Roth was rattling the marble urns and the fake busts of Roman emperors. Someone spilled vodka on the Italian travertine flooring. A couple necked ferociously on one of the sofas. There was no sign of Lacy, or, for that matter, Dieter and Corinne. There was, however, the red-headed hooker from the Carlton bar. Now what the hell was her name?

"Daphane," she said into his ear. She smelled of jasmine and roses.

"Daphane? It was not Daphane," Tom said vehemently. "It was Colette. It was not Daphane."

She smiled. "Tonight, it is Daphane. Tomorrow night, who knows? Maybe Celeste. I always like to be a Celeste."

"Every night I'm a Tom. It's boring, but there you go."

"You are Tom the producer?" Daphane said hopefully.

"No, I'm Tom-not-the-producer."

"I remember you bought me and my little friend champagne, and the waiter knew your name. So we thought for sure you must be a producer. But then you would not sleep with us. Very curious. We talked about you later. My little friend thought you were cute."

"And what did you think?"

She touched the end of his nose with a lacquered nail. "I was sorry you did not have five thousand francs."

"I still don't have five thousand francs."

"Tonight, it is not necessary," Daphane said. She wrinkled her nose. "Tonight I am not on duty."

"Let me buy you a drink," Tom said.

"Are you sure you are not a producer?"

"Positive," Tom said.

"If I meet a producer, I may say bye-bye, even though I like you. My ambition is to be a famous actress."

Tom shrugged. "Welcome to Cannes."

An hour later, Daphane still had not met a producer. She had Tom in a corner somewhere in the house. She was kissing him feverishly, one hand running through the hair at the back of his neck, the other hand gently clenching and unclenching between his legs.

"Please," she murmured, "tell me you are a producer."

"Daphane, for Christ's sake, I am not a producer. Mmm. Do that a little harder."

She increased the pressure. "Is that better?

"Much."

"Tom," she said. "You don't have to lie anymore. I know you are reluctant to reveal yourself to me. I understand that. You don't want a lot of women taking advantage of you. But I'm your friend. You can tell me."

"Tell you what?"

"Tell me that you really are a producer."

"I am not a producer," he said.

"I don't believe you," she said, resuming the feverish kissing. "Now," she said breathlessly, "I have something to show you."

"What are you going to show me?"

"You see, my little friend and I, we have been here before. "

"On business?"

"Very much the business. This villa is owned by an Italian count with very interesting tastes."

"What kind of tastes?"

"Kinky," she said. "What other tastes are there?"

"I can't imagine."

"Come with me."

He found himself being led up to the second floor, along a corridor to what appeared to be a closet door. The door opened on a narrow winding staircase. "This way," she said. They went up the stairs and into a small studio with lacquered black walls. One of the walls was on a slant with a large window built into it. The window looked down into one of the bedrooms.

"The glass is one-way," Daphane whispered. "On the other side, it appears that there is a mirror in the ceiling."

Several easy chairs were placed strategically in front of the window. There were also two video cameras mounted on tripods. They were aimed down into the room, presumably to record the sort of action that was now unfolding on the a circular bed. The lighting was low and indirect. But there was enough so that onlookers as well as the cameras could clearly pick out what was happening. Daphane came up behind Tom and snuggled against him.

"Well," she murmured, "what do you think?"

He didn't know quite what to think. On the bed below the window two women were intertwined with each other. They were naked. Except for the lace gloves. And the black masks. One of the women lay on her back, while the other kissed and kneaded her breasts. Daphane turned her hips against Tom. Her hands snaked around to his crotch, and she kissed his neck.

"Tom the producer, do you like that? Do you like to watch two women make love? Does that turn you on?"

On the bed, one of the women removed the other's mask. Tom started as he recognized Lacy Bergen. The other woman, still masked, ran her gloved hand down Lacy's belly and into her crotch. Lacy threw her head back and bared her teeth.

The anger was there before he quite realized it. If he had thought about it, he might have controlled himself. Instead he pushed Daphane away, fumbled with the cameras until he freed the tape cartridges and stuffed them into his pocket. Then he picked up the nearest chair, and smashed it through the glass. He dimly heard Daphane scream and demand to know what he was doing. He ignored her, used the chair to clear the remaining glass out of the window frame, and jumped down into the bedroom.

He managed to land on his feet. The masked woman was getting off the bed. Tom grabbed her, swung her around and ripped off the mask. It was Corinne.

"Tom," she said. It was all she had a chance to say before he slapped her across the face.

Then he saw Dieter Voss, naked, slumped down on a straight-backed chair, his head lolling forward. Tom went over to him, and Dieter managed the ghost of a drugged smile before Tom slugged him. Dieter flipped back in the chair, that inane little smile still glued to his face.

Lacy, only semiconscious, had not moved on the bed. Tom pulled one of the sheets loose and wrapped it around her. Then he unceremoniously slung her over his shoulder and hurried out of the room.

He found Alvin wandering around out by the pool, looking miserable. "I've lost Gina, my Italian starlet," he said forlornly.

"Forget Gina, Alvin," Tom said. "The shit's hitting the fan here. Have you got a car?"

"Of course, I've got a fucking car. Why?"

"I need you to get us out of here."

"I assume you mean you and the girl on your shoulder. What happened to her?"

"I'm saving her from a fate worse than death."

"Okay," Alvin said. "Then I guess we'd better get the hell out of here."

They found Alvin's Ferrari Testarossa, bundled Lacy into the back and started back to the du Cap. Once they were on the road, Tom filled Alvin in on what had happened. In the backseat, Lacy Bergen tossed listlessly.

"What'd they do, dope her up?"

"Probably cocaine and champagne," Tom said. "I don't think it would take anything more exotic than that. She is not exactly a woman of the world."

"Unlike us globe-trotters." Alvin kept his eyes on the road. "Dieter really is such a lovely man."

"How the hell am I going to get Lacy into the hotel?" Tom wondered. "The concierge already has my number drawn. All I have to do is walk into the du Cap with a naked movie star over my shoulder, and I'll be spending the rest of the festival at a youth hostel."

"Do you ever stay in a hotel where they aren't on the verge of throwing your ass out?"

"Never. It would rob life of its adventure."

The question of how to get a naked, unconscious movie star into the world's best hotel without causing a stir occupied their conversation for the rest of the trip. Alvin favored the cry-wolf approach. He would enter the lobby and announce that several poor people were about to invade the premises. Everyone would rush out in panic, leaving the way clear for Tom to get Lacy upstairs. Tom, however, vetoed that idea. He promoted the direct approach. Just walk in and carry her upstairs.

He almost got away with it. In fact, he actually had put his foot on the stairs when Louis came along.

"*Monsieur* Tom," the concierge said as calmly as possible, considering the circumstances.

"*Bonsoir*, Louis," Tom said.

"*Monsieur*, are you aware there is a woman over your shoulder?"

"Yes, Louis," Tom retorted. "I am aware of that."

"She does not appear to be wearing any clothes."

"True, Louis. However, in deference to the reputation of this hotel, I have covered her with a sheet."

"This hotel appreciates that, *monsieur*, believe me. May I ask one more question?"

"Of course."

"Where are you taking this young woman?"

"I am taking her to my room."

The concierge nodded. "Ah. Your room. I see."

"I know this doesn't look particularly good. And I know you have given me only one more opportunity, and a less generous man would say that this is that opportunity. But I beg your indulgence. Believe me, there is a satisfactory explanation."

"I'm sure there is, *monsieur*, And if you were any other guest, I would listen to it most sympathetically. However, you are not any other guest. Therefore, I am not in the mood to hear it. Tell me just one more thing."

"Certainly."

"Have you ever been asked to leave a hotel before this evening?"

"It has happened on occasion, yes," Tom conceded.

"Then given your experience in these matters, it will not come as a great shock when I tell you that you are to be asked to leave this hotel." The concierge raked Tom with a look of pitying disgust. Then he turned on his well-polished heel and headed across the lobby. The weight of Lacy Bergen on Tom's shoulder was suddenly very heavy indeed.

13

Tom awoke the next morning with a startled grunt. In the black pit of his nightmares, Ginger Shane was transformed into Corinne Voss. And Corinne Voss became Ginger Shane. And Rakko, his body streaked with blood, was slowly bending him in two. The two women became a single shrill monster screaming delight at Tom Coward's agony. His body was beginning to come apart at the seams. No wonder. He was folded uncomfortably onto the sofa in his room. He had retreated here after holding Lacy Bergen's famous head over the toilet in the black marble bathroom. With the sunlight pouring in and birds making ungodly noises, his body angrily reminded him of what he had put it through the night before. He was sore everywhere.

Lacy was already awake. She was sitting up, wearing one of Tom's shirts, knees tucked forlornly under her chin, hands clasped tightly around her legs. Her face was pale and childlike. There were dark smudges beneath her eyes. She stared at him.

"I feel just so awful. Tell me what happened last night."

He told her. She began to cry.

Tom struggled off the sofa. He wondered if it would be seemly to pour himself a little Mumm's and orange juice. Probably not. Mustn't corrupt the innocent. Any more than the innocent already had been corrupted, that is. Instead, he went over and sat beside her on the bed.

"I'm ruined," Lacy said between sniffles. "They'll sell those pictures to the *National Enquirer*, for sure."

Tom got up and went over to the chair on which he had flung his jacket. He retrieved the cassettes and handed them to her.

"What's this?" She looked up at him. The black circles were complemented by red rims.

"This is the incriminating evidence."

She threw her arms around him and cried some more. With relief this time. "Why would they do that to me?"

"I suppose they wanted to make sure you would sign a movie contract. The tapes were a little insurance. You threw a wrench into their scheme when you invited me along. That's why Dieter looked so displeased. He must be getting pretty desperate to pull a stupid stunt like this."

"I don't know how to thank you." She sobbed.

"You probably saved my life yesterday. It was the least I could do in return. You're, uh, a terrific kid, Lacy." It didn't sound right, and he knew it.

So did she. There were more tears. "I'm not just a kid," she said.

"What are you then?"

"I'm the woman who loves you."

Tom quickly changed the subject. "Let's talk about last night. Why would I have seen your mother getting her hand kissed by an Egyptian gentleman with a big yacht?"

"Didn't you hear what I said?"

"I heard it. I still want to know about your mother."

"She was having dinner with him. His name is Mehdi Abbas. He's very rich. I think Mom likes him."

"Do you know he's involved with Dieter?"

"I heard something about that, I guess. I think that's why Mom wants me to sign the movie contract with Dieter. She knows it would please Mehdi."

"Where did you meet him?"

"Mehdi? In New York, a couple of months ago. He took us to dinner at the Café des Artistes. Mom thought he was the most charming creature imaginable. I thought he was a little oily, myself."

"You speak and read French, don't you?"

"What's that got to do with anything?"

Tom got the manila folder off the desk where he had thrown it the night before. He pulled out the French magazine article about Ginger Shane and handed it to Lacy. "Translate this for me, will you? It doesn't have to be word for word. I just want a rough idea of what it says."

She looked at the story for a moment, then up at Tom. "I don't understand you at all. Why would you want to know about *her*?"

"Just humor me, will you?"

She sighed. "All right." She studied the page then said, "Well, it says Ginger Shane was a legendary porn star in Los Angeles. She was killed under very mysterious circumstances in Egypt in 1975. According to this, her beauty was, you know, incredible. Everyone was mad for her. She transcended the sleaziness of adult movies. That's what it says here. But, Tom, this is a load of crap, it really is. No one transcends the sleaziness of adult movies."

"Just keep reading, will you?"

Okay. But it's ridiculous. Anyhow, today her videos are hot sellers, and years after her death she remains a really big star in porno theaters, as big as Seka and Traci Lords and Ginger Lynn. Then there's a lot of stuff about her movies, and quotes from the people who knew her, how she could have been a great actress, except once she somehow got trapped in the porno business she was typecast and could never go legitimate. This story says it was a tragedy, that she could have amounted to something much better. Apparently, that's part of the continuing fascination with her. She's regarded as a kind of Marilyn Monroe type figure in the industry, someone who was used and abused by porn in the seventies, the same way Marilyn was by the studio system in the fifties. According to the article, she was always something of an enigma. No one was quite sure where she came from. Like a lot of people in the business, she created myths about herself that just weren't true. First of all, Ginger Shane was not her real name. But no one knew what her real name was. She told some of her friends that she came from the Midwest, Nebraska, where her father was a farmer and her mother was a schoolteacher. She said her parents had disowned her because someone showed them a picture of her in one of the skin magazines. But then she told other people that she came from Canada, and that her mother had been a journalist who moved to Paris."

Lacy looked up from the magazine. "I'm getting tired of this, Tom. Do you want me to go on?"

"Yes," he said. "Finish it up. Please."

She studied the article. "She never went out with the guys in the porn industry or anything like that. Toward the end she was doing a lot of cocaine and uppers, and drinking a lot as well. She was unhappy, but no one quite knew why. She was making tons of money and seemed to enjoy her work. Yuck. How could you enjoy a lot of strangers sticking their things into you while someone takes pictures? Anyhow, there were rumors that she was seeing a famous director. Someone named Welles Carpenter. I've never heard of Welles Carpenter. Have you?"

"He was famous," Tom said. "But way back in the fifties. I don't think he's made a movie for years."

"According to this article, he was making a movie in Egypt. Ginger went there to visit him. A few nights later, they found her nude body out by the pyramids. She had been shot once in the head. At first, the police thought it was murder, and they even arrested the producer of the movie. Good grief." She looked up from the article. "Do you know who the producer was?"

"Who?"

"Dieter Voss."

Tom raised his eyebrows and made a whistling sound. "Well, well. Someone said they heard he was once arrested for murder."

"He's just the type of guy who would kill a woman. She probably wouldn't sleep with him or something. Hmm. Listen to this. A hotel employee saw her stumble into his room, dressed only in a robe. The next thing, she was found dead. So the Egyptian police arrested him. Dieter denied she had been in his room. Said the hotel employee must have been mistaken. He was released after a day or so."

"Does it say why?"

"Hold on a minute. Let me read this. Yes. Welles Carpenter provided him with an alibi. He told the police that he and Dieter spent most of the night talking over production problems. There was no way Dieter could have killed her. Carpenter said that Ginger was emotionally distraught. She had been drinking and taking drugs, talking about killing herself. They had dinner together at the hotel the night she died. Welles thought she went to her room and fell asleep. But apparently she got up again, and somehow got out to the desert. The Egyptian police eventually concluded that she committed suicide. But since there was no gun beside the body, that seems unlikely. Unless, of course, someone came along, found the body and decided to take the gun. The Egyptian police think that's what happened. Anyhow, the case was closed. The movie was never finished, and shortly after the production closed down, Welles Carpenter disappeared. No one's seen him since."

She looked at Tom. "This is kind of sad, actually."

"Is that it?"

"Just about. The article ends by saying that her life and her death remains a mystery. Hm. That's really a fascinating story." She handed the piece back to Tom. "You know what I think? I think Dieter Voss murdered her. Is that why you're so interested in all this, Tom? Because you think Dieter is a killer?"

He flipped through the cuttings in the folder. Mostly they were stories from Egyptian newspapers about the death of Ginger Shane. There were a couple of clippings from the *Herald Tribune*. "Porn Actress Found Dead In Egypt" was the headline of one of the stories. It contained nothing that was not in the magazine piece. Tom closed the folder.

"There is something going on here," he said. "I'm not sure what it is. But somehow Ginger Shane is involved in it."

"You mean you think she's still alive?"

"No, I don't think she's alive."

"She's a ghost," Lacy said melodramatically. "A ghost who has come back to haunt everyone who was mean and cruel to her."

"There are no ghosts at the Cannes Film Festival," Tom said. "The hotel rooms are too expensive for them."

"All I know is, I feel absolutely rotten."

Tom started to get dressed.

"Where are you going?" she asked.

"Into Cannes."

She fell back across the bed and allowed the shirt to ride up her thighs. "Why don't you stay here with me?"

He threw the bedsheet over her. "Because I've got business in Cannes."

"You know what you are?"

"What am I?

"You're Scaramouche," she said. "'Born with the gift of laughter and a sense that the world was mad.'"

"That's me all right."

"There. You see? I know you, Tom Coward. You don't think I do, but I do. You're chasing something. You've got some crazy idea that if you can just get to somewhere you're not, or be with someone you don't know, then everything will turn out all right. But, Tom, my darling, that's not how it works at all."

"Oh? And I suppose you know how it does work?"

She rolled over on her stomach, her gaze fixed lovingly on him. "I've got some idea of how it does work, yes. It works on commitment and caring. It doesn't work on fantasies and dreams. You're always trying to chase the dreams and turn them into reality. For a change, you should try planting your feet down for a couple of minutes and looking around you. You might discover something interesting."

"What is it that I might discover?"

"Me," she said soberly. "I'm not an elusive dream, Tom, I'm real. I'm in for the long haul. I'm what it's all about, the commitment and the caring. I'm the great love of your life. I truly am. Just wait. Wait and you'll see."

He was going to say something smart and dismissive. But then he looked at her and he couldn't say anything. He was not sure what to make of her. But then, these days, he was not sure what to make of anything.

Downstairs, Tom encountered Dieter Voss. For once, he was not surrounded by security guards and acolytes. He was dressed in white, exuding health and good cheer. If there were uncomfortable memories from the night before, he refused to acknowledge them.

"Tom, a beautiful morning. I just took a lovely stroll down to the sea. The air is full of roses. It's so wonderful to be alive on a day like this. Don't you think?"

Tom hit him on the end of the jaw, and Dieter plopped down on one of the bright yellow sofas.

"You're a sleazy fuck, Dieter."

Dieter rubbed his jaw. His eyes glinted dangerously. "You may have hit me for the last time, Tom."

"Maybe not."

"Don't be so harsh. Who are you to judge? Lancelot on his white charger? I hardly think so. You are down here in the gutter with the rest of us, my friend. You drink the champagne and sell out just as fast as anyone at this festival. Only for you, the stakes are not so high. What is it? A free airline ticket? A first-class hotel? Some of us are not quite so fortunate. Some of us are playing a much bigger game. We risk much more."

"So you tricked Lacy Bergen into going to a party with you. You got her high on cocaine, and took some compromising pictures. Of course those pictures would never have been made public – not as long as Lacy signed a contract and saved your ass. That contract would have kept you from going down the toilet with a forty-million-dollar turkey called *Saudi*."

Dieter was on his feet now. "I will leave you with one final suggestion, Tom. Stay out of these affairs. They do not concern you. Be content with the little perks of the high life. For now, rich people are nice to you and put up with your ridiculous behavior. You would be surprised at how quickly the rich can desert you, at just how fast a small person like you could get hurt."

"You're absolutely right, Dieter. I could get hurt because I am a small person and it is a big world. But right now you're beginning to look like a pretty small person yourself. Mehdi Abbas is furious with you. And Mehdi Abbas is in town with a killer named Rakko. Who do you suppose Rakko is after? Could it be you? What did you do to Ginger Shane all those years ago, Dieter? Did you kill her? Is that why all this trouble is about to rain down on you?"

The tadpole eyes went blank. "I don't know what you are talking about. Ginger Shane has nothing to do with this."

"She doesn't? I wonder about that. We'll just have to wait and see, won't we?"

Dieter Voss looked at Tom in amazement. Then, without another word, he turned and stalked off across the lobby.

Tom was about to head out the door when he spotted Jean-Claude Irondelle hurrying toward him. He did not look happy. "*Pardonnez-moi*, Monsieur Coward," he called out. "Could I have a brief word with you?"

Monsieur Coward? What happened to Tom? Oh, God, Tom Coward thought. It was going to be one of those days.

Corinne found Dieter trembling in the suite. It was time to end it all. She came over and held his head against her breast.

"I don't dislike you, I really don't," she murmured. "You are a small boy. It is a shame you had to grow up."

He closed his eyes and snuggled more closely against her. The tears ran down his cheeks. "I don't want to die," he said, his voice full of desperation.

She pulled away and held his head between her hands. "You are not going to die. I have Mehdi Abbas's word on that. I wanted to hurt you as badly as I could, Dieter. But I never wanted to kill you."

His tear-stained face betrayed the confusion. "But why? What did I do to you? We never had anything but fun together. Not a cross word, nothing. I loved you, for God's sake."

"But you don't understand, Dieter. I never loved you. I hated you, in fact. At least at the beginning. Now there is no longer hate, only pity. I am so sorry for you. I am sorry that you had to kill someone who was very close to me."

"Ginger Shane? Oh, my God, you're not talking about Ginger Shane?" When she did not answer, he buried his head in his hands. "Oh, Jesus, Jesus. All this because of her? It's not possible."

"I am afraid it is, Dieter."

"You think I killed Ginger? Well, let me tell you something, darling. Let me tell you from my heart. No lies. No deceit. I have lied and cheated all my life, God knows. But I have never lied to you. I don't lie now. I did not kill her."

"Then who did?"

"Welles Carpenter. He was the murderer. He took her out on the desert and he killed her. That's why he provided the alibi for me. He had to, otherwise he would be implicated himself."

She walked away from him, as though wanting to escape the force of his words. No. It couldn't be. Not after all these years, all the planning.

Dieter babbled on. "Why do you think he disappeared after the movie folded in Egypt? Did you ever ask yourself that? He disappeared because he was the killer. He changed his identity so that no one could ever find him and arrest him for the murder."

"Do you know where he is?"

"No. If I did, I would tell you. I really would. Years ago, I heard he might be in Paris. But only rumors. I know Welles was crazy about the city. But he could be anywhere."

She came and sat beside him, speaking very quietly. "I am going to leave you now, Dieter. Our marriage is over."

He again buried his head in his hands.

She stared at the floor. She did not like the sound of a man crying. Curious. She had wanted him broken more than anything else in the world, and yet having accomplished it, there was no satisfaction.

"Please. Listen to me," she said. "It's important that you get out of Cannes as soon as possible. Tomorrow at the latest. Don't go back to Paris. "

"It doesn't make any difference," he said in a desolute voice. "Mehdi Abbas will get me. If Rakko is working for him, he will get me. I'm afraid you underestimate him terribly."

"I don't think so," she said. "You're not in danger as long as you return the five million dollars you and Sir Cecil stole. I know the money was deposited into a corporation set up in the Netherland Antilles. Dissolve the corporation and give the money back to Mehdi."

"But then I will be penniless."

"Yes, that is true," she said grimly. "But at least you will be alive."

She left Dieter slumped in the chair. She collected only a few things in a straw bag. Corinne Voss would be left at the Hotel du Cap, held in the lingering scent of expensive perfume and the memory of her weak, scared, distraught husband. Corinne would also remain behind with the French underwear and the Dior stockings. Well, not quite. There was one final use to be made of her. She went down to the lobby and had them bring her car around. Then she drove down the road until she found a telephone. The receiver at the other end was picked up on the second ring.

"*Oui?*"

"Mehdi," she said.

"My love." His voice sounded ebullient. "I have been waiting for your call."

"It's over," she said. "Dieter knows everything. About us. Our affair. He has agreed to return the five million he stole. He's finished. He has no movie. No money."

"We must drink champagne and make love," Mehdi said merrily. "There is much celebrating to be done, my darling."

"At the yacht in St. Tropez. We can be alone there."

"I can hardly wait. But there is a small complication. It will take me until tomorrow morning to clean up some loose business ends. I tell you what. Why don't you go the yacht and wait for me there?"

"All right, darling. But alone. I must have you alone."

Mehdi chortled. "So hot, my love. You make me so hot. Alone you will have me."

She made a second phone call. She spoke slowly into the receiver to ensure that there was no confusion. Then she asked that the whereabouts of a Welles Carpenter be checked into. There was a possibility he was in Paris, using an assumed name. She needed the information as quickly as possible. The voice on the other end of the phone assured her she would have it. The voice inquired if she was all right. Yes, she said. She was fine.

She hung up the receiver and stepped out of the phone booth. She thought of Tom Coward.

Tom had one of the attendants at the Hotel Majestic park his car, then he made his way up to Touch Lathrop's suite. The Shree Ramana opened the door. This morning he was in a snowy white caftan.

"I must speak to Touch," Tom said.

"That will not be possible," the Shree said coldly. "Touch is not here."

"Do you know when he will be back?"

"I'm afraid he left without saying a word."

"Look, could you tell him it's important that we talk? Tell him it's about Ginger Shane."

"We have spent a great deal of time meditating with Touch, trying to get him to forget that name. Now why don't you just fuck off, Coward, and leave him alone?"

"What happened? Did you get up on the wrong side of your bed of nails, Shree? We do not sound very gurulike this morning."

The cultured tones of Shree's voice had roughened a bit. "When I encounter assholes like you, I don't feel much like a guru. Now get lost."

Shree slammed the door in his face.

Tom kept an eye out for Touch among the crowds along la Croisette, but there was no sign of him. He wasn't on the Carlton terrace, either. It was now eleven-thirty in the morning. Alvin Jarvis came out of the bar. He was wearing a windbreaker and jeans. The glasses were back on the bridge of his nose. They sat down at one of the tables, and Tom told him about what had happened at the du Cap.

"If it's any consolation," Alvin said, "you are probably the first person in the history of the festival to be kicked out of the du Cap. It's something of a distinction, I'd say."

"That's what I'm trying to tell myself," Tom said. "Except there are only so many first-class hotels in the world, and I'm quickly running out of them."

"We're both going to have to make some drastic changes in our lives."

"What's that mean?"

"It means no more looking for contact lenses," Alvin announced triumphantly.

"I'm not sure I understand."

"It means Lea has gone back to New York. It means there is Canadian money desperate to finance *Buns II.*"

"Jesus, Alvin. I can't believe you're really going to do it. You're going to throw over a perfectly good marriage for *Buns II*?"

"You can't believe it? That's why I'm a movie producer, and you're not."

He looked as though he was ready for a fight.

Tom didn't have the time or the enthusiasm. "I've got more pressing problems. Touch Lathrop, for example. I don't suppose you've seen him."

"Not a sign of him." Alvin glanced around the terrace. "Now that's curious."

"What's curious?"

"The Director. He's not at his usual table."

At noon, Tom drove the Renault up Le Suquet and parked beside the church in the Place de la Castre. In the cool dimness of the apartment, the marmalade cat blinked a welcome from the sofa. He went over and sat next to the cat. After a few moments it slinked up on his lap, curled there and began to purr contentedly.

An hour passed. Then two. Still, he sat there. The marmalade cat never moved from his lap. He could hear the dim sounds of children playing. A woman's high voice scolded in French. A truck with a faulty muffler passed. Someone laughed. Then he heard the footsteps, a scrape against the cement just outside the apartment. The cat jumped off his lap and Tom hurried into the closet, closing the louvered door behind him.

Corinne Voss stepped into the room. She carried a large straw bag. She wore shorts and a white peasant blouse. She bent down and stroked the marmalade cat. Then she went into the bedroom.

Five minutes later the curtain across the entranceway parted, and Catherine Bujold stepped back into the living room. Her long hair fell past her shoulders and her face was scrubbed clean of makeup. She looked sleek and healthy. She wore a short blue dress that accentuated her uncomplicated beauty. It was her. His woman of mystery. She was Corinne. And she was Catherine. Two totally different women. But the same.

She stepped forward and stood in front of the closet. She removed the wig she was wearing.

"Please, come out, Tom. I presume you have my passport."

14

"There is no devil and no hell," Nietzsche said. "Thy soul will be dead even sooner than thy body: fear, therefore, nothing any more!" When Rakko was a little boy, everything scared him. His father was a green-eyed whiskey-breathing monster who could not bear to look at his own son, but who could beat him with an almost nonchalant ease for the most minor misdeed. His schoolmates were the devil's henchmen, tirelessly teasing and taunting him about the way he looked. His teachers were shadowy shamefaced creatures, constantly averting their gazes from him. The doctors, stern apologists. Yes, his head was misshapen, an accident of nature brought on by a condition known as neurofibromatosis. Simply put, it meant that fibrous tumors had developed within the network of nerves in the skin on his head. Not a severe case, the doctors assured him. He was then summarily dismissed from their dark and gloomy offices. Not a severe case? He would be ridiculed for the rest of his life, but it was not a severe case.

Then he killed someone. What a feeling that was! The killing changed everything. If you know you are capable of murder, then there is absolutely nothing to fear. He was only twelve the first time he killed. His father had sent him to the corner for a bottle of wine, and he had been ambushed by a foul young punk named Tito, who laughed as he ripped open Rakko's pockets and took the ten francs his father had given him. For his carelessness, Rakko's loving *père* kicked the hell out of him. He lay awake all night. By morning he had decided to change things.

The next night, Tito was returning home to his parents' two-room apartment when Rakko grabbed him and stuck the paper spike he borrowed from his father's rolltop desk through Tito's neck and out the other side. Rakko then shoved the point of the spike into a nearby wooden post. Tito dangled on his toes as the blood gushed out and he bled to death. Rakko found two hundred francs in the dead boy's pockets. A good night's work. Rakko felt nothing, except a satisfaction that the job had been accomplished with unexpected professionalism. He was never afraid again.

He joined the Foreign Legion when he was seventeen. He had read all about the legion in French comic books and loved the idea of becoming a soldier. He was recruited at Marseilles then shipped to Africa, to the temple of the Foreign Legion at Sidi-bel-Abbes, where he had first worn the white kepi and heard the legion anthem,"*Tiens, voilà du boudin*." It was at Sidi-bel-Abbes that he began to experience real pride in himself. He had found a place that he could truly call home.

A month later, he was shipped to Algeria to help contain the rebellion that had broken out among the partisans of the National Liberation Front. Algeria was his trial by fire. The killer in him emerged, and took over his life. During this period he became involved with the *Organisation Armée Secrète*, the OAS. The group was mostly made up of disenchanted officers who organized themselves following a failed *putsch* among members of the French army in Algeria. The OAS concluded that drastic and violent action was necessary in order to preserve Algeria for France. Therefore its members began to carry out *operations ponctuelles* – the euphemism the OAS liked to use for murder. Rakko had no strong political views either way, but he was a soldier, a man of action, and here was the kind of action he enjoyed. His first victim was Commissaire Gavoury, the senior police officer in charge of hunting down OAS members. Rakko stabbed him to death outside his apartment. It was quick, satisfying work, and it led to more of the same. The killings usually took place in out-of-the-way cellars and were performed at leisure, after extracting as much information as possible from the victim. Other OAS commandos were, for the most part, happy to drive past a crowd on the street and fire into it or to plant plastic explosives in bistros. On the infamous "blue night" of 1962 there were forty such explosions in Algiers. But Rakko preferred to work more precisely, to target certain *fellaghas* and eliminate them as ruthlessly and violently as possible. He started using a specially manufactured Gurkha Kukri knife, twenty inches in length. Rakko learned to take a man's head off with it. The headless corpses of his victims became a signature. He was feared and highly respected. He got things done effectively. No questions. No nonsense.

By then he had discovered the writings of the German philosopher Friedrich Wilhelm Nietzsche. He read Nietzsche to find an explanation for the violent world he now inhabited and to learn the reasoning for his role in it. "I preach not contentedness, but more power; not peace but war; not virtue, but efficiency. The weak and defective shall perish." Yes, yes, Rakko thought. And he killed with a new zeal. To win one must be strong. There was no place for sympathy or understanding. "Sympathy," Nietzsche wrote, "thwarts the law of development, of evolution, of the survival of the fittest. It preserves what is right for extinction."

Then everything fell apart. Following the murder of an Arab tradesman who was known to be a collector for the FLN, the Algerian police arrested Rakko, who was charged with murder. However, sympathetic jail guards helped him escape before he came to trial, and the OAS arranged to have him transported secretly by ship to Marseilles.

It was in Marseilles that he met Luc Delon. Luc's younger brother was a member of the OAS and had recommended Rakko highly. Luc Delon had become quite powerful importing raw opium into Marseilles from Turkey and running the factories that processed it into heroin. But he was having trouble getting his product distributed in Paris. The Moroccans, who had established their own successful drug trade in the rough and tough Belleville district, were giving him a bad time. Delon was basically a businessman. He was not particularly adept at handling himself in violent situations. Perhaps Rakko could help him. In short order, Rakko had found a new career, no longer as a soldier for France, but as a soldier for organized crime.

That career was almost short-lived. Rakko had no sooner arrived in Paris than three Arabs jumped him as he left a bistro in the Pigalle area late one night. They took him to a cellar where they used a stiletto to cut out his tongue, and gouge out his right eye. He was left for dead in the street. It took Rakko just three weeks to recover. It took him another month to wipe out the Moroccans and clear the way for Luc Delon's heroin on the streets of Paris. By the time the war with the Moroccans was over, Rakko had become a figure of almost mythological proportions in the Paris underworld. "In itself," Nietzsche wrote, "an act of injury, violation, exploitation or annihilation cannot be wrong, for life operates, essentially and fundamentally, by injuring, violating, exploiting and annihilating and cannot even be conceived of outside of this character." Precisely, Rakko thought.

He had sat cross-legged and motionless in the empty room for two days, reshuffling the details of his life, repeating the words of Nietzsche in his head, preparing himself for what was to come. The bloodbath, as usual, would be swift and dramatic. The conscience that occasionally nagged had been cleared. Man must kill. It is his destiny. It was, by extension, Rakko's destiny. "Live dangerously. Build your cities on the slopes of Vesuvius." Rakko recited the words of Nietzsche, and the excitement began to rise in him.

"Why St. Tropez?"

"Because I want to get away. I want to walk in the sun and drink some wine and not worry. St. Tropez is perfect for that. It is the perfect escape. And the sun there is so wonderful."

"You can get the sun in Cannes," he said.

"The sun in St. Tropez is special, Tom. You see, Cannes faces south, so you get the best sun there in the morning. In the afternoon when the sun goes down, it is all very melancholy. But in St. Tropez, the port faces the opposite direction. Therefore, the sun is an afternoon sun, and the colors of the town are at their best late in the afternoon. There is no afternoon melancholy. I like that very much."

In the early afternoon, not even a wisp of cloud marred the azure blue of the sky. Tom's Renault slid smoothly along the autoroute as it cut around the northern tip of the Esterel mountains. Through the ash and cork trees there were glimpses of spectacular ravines tumbling away into the lower valley of the Argens.

She put her head back on the seat, closed her eyes and inhaled deeply.

"There is an east wind in St. Tropez," she pronounced.

"How do you know?"

She laughed. "Because I can smell it. There are two winds. One is the mistral. A very dangerous wind, sometimes. It blows down from the Rhone Valley, bringing dry, cool air. The sea darkens, and all the colors have a kind of clarity that is frightening. You think you can see everything, but it is misleading because you can see nothing. The east wind, on the other hand, that is a very happy wind. It draws out the scents around St. Tropez, and it casts everything in a soft light, a light you can dream in. A light that makes everything okay for a few hours."

"You know, I don't even know what to call you."

"Call me whatever it pleases you to call me."

"Your passport says you are Catherine."

"Then call me Catherine."

"All right. Catherine. Tell me how you knew I was in that closet."

She laughed softly. "It was not difficult. No great detective work. I watched you go into the apartment."

"Aren't you curious about how I got the key?"

"Not particularly."

"It fell out of Jerry Alt's pants a moment before he died."

She said nothing. They drove in silence for a time.

"I've figured out a lot of it," Tom said finally. "At least, I think I have. I know that you somehow were close to Ginger Shane, and that Dieter was arrested in Egypt for her murder. You must have known that when you married him. So I assume you were after revenge, although I have no idea why. Anyway, I can't tell you how much I admire what you've accomplished. Anyone who can engineer a movie disaster the magnitude of *Saudi* deserves a tip of the hat."

She allowed a small, ironic smile. "I'm afraid I can take no credit for that. Dieter created *Saudi* all by himself. The more I got to know him, the more it became apparent that he could mess himself up much faster than anyone else could."

"But you decided to make sure."

"Let's say I held his hand while he did it."

"But maybe you got yourself in a little more deeply than you intended. Maybe you didn't expect Rakko to come jumping out of the woodwork. You could be in a lot of trouble."

"And you are going to protect me?" There was a mocking tone in her voice.

"When you called that night, you said I was your knight in shining armor. Do you remember that?"

She put her hand on his arm. "Please. For the next few hours just be my boyfriend. Don't ask me a lot of questions. I want to be very romantic with you. I want you to hold my hand and buy me champagne. I want you to whisper in my ear and kiss me on the neck. I want you to kiss me in a lot of different places. I want you to make me forget everything, make me laugh. St. Tropez will help. It always does. Can you do that much for me?"

"Yes," he said. "I shouldn't. I know better. I really do. I suppose you are used to men making fools of themselves. I don't want to let the side down."

"You are many things, Tom," she said seriously. "But I doubt very much that you are a fool."

"Oh, yeah?" he said. "Stick around. I may surprise you."

They parked the Renault in one of the lots just below the old town of St. Tropez, then spent three-quarters of an hour wandering around the harbor.

And he held her hand. They inspected the yachts, took note of the tourists. And he whispered in her ear. They considered the paintings depicting the pink and yellow facades rising up around the harbor. The works were mounted on easels, created by artists who interrupted art long enough to conduct commerce, then went back again to the art. And he kissed her neck. And he made her laugh.

They wandered up through the narrow cobblestone streets of the town and window-shopped along Rue Clemenceau.

"Let me tell you about the legend of Tropez," she said.

"Who was Tropez?"

"He was a Christian centurion who was beheaded by the emperor Nero. His body was placed in a boat along with a pig, a viper, a cock and a dog, who were supposed to devour his remains. The boat was set out to sea. The pig and the viper disappeared. But the dog and the cock did not eat the body of Tropez. It is said that the boat was washed ashore here."

"So a headless dead man founded St. Tropez. I thought it was Brigitte Bardot.

"Actually, it was a novelist. Guy de Maupassant. He arrived here and wrote that St. Tropez smelled 'of fish and burning tar, brine and boat.'"

"I'll bet there wasn't even a Benetton store here in those days."

She laughed. "He said sardine scales glistened like pearls on the cobblestones. After de Maupassant, everyone started coming to St. Tropez. Before that it was just a little fishing village no one ever paid much attention to."

They searched everywhere and could not find sardine scales on the cobblestones. Which was fine with Tom. It was sundown now, and the colors of the town were indeed very bright. Tom wanted a drink. They found a tiny bar where the patrons spilled out on the street, leaning against Ferraris and Mercedes Benz to sip Moët et Chandon champagne from long-stemmed glasses. Inside, waiters hurried about, pouring from champagne bottles jammed into large silver ice buckets stationed at intervals along the bar. The atmosphere was rich and casual. He kissed her lips after they finished the first glass of champagne. And after the second, she opened her mouth for him. They were oblivious to anyone else.

Later, she led him down to the harbor. She climbed into a blue-and-white Donzi speedboat. Tom was confused.

"Where are we going?"

She kissed him. "I want to take you for a ride."

"Where?"

"You'll see. Come on. Hop aboard. It's all right. I'm a very good driver."

She handled the Donzi superbly, in fact, sweeping past a Nauticat Motorsailor, heading out of the port. The Gulf of St.-Tropez was turning gray and choppy as the sun lost itself behind the Maures. There was a cool wind, and Tom shivered. He was not sure whether it was the twilight air that made him shiver, or the fear. Was he afraid? He looked at her fine profile silhouetted against the distant background of the resort town of Ste. Maxime. He wanted to love this woman, not fear her. But he was not sure he was in love. He was pretty certain he was afraid.

She cut the craft to the west past Pointe de la Rabiou. The headland was behind them. He could see the last sailboats heading east to make their way into the harbor. Ahead, the Mediterranean darkened even more. The yacht stood out on the horizon like a lone black sentinel. They were very close before Tom realized that it was the *Furyo*. This is where he had seen Mehdi Abbas, where he had encountered Rakko. So that was it. She was with Abbas and had tricked him after all.

"Please, be calm," she said. "This will all be over very soon."

15

Rakko prepared to kill. He stripped naked, then climbed into the black bikini bathing briefs. He set out necessary tools: the twenty-inch Kukri knife, a lock-back knife with an eight-inch stainless steel blade and, most importantly, the Mauser Schnellfeuer machine pistol and a dozen stick magazines each holding twenty rounds.

He placed all the weapons into the waterproof pouch. He blackened his face with shoe polish, then carefully oiled his entire body so that it glistened. As he made his way down the rocks to the motor launch he had stolen the day before, he ran over the plan once more. It was simple enough, yet it would get the job done, and it would create a sensation. Rakko saw no reason to kill simply, quietly. If you are to take a life, he reasoned, it must be accomplished with great drama. The police would be no wiser simply because the production was grandiose. He was an artist, and an artist does not perform anonymously.

The motor purred to life. He nosed the boat out of the tiny inlet. The stars blazed in the heavens. Rakko pushed at the throttle, and the boat picked up speed.

She laughed when she saw the concern on his face. "Oh, Tom, don't worry. You are quite safe. The yacht is empty. Mehdi Abbas will not return for a couple of days, if then."

"I'm the nervous type," Tom said.

The motorboat slapped against the *Furyo*. She cut the engines, then, grabbing a line, hopped on the aluminum stairs that ran down to the water from the deck.

"Well? How do you like it?" she said once they were up on the deck. "Isn't she something? One hundred and thirty feet long with twin diesel engines that allow her to cruise along at twenty-seven knots. If you want to push it a bit, she can do thirty. There is a main salon and a dining room, five staterooms. There are all sorts of state-of-the-art navigation equipment, including a gyrocompass, a Loran C, an interfaced autopilot, an echo sounder, sonar and even color radar."

"But is there anything to drink?"

"*Mais oui*, Monsieur Coward. I'll be back in a few moments. Make yourself comfortable. We will sit out on the upper deck."

She returned with a couple of bottles of white wine. "There is fresh loop in the refrigerator," she said. "It's my favorite fish. I will grill it with fennel. Magnificent. We can do that later. First I want to drink wine and sit on the deck and watch the stars."

There were questions he wanted to ask. The questions filled his brain. But then there was the wine, and before he knew it, the questions flew up to the stars, and were lost there. He was with her, and that was all that counted. This was what he had been after from the first night he met her. Wasn't it? His dream was reality. And reality was a dream. The dream cradled him in her lap, and possessed the softest lips in the world. He was hungry for them. They darted and pecked at him, then captured his mouth, held it, kissed it. The dream ran her tongue behind his teeth. He touched her breasts through the material of the blouse. The dream opened her blouse for him. Her naked brown breasts pointed toward the stars where the questions had fled. Ah, yes. The questions. There should be questions. Maybe one question. "Why?" It echoed across the blackness of the Mediterranean. Her laughter followed.

"What do you mean, why?"

"Why me?"

"Come here, you idiot," she said. "Come here and kiss me. I want to be kissed."

He kissed her again, and she said, with her lips against his, "Perhaps you really are my knight in shining armor, darling Tom. Perhaps I like you because you are a hero without ever intending to be heroic. Maybe I should be asking you – *pourquoi*? Why run off with a perfect stranger?"

"At the time, it seemed terribly romantic," Tom said.

She smiled. "There you go. You want to know why. That is why. At this moment, this seems terribly romantic."

He touched the edges of her mouth. "Or maybe you want me out of the way."

"Why should I want you out of the way?"

"You said something about things coming to an end."

"Did I?"

"You did."

"Maybe I was being merely melodramatic. Maybe this is just the beginning. Now please, darling. Kiss me some more. I love it when you love me."

The figure was not seen as it came out of the sea. It climbed easily up the rock face to the pool terrace. At that time of night the terrace was deserted, and the figure was able to stand there a few moments, undetected, regaining his breath, taking his bearings. He then hurried past the Eden Roc pavillion to the path that led toward the hotel. The first guests to spot him were discussing the possibilities for the evening meal. Joel Adler, an independent producer who had just signed a three-picture deal at Columbia, was anxious to try the crayfish. His date for the evening, a quite ravishing secretary from Chicago he had met at a disco the night before, wondered if it might not be possible to get a hamburger. Joel Adler, at that moment, was beginning to think he had made a dreadful mistake in his choice of dinner companions. Then he saw the man coming up the walk and, as he later told a reporter from the *International Herald Tribune,* "nearly crapped my pants" (actually he used the word "shit," but, of course, the *Trib* wouldn't print that). At first he thought the guy was naked, but then he noticed the thin strip of black bikini. He had some sort of bandolier around his torso. His face was smeared with black, and his head was shaved, except for a long fringe of weirdly colored hair. He seemed, Joel later recalled, to emerge from some punk nightmare. One thing was sure, the producer was quoted as saying: he didn't look like any guest at the Hotel du Cap. Then Joel saw the gun, a machine pistol of some sort, and he grabbed the ravishing secretary from Chicago and tossed her off the path, then leapt after her.

Rakko never even noticed. He flipped the safety off the Mauser Schnellfeuer and continued up the walk. Other guests, intent on a languid evening of luxurious dining, started when they saw him coming toward them, and understood suddenly that there was evil in the world and that it did not necessarily pause at the gates of the du Cap. They fled as hurriedly as possible.

Dieter Voss was upstairs, carefully locking the door to his room. He had done a little cocaine, and it had snapped his confidence back into place. Tomorrow, he would leave Cannes. Mehdi, that bastard, would get his money back. The corporation he and Sir Cecil House set up had made some American real estate investments that had done very well. So even without Mehdi's money, he would still have perhaps a million dollars. Enough to get started somewhere else. Canada perhaps. Canada seemed a long way from Mehdi Abbas. They made movies in Canada, did they not? After a time there might even be a reconciliation with Corinne. Anything was possible.

He walked down the corridor and was delighted to find the glass elevator awaiting him. Cinderella had had her glass slippers. He, Dieter Voss, had his glass elevator. Life could not be too bad as long as a man could take a glass elevator to dinner. Fuck Mehdi Abbas and his killers. He swung the gate closed. Someone once said that the movies were the only business where it helps to be crazy. He was crazy. If he could keep smiling under these circumstances, he could only be crazy. He cackled to himself as the elevator began the short descent.

As the lobby came into view, he saw the curious-looking figure with the oiled body and the black face, dressed only in a bathing suit. What a vulgar man, Dieter thought. Surely such a man was not a guest of the Hotel du Cap.

Rakko spotted the elevator with Dieter Voss inside. He raised the machine pistol and let loose a burst of fire. The glass around the elevator shattered. Dieter was thrown back, clawing at his chest. The elevator continued to make its descent. Rakko fired off another burst. Bullets ricocheted off the brass and the iron gate. But they also caught Dieter in the head and the neck, so that by the time the elevator disappeared from view, going down toward the lower floor, the producer of the forty-million-dollar disaster, *Saudi* was a dead man.

Rakko was vaguely aware that there were others – guests and employees – in the lobby. Their cries and whimperings were like vague, distant sounds. They made no difference. They were civilians; they would do nothing. With any luck, they would not even consider calling the police until he had left the hotel.

Outside, a dark green Peugeot was pulling up to the steps. Rakko hurried down. The driver already had thrown open the rear door for him. He dived inside. A moment later the Peugot was careening out of the courtyard.

They both were naked. She ran her fingers along his stomach, brushing his groin, touching his cock.

"I want to know all about you," she said.

"Isn't that curious?" Tom said kissing her breast, tasting the hard brown nipple in his mouth. "I want to know all about you."

"Mmm. You...first, *chéri*." She wrapped her hand around his penis. "Oh, that is so nice."

He was speechless, luxuriating in the feel of her.

"Tell me, Tom," she said gently. "Tell me about your parents."

She brought her second hand into play.

"That's – oh, Jesus, that is nice.... My father was...a diplomat with the External Affairs department in Canada. We moved around constantly. I've got a Canadian passport, but Canada was never home. I've never felt at home anywhere, come to think of it. Which may account for a certain nomadic restlessness on my part."

Her hands kept busy while she leaned forward and caressed his chest with her lips.

"And your mother. What about her?"

"My mother...oh, Jesus, I'm lying naked on a boat deck while a beautiful woman plays with my.... I think my mother always suspected this fate would befall me.... Anyway, my mother. She made sure the hors d'oeuvres trays were properly served. She fretted a lot. She fretted a lot about me, as a matter of fact. My father never paid too much attention. I don't think he ever got over the fact that I didn't like sports and could not be displayed in public."

He put his hand gently between her legs. She was soaking wet.

"Why not? Oh...don't stop that. You know exactly what to do with your fingers."

"I liked to fart. It livened things up considerably in diplomatic circles."

She laughed and opened her legs wider for him. "There. *Voilà*! Go as deep as you can. Ooh.... Now, tell me.... Where did you go to school?"

"You are so wet and lovely.... School, where did I go to school? Oh, God. Everywhere. I was kicked out of some of the best places in Canada and England. I was not fit for anything."

"Except journalism." She rose up momentarily, then lowered herself again, caressing the tip of his penis against her face.

"Uh.... Exactly."

"You are so hard, Tom.... So you are a wanderer, and now you have wandered here and you have found me...and I have captured this beautiful hard cock."

"Oh, God, you have captured it. Don't stop... capturing...it."

"Darling Tom, I won't stop. I promise. Soon, I must kiss it. Do you mind if I kiss it?

"Be my guest."

She bent to him. He groaned.

After a moment, he said: "There is...an old man who hangs around on the Carlton terrace. He is known as the Director. Do you know him?"

She lifted her head. "Should I?" She licked the top of his penis with her tongue.

"He fits...oh, that's so sweet.... He fits into this somewhere...."

Her hand was stroking him gently. "And where does he, as you say, fit in?"

"I'm not sure. He's suspicious of me.... Umm.... He thinks I'm after a story. So he's – very cagey. But it wasn't the story I wanted."

"What did you want?"

"You. That night at the Carlton. Then on the beach. The way you kissed me. I had to find you again...find out if you were real...."

She rose up and moved along his body until she was straddling his chest, pendulous breasts dangling over him. She moved up so that her vagina was poised above his face. He buried his mouth into the juncture of her legs. She closed her eyes and began to thrust her pelvis back and forth.

"I am very real." She groaned. "Flesh...and... blood.... Ohhhhhh...*ne t'arrête pas....ne t'arrête pas!*"

Eventually, Tom fell into a deep, open-mouthed sleep. She sat up and ran her hands through her hair. In the morning, she would take him back to shore, then return to the yacht to await Mehdi's arrival. After that, it really would be over. The thought failed to spark any emotion. She had traveled a long way beyond satisfaction or happiness. She was now in a desert land where there was no feeling, only steely determination. She had come through this only to be left alone with her obsession. In destroying Dieter, she had destroyed herself.

She looked down at Tom Coward. It had been a risk to bring him here, she supposed. An unnecessary indulgence. But one she needed desperately. The thought of spending the night alone had scared her as much as anything scared her. It was not that she cared about him, she told herself. It was that she could use him.

Perhaps in more ways than one. She smoothed the damp blond locks off his forehead, bent down and kissed his face, then his neck and then his nipple. There was a reckless, unkempt charm about him, no doubt about that. The recklessness and the charm she must resist, of course. There was no future here. Not for her. Certainly not for him. But if there was no future, there was the present. And there was the sex. She could lose herself in the sex. Suddenly she wanted him again, more urgently than before. She wanted to float on this yacht, lost among the stars, fucking and fucking and fucking....

16

She awoke hearing the approach of the powerboats. That was not right. That was not a sound she should hear. Not yet. Tom Coward tossed restlessly beside her but remained, thankfully, asleep. She arose quickly and dressed, trying to stave off the feeling of panic that even now was numbing her.

The two launches, powerful 38 Scarabs, were already coming alongside the *Furyo*. There were six men, all of them naked to the waist, tough-looking, burned a deep brown by the sun. They carried automatic weapons. Pistols jammed into their belts. Rakko, wearing only a black bikini, swung up the stairs just as she came to the railing.

"*Qu'est-ce que c'est?*" She demanded curtly.

"There has been a change of plans," one of the henchmen called out. "We are to take you to shore."

Rakko stood very still on the deck, seeming to sniff at the wind. He did not look at her.

"Abbas wanted me to wait for him here," she protested.

"Abbas now wants you on shore. These are the orders."

She had no choice. If she objected, they would come aboard. If they found Tom, they would almost certainly kill him. It was so stupid to have brought him here in the first place.

"*D'accord,*" she said. She turned to Rakko, touched him on the arm. "Come," she ordered. "We must go."

He advanced a few paces across the deck. She was sure he was going to look below.

"Rakko!" she called out sharply.

He swung around to face her. His face was impassive.

"We must go. *Vite!* I don't wish to keep Mehdi Abbas waiting."

He came slowly back across the deck, then hopped down into her Donzi speedboat. She gave a silent sigh of relief and followed him. Tom would hate her for deserting him. But she had no choice. At least he was alive. Someday, perhaps, he would be thankful. Then she got into the boat and pushed him out of her mind.

As the boats picked up speed, moving away from the yacht, Rakko studied the woman. She made a point of ignoring his scrutiny. He disliked women intensely. They caused men to do foolish things, to be weak when they should be strong. It was safer and less complicated to exercise passion with men rather than women. Women complicated everything. This one, for instance. She had Mehdi Abbas wrapped around her little finger. A careful man, Abbas, made careless in the face of passion. But she did not fool Rakko. She was lying to him. There was someone onboard the yacht. He was certain of it. He would send the second boat back for whoever it was. Mehdi would have his play toy alone for a time. Then he would kill her. Just to be safe.

The howl of the five-hundred-horsepower engines yanked Tom out of his sleep. He sat up groggily, stared around the cabin, then called out for her. There was no answer. Only the engines fading into the distance. He rushed up on deck. No sign of her. No sign of the boat that brought them here. The coast was a sketchy outline in the morning haze. Three powerboats were outlined against it, moving very quickly in the direction of St. Tropez.

"Oh, shit," he called out. "Oh, shit. Shit." Another goddamned trick. But why lure him to this yacht only to leave him stranded? He went back down to the stateroom, dressed, then made his way up to the bridge, mumbling angrily to himself, mimicking her voice: "Oh, Tommeee, could I suck your cock, *s'il vous plaît*? But of course, *mademoiselle*. You may suck my cock and make a horse's ass of me to your heart's content! *Shit!*"

He inspected the bridge and quickly decided that even if he could find the ignition key, never in a million years would he ever be able to drive this baby. He would have to swim back to shore. He slumped down on a deck chair and stared out at the sea. The sky opened up a bit over the Maures and a shaft of sunlight fell through to the water. A powerboat cut across it. Tom sat up. The boat was heading toward him. Someone was coming. Or more to the point, someone was coming back. Now why would they do that? He got up off the chair. There was one pretty goddamned good reason somebody might come back. Somebody might come back to get him.

The powerboat was even closer now, a black Plexiglas knife blade cutting through the waves. What was their hurry? He wasn't going anywhere. He went below through the main salon and into the dining room. He pushed open the door that led to the galley. Above him, he heard a thump as something banged against the hull of the *Furyo*.

The galley was narrow. Brass pots and pans were clustered above a butcher-block table. Everything was spick-and-span and shipshape. Okay. Here he was. What was he to do? Try to catch them by surprise? That would be interesting, since he had no idea know how many he had to catch by surprise. And what if Rakko was among the boarders? He would have a great time attempting to catch Rakko by anything, let alone surprise. But there was not a lot of choice. He could go up on the deck, offer himself up to them and pray they were in a good mood and would get it over with quickly. Or he could do something.

An array of stainless-steel kitchen knives protruded from an oak block. A meat cleaver lay beside it. That was a start. He began tearing through the cupboards. Below the sink, he found a plastic container of liquid ammonium chloride. There was a roll of thin steel cable in one of the drawers. He unhooked one of the hanging brass pots and filled it with the ammonium chloride.

There were four of them up on the deck, each armed with Mac-10 machine pistols. They were professionals, not young, not old, but secure in themselves and the knowledge that out here, as they went about the task at hand, they were not going to be interrupted.

"*Monsieur,*" the eldest of the quartet called out as they spread out across the aft deck. "*Où êtes-vous, monsieur*? We would like to *parler avec vous*." The other three cackled with laughter. The speaker was known as something of a joker. The youngest of the gunmen, the one with the thin French gangster's face and hair that fell to his shoulders, started below.

The first helicopter swooped in, coming low across the port side of the yacht. The joker of the quartet reflected upon his own carelessness. He had not even heard the sound of the chopper until it was too late. The helicopter sprayed the aft deck with machine gun fire, catching one of the gunmen as it chopped up the teak deck and smashed the glass in the windows along the bridge.

Below, Tom heard the whoosh of the helicopter a moment before the galley door was kicked open. The gunman with the French gangster's face came through, teeth bared, machine pistol at the ready. Tom was backed against the wall, adjacent to the door. He stepped out and tossed the potful of ammonium chloride directly into the gunman's face. The man screamed in pain, dropped the pistol and clawed at his eyes. When he stumbled forward, he tripped over the wire cable Tom had strung taut between the two bulkhead walls. He spilled across the butcher-block table. Tom stepped over, raising the meat cleaver. He paused on the upswing. Oh, Christ, could he kill a man with a meat cleaver? The gunman swung his arm wildly and hit Tom in the stomach with the hard edge of his hand. The cleaver fell from Tom's fingers and bounced across the table as Tom exhaled loudly and collapsed to the floor. The gunman groped around blindly, issuing shouts for help.

Back on the deck, the joker recovered somewhat as the helicopter swung around the *Furyo*'s aft end, and came back for a second pass. He noted the position of the second helicopter, which hovered beyond the port side of the craft. The joker reached the top of the aft deck directly behind the bridge. He called to his henchman that there was a second helicopter coming in on them. At that moment, the first chopper opened up. The joker caught a glimpse of a young hotshot leaning out the open hatch with what looked like a German HK 11 light machinegun. He knew the HK 11 could fire 850 rounds per minute, and that it could chew the hell out of this yacht. The joker opened fire at the bubble of the helicopter's cockpit. He saw the young hotshot drop the AK 11 and slump forward. For a moment – the last one he ever had – he thought he had won the encounter. But the helicopter was coming straight at him, and he realized he had shot the pilot and the craft was out of control.

The gunman with the French gangster's face reached out blindly. His fingers found the handle of the discarded meat cleaver. He swung it in a wide arc. Tom, on the floor, pulled at the kitchen knife he had taped to his leg. He rose to his feet, trying to gauge the arc of the gunman's swing. For a moment, the gunman's naked torso was exposed. Tom lunged. The kitchen knife sank smoothly into the man's hard brown stomach.

The first helicopter skimmed along the aft deck and smashed into the cavity of the bridge, taking the joker with it. A moment later, the entire upper section of the yacht exploded.

Tom was still holding the kitchen knife. The dead man was thrown against him by the force of the helicopter slamming into the bridge. The entire boat quivered as though in pain.

Tom was dazed but unhurt. He somehow got to his feet, picked up the gunman's machine pistol and began looking for the way of escape.

That was not so easily accomplished. Flames were everywhere. As Tom made his way into the main salon, the entire upper section of the yacht seemed to be coming down into the cabins.

The fourth gunman lurched at him. His face was blackened and consumed with madness. He held a knife in his hand. Tom raised the machine pistol and pulled the trigger.

Nothing.

He looked down at it in panic. "What the hell?" he exclaimed out loud to his assailant. "How the fuck do you fire one of these goddamned things?" The fourth gunman paused at this, as though stymied by the question. Then he crashed to the floor. It was only then that Tom saw the long shard of fibreglass protruding out his back, one of the explosion's more grisly side effects.

He reached the deck and found a life preserver. The remains of the helicopter lay cradled at a grotesque angle in the housing of the bridge, flames shooting around it. The yacht could not hold the weight of the chopper. It was listing badly, and Tom realized that at any moment it would flop over into the water. He flung himself off the railing into the sea. There was a second explosion, and the yacht, like some great flame-gouged whale, flipped onto its side.

Tom bobbed up in the water and began swimming away from the burning corpse of the yacht. Did sharks roam the Mediterranean in search of hapless journalists? he wondered. Perhaps. But the helicopter was a more immediate danger. It was outfitted with pontoons and was swinging around the burning yacht. Then it came low through the smoke and burst over Tom with a whoosh and a clatter of chopper blades, speckling the sea around him. He caught a glimpse of a face in the cockpit door, leaning out to inspect him. The helicopter banked sharply and came around again. They had him if they wanted him. A burst of automatic-weapons fire and the sitting duck in the water would be no more.

But the men in the helicopter did not open fire. Instead, the chopper settled gently on the sea. A Plexiglas door opened, and a man wearing mirror-lensed aviator glasses leaned out. He wore white jeans and a navy-blue pullover, its sleeves shoved up to his elbows. He put a megaphone to his mouth.

"*Monsieur* Coward," he called. His voice sounded programmed and unreal, as though he were making announcements at a sporting match. "We are not going to hurt you. Please. Swim over to the chopper. We will get you safely back to shore."

There was nothing to do but comply. Tom floundered over to the helicopter. The man with the mirror-lensed glasses bent down to help him hoist himself up onto the pontoon.

"Are you all right?" he inquired politely. There was a second man, the helicopter pilot. He wore a baseball cap and the same kind of mirror-lensed aviator glasses.

"I'm all right," Tom said. "Who are you?"

"Let's just say we mean you no harm," the man said. "We'll get you to shore."

Tom climbed into the helicopter and noticed the machine gun lying across the passenger seat. He strapped himself in behind the pilot. The helicopter lifted off, and Tom had a bird's-eye view of the yacht, now a black smoking hole against the aqueous blue of the Mediterranean. Tom leaned forward and tapped the man with the mirror-lensed glasses on the shoulder. He strained around. He had a fine, straight jawline, cleanly shaved. He smelled vaguely of cologne. Tom could imagine him slapping the cologne against that jawline just before going forth to machine-gun a yacht.

"*Oui?*" the man inquired politely.

Tom pointed toward the yacht. "Did you guys do that?"

The man nodded. "We did. Unfortunately, we missed our target."

"Who was your target?"

The man turned and stared straight ahead.

The shore jumped up in front of the chopper, a mass of sea pine and olive trees. The chopper veered to the right and nestled down into a quiet inlet. The man with the mirrored glasses turned once again to Tom.

"I'm afraid this is where you have to get off, my friend. You are not too far from St. Tropez. It doesn't make that much difference, I suppose, but it's probably just as well if you don't say anything about this."

"Can't you tell me who you are? What about Catherine Bujold? Are you involved with her?"

"*Bonjour,* Monsieur Coward. Have a good day. I am sorry. But you must once again get wet."

He waded ashore amidst a gentle surf as the helicopter rose and lost itself behind the hills of the Maures. He found the highway beyond the narrow beach and a copse of sea pines. Around a bend, and he encountered the welcoming façade of the Résidence de la Pinède. If nothing else, his luck was impeccable. He had stayed there quite happily a couple of years before.

The bartender was a gentleman who understood that if you were good enough to be in the Pinède in the first place, it did not matter that you happened to be soaking wet. He good-naturedly poured Tom a double Napoleon brandy. He downed three double brandies, and afterward felt perky enough to hike the one kilometer that lay between the hotel and the parking lot where he had left the Renault.

However, by the time he reached the car and slumped against it, the effects of the brandy had worn off. He was exhausted, able only to frisk himself half-heartedly for the car keys. He got in behind the wheel, put his head back on the seat and closed his eyes. God, he was tired! He needed another drink and some sleep. He had made love all night, fought the bad guys, swam the high seas, walked a kilometer. Errol Flynn could not have acquitted himself more nobly. Maybe Flynn might have been a little smoother in the sack.

And he would not have stumbled around so much performing the rough stuff. But even so.

His reverie was interrupted by certain nagging questions: Who were the guys in the powerboat? Did Catherine send them? After all they had been through the night before, had she tried to kill him? And who were the guys in the helicopter?

A voice whispered into his ear but it offered no answers. It merely said, "Better hold it right there, buddy boy." Then the voice was gone, and in its place something cold and metallic was pressed against his ear. He turned enough so that he could see the barrel of the gun.

17

"Okay. Now just put those hands up there on the steering wheel where I can see 'em."

Tom would have recognized that drawl anywhere. "Touch Lathrop," he said.

"You're not packing a hog leg or anything like that, are you, Tommy?"

"What the hell is a hog leg?"

"Jesus, Tom," Touch said, sliding around into the front seat, and managing at the same time to keep the gun trained on Tom. "Where the hell have you been? A hog leg is a gun."

"Oh," Tom said. "Well, I'm afraid I'm fresh out of hog legs."

Touch slapped his palm along Tom's shirtfront. "Can't be too careful, Tommy. From here on in I've got to watch myself very carefully. Hey, you're all wet."

"Didn't I tell you? I like to swim with my clothes on."

"Okay, now let's get down to business. Where is she?"

"Where is who?"

"Catherine. Catherine Bujold. You spent the night out there on the ocean with her."

"How do you know that?"

"Because me and the Shree followed you here. The next thing I know, it's morning and she's coming back with some real rough-looking characters. They looked like the kind of guys I took on in *Brute Violence.* That thin, white dude, especially. The guy with the funny hair. Whooee. What would she be doing with a character like that?"

"Don't ask me." Tom sighed. "I'm just the pawn in the game here. I'm present for certain events, but I'll be damned if I know what they mean."

Touch shoved his pistol into a shoulder holster under his linen jacket. "It's time you and me had a talk. Is there a place we can get a drink around here?"

"Ah, Touch, I'm dead tired."

"You been sticking your wang into that girl all night, I suppose?"

"Look, Touch, I don't want to talk to anyone. Some guys just tried to kill me. A helicopter crashed into the yacht. I had to kill someone with a kitchen knife."

Touch gave him a crinkly smile and shook his head. "You are a funny one, Tommy, I'll give you that. And you got one hell of an imagination. Maybe I should get you to write a script for me."

Tom gave up. "All right, Touch. Let's get a drink. You can tell me your life story."

"Well," he said seriously, "that's about what it comes down to."

At that hour of the afternoon, La Romana was pretty much left to the exotic fish in the aquarium. The long-haired beauties who came in late at night were not yet awake, let alone thinking of the fresh pasta or the fish that was grilled on a wood fire. A surly waiter, furious that there should be such a thing as a customer at this time of day, reluctantly served them beers.

"Brigitte Bardot used to come in here," Tom said.

"Too bad she's old now," Touch said.

"We're all old now," Tom said. "Only the young aren't old. What's the story, Touch? Is this the point where you tell me you know a lot more about Ginger Shane than you've been letting on?"

He looked at Tom, genuinely abashed. "Now how the hell did you know that, Tommy?"

"I've put two and two together. It equals about two hundred and fifty thousand."

"It's complicated, all right," Touch said.

A big red fish in the aquarium behind Touch seemed ready to nibble his ear and whisper sweet fishy nothings into it.

"You didn't discover Ginger Shane watching her old videos, did you? You met her somewhere along the line."

Touch was uneasy, glancing furtively around as though Brigitte Bardot might overhear him. "Jesus H. Christ, who's been telling you all this stuff? You are a regular detective here." His eyes narrowed. "You're not doing a story, are you?"

"For Christ's sake, I'm not doing a story. I made a mistake one dark and stormy night. I met a woman. My life is full of such mistakes, believe me."

"And that woman turned out to be Catherine. Right?"

"Right. Except I didn't know who she was."

"I wonder if it's possible to get another beer here," he said.

Tom signaled for the waiter. He skulked over and took away the empty bottles. Touch drummed his fingers once along the tabletop.

"You know, Tommy, ten years ago I wasn't Touch Lathrop at all."

Oh, God, Tom thought, he really is going to tell me his life story. He tried to look interested. "Yeah? What was your name?"

Touch looked uncharacteristically sheepish. "I was Edgar. Edgar Lathrop. I was from Detroit. And my old man worked at the Chrysler plant in Pontiac. Tough old fella. He was the one who hauled me off to the Marine recruitment center. He was a Marine in World War II, you see. It kinda changed his life around, and he thought it might do the same for me. See, I was just hanging around the streets, looking for ways to get into trouble. Nothing serious. Course it didn't get serious because Dad didn't let it get serious. The next thing I knew I was a Marine. Just like my dad."

By 1968 Edgar Lathrop was in the jungles outside Da Nang trying to shoot North Vietnamese. They were not, it turned out, easily shot. But he enjoyed the combat situations immensely. He was, he discovered, one hell of a soldier. Perhaps a little too gung ho for his own good. On a recon patrol, he was hit by enemy fire and suffered shrapnel wounds. After three weeks in a Saigon hospital, he was shipped out to Hong Kong, where he was discharged. It all happened so fast. One moment he was a soldier in the field; the next he was a civilian with no money and nothing to do with himself. He was a fighting man. Except now there was no one to fight. He went looking for another war, and it did not take him long to find it. He was recruited for mercenary work in London, England, by a company that acted as a go-between for African countries looking for professional fighting men and professional fighting men looking for a fight. He saw action in Biafra and the Sudan and participated in a coup in Niger in 1974. But it was all pretty discouraging. Often he was not paid, conditions were terrible, and by the time he was offered a job training Idi Amin's soldiers in Uganda, Edgar Lathrop had had enough of war. He ended up in Cairo, nearly broke, trying to figure out a way to hitch a ride back to the States. Then he had a stroke of good luck. He was hired on as a stunt man and bit player with an American movie company that was shooting a thriller at Giza, near the pyramids outside Cairo. The company was quartered at the nearby Mena House. When Edgar Lathrop was hired on, he was put up at the hotel as well.

"I tell you, Tommy," he said over his second beer, "I swear I thought I had died and gone to heaven. This guy, this casting director, just walked up to me on the street, asked if I was American. I said I'd be glad to sing 'The Stars and Stripes Forever' if it would convince him. Then he tells me they're shooting this thriller movie, and that they're short of American faces. And hell, Tommy, I've certainly got an American face. They hired me right away. I'd always loved the movies. What's more, it looked easy. It *was* easy. Movie acting, Tommy. Nothing to it. You squint. You look tough. Big deal. Hell, I *was* tough by that time. You had to be tough to survive what I survived. I didn't have to pretend anything. Except that I had to get beaten up by assholes who wouldn't have been able to land a punch. But I didn't give a damn. The pay was fine."

He took a long drink of his beer before continuing. "Anyway, it was one night after I'd worked there about two weeks. We'd been shooting right around the pyramids. Everybody sort of pitched in and did everything. There was no real big budget on this job or anything. So I'm there late, packing up some of the stunt equipment. I'm all alone, and it's one of those beautiful, empty desert nights where you don't think there is another soul in the world, and that's just fine. I had a Jeep with me, so I decided to go for a spin. My headlights picked her up. And don't think it didn't shock the hell out of me when I saw her. She didn't have any clothes on at all. This incredible-looking woman, as beautiful as anything I'd ever seen in my life. And here she is naked in the desert. She was just sitting there on the sand, cross-legged, calm as can be, as though she was waiting for something. I stopped the Jeep. I didn't know what to make of it. I called out to her, and she seemed to come out of a trance or something. I went over to her and asked if she was all right. She didn't say anything at all. Just stared straight ahead. I said that it was going to get pretty cold, and that she shouldn't be out here because it was dangerous. Which was not exactly a lie. I offered to give her a ride back to the hotel. But she said no, she was all right. Welles knew where she was. Welles, I thought to myself. Shit. Welles was more than likely Welles Carpenter, the director of the picture. And, I think to myself, this is some chick he's gotten all doped up in his room or something, and now she's wandered out here, and I'd better get her back."

"So you took her back to the hotel?"

"Yeah, only she didn't want to see Welles. Not like this, she said. So I got her back to my room, and it turned out I was right about the dope. She had taken all sorts of pills and was not feeling at all well. But she wanted to talk, Tommy. She said her name was Ginger Shane, and she'd flown in from New York to be with Welles. Now you have to understand about Welles. Back in the fifties he was pretty much of a hotshot director. He did all this what they call film-noir stuff, and a lot of people thought his movies were masterpieces. I don't know about that. But they were pretty tight and very gritty. Welles shot on location when everyone was still shooting New York streets on a studio soundstage in Hollywood. That sort of thing. But the point here is, he hadn't worked for a long time. This Egyptian thing, well, it was supposed to be a comeback for him, the movie that was going to get him back on the track again.

"Anyhow, he had filled Ginger with the usual director bullshit about how beautiful she was. And how talented. But here's the thing: Ginger had talent all right, but she was an actress in what they call adult films. At least she called them adult films. Insisted on calling them that. Got really pissed off when I called them porn. What's the difference? she demanded. Acting is acting. If you do a love scene in the regular movies, is that pornography? The love scenes in adult films were just more honest, that was all. Sure. Yeah. Everyone waving their dicks around, sucking and fucking away, just one step removed from Larry Olivier himself. But I didn't argue the point. To tell the truth, Tom, I was kind of, well, mesmerized by her."

"No kidding," Tom said.

"I tell you, it was like having Grace Kelly's twin sister in the room with you. I'm sitting there listening to this, Tommy, finding out she is a porn actress, and I can't believe it. Welles was going to hire a porn actress for a regular Hollywood movie? Not very likely. She no sooner arrives in Cairo than suddenly there's no part. The executive producer got wind of what Welles was planning to do and had a fit. He went screaming around, saying that all they had to do was cast a porno actress. Then for sure there would be no U.S. distribution for the movie."

"The producer was Dieter Voss."

"That's right," Touch said. "Dieter Voss." He looked impressed. "You know a hell of a lot more about this than I figured."

By the time Edgar Lathrop found Ginger, she had done a lot of coke and pills and drunk a good deal of whiskey besides, then decided to wander out onto the desert. Her intention was to die there. Now, in Edgar Lathrop's room, she broke down and began to cry. The way Touch told it, he tried as best he could to console her. He was a young kid. What did he know? Before long, he had stopped her tears. They found themselves in bed, making love. For Touch, it was something right out of fantasyland, but for her sex was just a way to block out the pain. When the sex was over, Ginger grew restless. She wanted to talk once more to Welles. Touch thought she should get some rest. Maybe he was right, she said. He wrapped his arm around her, she curled against him and he fell into a deep sleep.

When he awoke the next morning, Ginger Shane was gone. He thought it was all a dream.

"But you weren't dreaming," Tom said.

The shiny blandness of Touch's face drooped into sadness. "No, Tommy, I'm afraid I wasn't dreaming. They found her body the next day, way out in the desert beyond the pyramids."

"So she committed suicide after all."

"Well, that's what I thought all right," Touch said. "But then there was this tiny little bullet hole in her head. And no sign of any gun. The police, as we like to say in the movies, suspected foul play. I did, too. The next thing I know, they had arrested Dieter for the murder. That took me by surprise. I had no idea how Dieter managed to get himself into the picture that night. But apparently a porter saw her go into his room. I'm thinking to myself, wait a minute. She never talked at all about Dieter. The guy she wanted to see was Welles. The guy who was making her nuts was Welles Carpenter. Then Welles is providing an alibi for Dieter, so he's released, and everyone is saying, well, she did in fact kill herself. It's just that some Arab wandered along and took the gun. Then the whole thing was forgotten."

"Did you go to the police? Tell them Ginger was in your room?"

"Are you kidding? How do you suppose they would have reacted? Ex-Marine, mercenary. Just the kind of fella who would put a bullet in Ginger's head. No sir, Tom. I was just young, not stupid. There's only one person I said anything to."

"Welles Carpenter."

"You got it. I popped around to have a little chat with Welles, the *auteur* himself. He was pretty morose, distracted, sort of. Anyway, I really laid it on him, told him everything I knew. To my amazement, Tom, this guy breaks down in front of me and begins to sob. Yeah, he says. He killed her all right. But it was a terrible accident."

"Welles Carpenter killed Ginger Shane?"

"In a manner of speaking," Touch said. "Let me finish."

"Okay. Finish."

"This is according to Welles now. The three of them had been together earlier that night. They all made love. Or tried to. Ginger got really pissed at Dieter, and started screaming and yelling. Then she stormed out of the room. That's when she must have stumbled out into the desert. Anyway, after she left my room, she probably tried to get into Dieter's suite. Maybe she did, maybe she didn't, but I guess that's when the night porter spotted her. Along toward dawn, she knocked on Welles's door, and he let her back in. He said she was awfully depressed, and fed up. She knew he kept a pistol in a bedside table. Welles claimed that before he could stop her, she grabbed the gun from the drawer. He claims he tried to get it away from her. The gun went off. And she was dead."

A few more customers had now drifted in. In the interest of commerce the waiter was forced to discard surliness. He actually smiled at a pretty American brunet who murdered the French language in the name of ordering a whiskey and soda. Tom finished his beer, and wished he were a pretty American brunet so he could get another quickly.

Touch was speaking again. "Welles somehow got her out of the hotel and dumped her body in the desert."

"He should have dropped the gun, too," Tom said. "It would have simplified matters considerably."

Touch shrugged. "What can you do? I doubt he was thinking very straight at the time. Personally, I'm amazed he got away with it."

"Let me guess at what happened next," Tom said. "You stood up, pointed at Welles Carpenter, yelled '*J'accuse,*' and turned him over to the Egyptian police."

The sheepishness returned to Touch's face. "Not exactly."

"Now why doesn't that come as a big surprise?"

"All the time he's telling me this story, he's begging me to keep it a secret, right?"

"Understandable," Tom said.

"You had to be there, Tom. You have to understand the scene. The more we talked, the more Welles started to calm down. No more tears. It was as though, well, there was a situation that had to be dealt with. I started to tell him a little bit about what I wanted out of life. I told him I was basically a professional soldier, only I'd recently decided I no longer wanted to be a soldier. This is not a world that takes kindly to soldiers, let me tell you. Welles started saying things like, 'You got a lot of presence, kid. You handle yourself well in front of a camera. The camera's very kind to you. You're a natural. Ever think about taking up the movies seriously?' Exactly the sort of stuff I wanted to hear. Right? And all of a sudden, out of nowhere, Welles said to me, 'How'd you like to be a movie star?' "

"What?" Tom said.

"That's exactly what I said, Tommy. I said, 'What? What the hell are you talking about?' He was speaking real quickly by then, as though he couldn't get the sentences out fast enough. He swore he could do it. He swore he could make me a star in the movies. I got everything it takes, he tells me. And, of course, I couldn't disagree with him there. I'd been sitting on that set for two weeks thinking the same thing. He had a friend in Hong Kong, he said. A bigtime producer there. He was looking for a good-looking young American, athletic, who could star in these chop socky movies he made. Because even though these things made big money in the Orient, he couldn't get into the American market with them. Americans weren't interested in seeing some Oriental guy beat up on a lot of bad guys. They liked to see Americans beat up bad guys. Even Bruce Lee never did all that well Stateside.

"Now I'd even had martial-arts training. Not a lot, but enough to get me through a fight scene. Anyway, Welles Carpenter was telling me he could get me into this stuff. It's a start, he said. You get your foot in the door. After that, it's up to you. I'm thinking about this, Tom. Heck, I'm only human. What else am I gonna do, for God's sake? That's what I was asking myself. I got no prospects, no trade. But here I was being handed prospects. And it was an accident, I think to myself. She was suicidal, God knows, plugged up to the eyeballs on dope and pills. Maybe it did happen the way he said. More than maybe. It probably did happen that way. What difference does it make, anyway, I told myself? I keep my mouth shut, and I'm a movie star."

"So you kept your mouth shut."

Touch Lathrop looked around for the waiter. "I wonder if we can get that guy to get us more beer."

Tom motioned to the waiter, who trotted over. He picked up the bottles and for the first time seemed to notice Touch. His face lit up. "I know you," the waiter said."You are the American actor, Touch Lathrop, am I right?"

Touch shook the waiter's hand and gave him a smile as reassuring as a Hershey bar in the hands of a Third World orphan. "Good to see you," he said.

"I love your movies," the waiter exclaimed. "You are the ultimate American tough guy. You know, with a kind face, but you cannot be pushed around. You are better even than Stallone."

"Why, thank you, thank you ever so much." Touch beamed. "I appreciate it." When the waiter went off, Touch said, "Yeah, Tommy, I kept my mouth shut. Tell me I made a mistake."

Tom said nothing.

"Anyway," he continued, "Welles Carpenter was true to his word. This guy in Hong Kong eventually did hire me. Maybe I did sell out. I don't know. Maybe we all have to sell out a little bit to get what we want in life."

"But what happened to the movie in Egypt? For that matter, what happened to Welles?"

"Welles was in pretty rough shape," Touch explained. "He really was shaken badly by this whole business. Maybe he cared more for the girl than he thought he did. He was on the set, but he really wasn't there. They started to fall behind schedule. Dieter was getting more and more pissed off and was threatening to fire him. Then about three weeks later, with only a few days of shooting left, Dieter ran out of money. The whole production was closed down. Dieter made the usual noises about starting up again, but everyone knew he wouldn't. The picture never did get finished. Welles Carpenter disappeared shortly after that.

Never did hear what happened to him." Touch paused. "By that time I was in Hong Kong. This Oriental guy thought I was a pretty lucky dude – which I was. He said I had the touch. So in the movies I became Touch Lathrop. I haven't seen poor old Edgar for a long time."

"But something must have gone wrong," Tom said.

"What do you mean?"

"Come on, Touch, you get a couple of drinks into you, and you're shoving a Ginger Shane porno movie into your VCR and moping around about this great tragic figure you're obsessed with."

"There you go, Tom," he said ruefully. "I fooled myself. I thought I was this hard case. After what I'd seen, what was one more dead body on the landscape? But I could never get her out of my mind. Then one day I started to buy her movies. Most of 'em are available on video. Most of 'em are terrible, except for her. She's wonderful. I watched her by the hour, and I guess I did start to get obsessed with her. I was in the movies because of her, and I began to think that her spirit had possessed part of me, that maybe in a crazy kind of way I was having the kind of career she could never have. Not that my career was any great shakes, or anything. But it has potential, which is something Ginger never had because of the porno thing.

"After a while, though, it started to get pretty scary. I mean that woman was literally never out of my mind. She was interfering with my whole life. I couldn't even get interested in other women. I was in love with a dead woman. Did you ever see that movie *Laura*? Where the detective played by Dana Andrews falls in love with the portrait of Gene Tierney? The same thing happened to me.

"I tried everything to shake her, even the guru. Actually, old Shree has done more for me than anything else. Can you imagine? If my old man heard I had some guy called the Illuminating Light trailing me around, acting as my spiritual adviser, he would be sitting behind the wheel of that big Buick he's probably driving in heaven, shaking his head. 'What happened to my boy?' he'd want to know. Well, I'd tell him, and I'll tell you. That boy disappeared a long, long time ago."

18

La Romana was filling up with the sort of young women the guidebooks swore came in here, and who would give the young Bardot a run for her money. Touch Lathrop did not notice them. He was a long distance away, lost in beer and memories. Tom decided to pull him back.

"All right," he said, "we have Ginger Shane and her mysterious death, although you seem to have cleared up the mystery. But I don't understand where Catherine Bujold fits into this."

"Catherine is Ginger's sister. Half-sister. It took me a long time to find that out, Tom, believe me. By then I had hired private detectives, for Christ's sake. That's how hooked I was on this whole thing. Some of the people who worked with Ginger in the porn business in Los Angeles recalled that she spent a lot of time in Montreal. The detectives managed to trace her in Montreal. They found out that her real name was Corinne Bujold, and that she had raised her younger sister, Catherine. Catherine's mother and her second husband had been killed in Israel. Corinne Bujold lived quietly in Montreal and took care of her sister. Every few weeks or so she flew to Los Angeles and became Ginger Shane, the hottest porn star in the business. In effect, she lived two lives. Since the sort of movie Ginger made was not exactly available over the counter in Canada, no one in Montreal was the wiser, least of all Catherine."

"Until Ginger died in Egypt."

"Well, I don't know what Catherine found out, but it must have been a hell of a lot, Tommy. Six months ago, the detectives finally found her living in Paris. It took them a hell of a long time. She had covered her trail pretty well, whether she meant to or not. Anyway, Catherine, by this time, had changed her name to Corinne Verneuil – a combination of her sister's first name and her father's surname. But that's not the real surprise. The real surprise was that Catherine had married. The groom was none other than Dieter Voss. For Christ's sakes, she had married the guy who was arrested for murdering her sister."

"So what did you think about that?"

"For a while there, Tommy, I didn't know what to think. Then I thought, well, maybe I was wrong. Maybe Dieter really was the killer. Maybe Welles was just providing him with an alibi, and he bought me off so I would keep my mouth shut about the whole thing. The more I thought about it, the more that became a possibility. Maybe Catherine felt the same way, and she married Dieter to get some sort of revenge. Well, then I find out that Dieter is going to be at the festival with his new wife. Fate has a way of working these things out. I was going to be at the festival. Finally I would get a look at the sister of a woman who had plagued my life for the better part of a decade. And what's more, she was going to be with the man who may very well have killed Ginger Shane. It was weird. Very weird."

"Did you meet her?"

"I've come real close a few times. But I keep getting cold feet. The Shree wasn't very happy about all this. He thinks I should forget it, put the whole thing behind me. He thinks I'll run into Ginger in the next life anyhow. But I wasn't paying much attention to what the

Shree had to say. I was being pestered by Jerry Alt, who wanted me to do a movie with him. Well, the guy was a loser, and I was trying to shake him. But then he started talking about what a pal this Egyptian financier named Mehdi Abbas is, and how crazy Mehdi is about this girl who is married to Dieter Voss. Jerry started to get very mysterious about Mehdi whenever he brought the subject up – which was constantly. I was intrigued, naturally. And it all started to get even more complicated. Obviously, Catherine was up to something. But what? I knew about the apartment in La Suquet. Jerry told me about it, trying to impress me, implying that he met Catherine there to screw her. Which I thought was absolute bullshit. It was all kind of crazy. Then you came around yesterday looking for me, mentioning Ginger Shane. So when I got back, the Shree and I decided to drive up to La Suquet and have another look at the apartment. That's when I saw you leaving with Catherine. We followed you to St. Tropez. Watched you walking around, holding hands and necking. Made me wonder where you fit into all this. Thought I'd better stick around and find out."

"I play the role of the fool who meets the beautiful girl on a moonlit beach and is swept away. It's a role I've played often in many parts of the world. You'd think I'd understand its nuances by now. But I never seem to learn."

Touch eyed him quizzically. "I got to be honest with you, Tom. Sometimes I'm not exactly sure what it is you're getting at." He looked at his watch. "Okay, now here's the thing. I'm to phone Shree just about now. He followed those guys when they took Catherine away. It looked like they were headed back for Cannes, but you never know."

Touch went to make the phone call. Tom wandered over to the bar and found a copy of *Nice-Matin*. The story of Dieter Voss's murder at the Hotel du Cap was splashed all over the front page. He understood enough French to make out that Dieter had been gunned down in the lobby of the du Cap and that, from the description, the assassin was Rakko. There was shock and outrage at this gangland-style assassination. So Catherine had engineered her revenge for her sister's death. Was Tom supposed to serve as the alibi? Maybe Rakko had decided Catherine didn't need an alibi and had dispatched his henchmen to finish off Tom on the yacht. Wait a minute. Why wouldn't she need an alibi? Because Rakko planned to kill her?

When Touch returned, Tom showed him the newspaper and explained his fears. "Catherine could be in a lot of trouble," he said. "I think we'd better get to the gendarmes."

Touch looked appalled. "The police? Are you kidding? What the hell are the police going to do? Listen to me a minute. I've been talking to the Shree. They went back to Cannes, all right. She checked into the Carlton. She's staying in a top-floor suite that's registered to Mehdi Abbas. The Shree thinks she's there alone but he's not sure. We go to the police, Tom, and we'll be making long explanations in a language neither one of us is good at. After that, providing we get our point across, it'll be search warrants and all that crap. Christ, by then they could have killed her and taken up residence in Switzerland."

"You may be right," Tom conceded. "But I don't think we've got an alternative."

"We've got the best alternative there is. We've got ourselves."

"What's that supposed to mean?"

"What does it sound like it means?"

"Aw, come on, Touch. Let's be serious here. You're not suggesting we try to rescue her ourselves?"

"I'm not suggesting we try anything," Touch said, his baby-blue eyes burning with the intensity of the true hero. "I'm suggesting we goddamn well *do* it."

19

It was dark by the time they got back to Touch's suite at the Majestic. The Shree was not in one of his caftans this evening. Perhaps the guru was taking the night off. He wore jeans and a Huey Lewis and the News T-shirt. His brown face grimaced when Tom walked in behind Touch.

The grimace became a look of abject horror when Touch began to fill him in on his plans to rescue Catherine Bujold. "From what you were telling me, the suite is just below the dome on the west side of the hotel. We've still got those nylon scaling ropes from the exhibition last week. Tommy and I rappel down the hotel face to the balcony and come in through the French doors. Catch 'em by surprise."

"This is madness," said the Illuminating Light.

"I agree," Tom said. "What's this rappel stuff?"

"It's a climbing term, for God's sake." Touch was exasperated. "Listen, you two," he said in his best commando voice. "I want you onside, and I want you onside *now*. There's a woman in danger here. And you guys stand around a cushy hotel suite whining. Now come on. Let's go."

The Shree glared at Touch. "This is a violent act. We will not participate in a violent act."

"You don't have to participate in anything violent. All you have to do is keep the motor running at the service entrance of the hotel. When we come out the door with the girl, you put your foot on a gas pedal and you drive away."

The Shree was grasping for an excuse, and Tom thought he came up with a pretty good one: "We cannot drive."

"Bullshit," Touch countered. "You were a chauffeur in London for three years."

The Shree's face flamed red. "How did you know about that?"

"I know a lot about you, my friend," Touch said. "A lot more than you think. For instance, I know that before you were a chauffeur you were in Shrublands prison, where you served three years for robbery."

"We are shocked," the Shree said quietly. "We have given up our past. It did not exist. Now you throw it in our face."

"We all get our pasts thrown into our faces, Shree," Touch said gently. "It's what this evening is all about. Now, will you drive?"

The Shree nodded. "Are you still my disciple?"

Touch put his hand on the Shree's thin shoulder. "You've done more to help me than any other human being on the face of this earth. But tonight I need you to drive."

"Then we shall drive." The Shree turned and snarled at Tom. "None of this would have happened if it wasn't for you. You are a most dangerous person."

"If I can ever afford a chauffeur, Shree," Tom said brightly, "I want one just like you."

"Come on, you two," Touch said crossly. "We're going to have to rely on each other for the next couple of hours." It was Tom's turn to have Touch's arm thrown around him. "Now, Tom, listen up. It's going to be your job to make sure the girl gets down to the car safely. I'll be running interference for the two of you. I may have to stay behind and mop up. Don't worry about me. If anything happens, Shree will drive you and Catherine up to Paris. I have an apartment at forty-five Rue Madame. Apartment number fifteen. You'll be safe there until we get things sorted out." He produced a key, which he handed to Tom. "Everything clear?"

"As clear as my future," Tom Coward said glumly.

For the occasion, Touch dressed in black, just as he had the day Tom saw him promoting *The Adventurer* in front of the Carlton. Their equipment for what Touch insisted on calling "the operation" consisted of two thick coils of nylon scaling rope with grappling hooks attached, a pair of leather gloves for each of them and Touch's .45 automatic pistol. It did not seem to be much in the way of firepower. But Touch was not to be deterred. It struck Tom that perhaps Touch had seen too many of his own movies.

Touch, of course, knew how to get into the back of the Carlton undetected. They clambered into the rickety iron skeleton of the service elevator. It shuddered and quivered its way to the top floor. There was a dusty stairwell leading to the roof. At the top was a padlocked steel door. It took Touch about thirty seconds, using a thin piece of wire, to pick the lock. It was a languid, starry night. Their feet crunched on gravel as they ran along the roof toward the cupola at the hotel's southwest corner.

Touch came to a stop at the point where the roof ran into the sleek curve of the cupola. Tom found himself staring down on the huge N of the Carlton's sign. The royal-blue letters that informed the world this was the Carlton were fitted around a narrow platform about ten feet below the cupola.

"We'll do this in two easy stages," Touch said. "First of all, we lower ourselves to the ledge, just below us. Then from there down to the balcony. Nothing to it."

"Nothing to it," Tom repeated dully.

From this vantage point, la Croisette was a thin golden ribbon festooned with palms stretching off into a wide panorama around the harbor. It was, Tom could not help but think, an awfully long way down.

"Look, Touch, I don't know how good I'm going to be at this."

Touch eyed him coldly. "Don't let me down now, Tommy," he said. "We've come too far to go back."

"Why is it that every time you open your mouth it comes out like dialogue from *The Guns of Navarone*?"

"Come on, let's go."

Touch yanked at the rope to ensure that the grappling hook was wedged securely. Then he swung a leg over the low parapet that decorated the edge of the roof and dropped smartly down onto the platform below. He balanced for a moment, then caught the N beside him and steadied himself. He turned and looked up at Tom.

"Nothing to it," he called out in a loud whisper. "Hurry up."

Tom followed suit. The rope raced through his clenched leather-gloved fists, and the white facade of the hotel flashed past him. Then his feet hit the ledge. He fought for balance. Touch steadied him.

"Easy. You're okay."

"Yeah," Tom said breathlessly. "I'm okay. Now what?"

"Part two." He freed his rope from its mooring, deftly caught the grappling hook as it whizzed down. Then he did the same for Tom. Next, he secured both hooks into points along the platform, tested them with hard yanks. They held. "It's an easy swing down to the balcony from here. I'll go first. You wait a minute or so, then follow. Got it?"

Tom nodded.

"Remember. It's surprise that's going to count."

"Surprise," Tom mumbled.

"Good luck," Touch called and disappeared into the darkness, arcing swiftly down to the balcony. His face looked ghostly white as it peered up. He beckoned to Tom.

Tom swung off the ledge, trying to play out the line slowly. But once again it got away from him, and he was shooting downwards. Tom's feet kicked against a balustrade, fought for some sort of purchase. He managed to hook a heel over the balustrade and pull himself in and down onto the floor of the balcony. He landed on his knees, out of breath. His hands, even with the leather gloves, were burning.

Touch was nowhere in sight. The French doors leading into the suite were partially open. Tom scrambled up and pressed his body against the wall. He listened. Nothing. No sounds. He tried to peer through the doors, but the gauzy curtains allowed him only a hint of light and a suggestion of pale blue. A voice called out. "Tom? Are you out there?" It sounded like Catherine. He pushed open one of the French doors and stepped gingerly inside.

Touch Lathrop lay on his face on the royal-blue broadloom. His gun was nearby. Catherine, wrapped in a black-lace and chiffon evening gown, stood over him. She stared blankly at Tom. The man from the helicopter with the mirror-lensed aviator glasses came out from the wall and held a gun with a silencer attachment to Tom's head.

"*S'il vous plaît, monsieur*. You must be very quiet."

From the other side of the room, a second man appeared. He, too, was armed with a pistol with a silencer attachment. This man was older, silver-haired, the years lending a heavy grayness that made him seem weary with life. He wore a rumpled tweed jacket and dark trousers.

"What are you doing here?" he demanded impatiently.

"I think we're here to rescue her." Tom looked at Catherine, feeling, curiously, a little embarrassed.

"Jesus Christ," the man said. "Can anything else go wrong with this? Perhaps we should invite the jury of the festival in for cocktails."

"He will be here any moment," Catherine said.

The silver-haired man shrugged. "What choice have we at this point? Let's play it out."

The second man nodded. The silver-haired man turned back to Tom. "I'm sorry you keep getting yourself involved in this matter, Mr. Coward. You have a quite remarkable knack for getting in the way. Now, if you will just step back against the wall and keep quiet, we will attempt to see to it that you get out of this alive, although I must tell you, if it were not for her" – he nodded toward Catherine – "I would probably have you killed. Not because I have anything against you. To the contrary. It's just that it would be more expedient to have you permanently out of the way. But Catherine here doesn't like killing. Which is too bad, because there seems to be a great deal of it going on."

There was a knock on the door. Catherine, in a gesture worthy of the worst romantic fiction, put her hand to her mouth. The silver-haired man, the stage manager for this production, took her by the elbow and placed her about midway across the room. The man with the mirror lenses needed no direction. He stood against the wall, just beyond the alcove where the door was. The silver-haired man, having checked the stage, moved back a few paces and readied his pistol.

Outside someone was fumbling with a key in the lock.

A moment later, the door swung open. Mehdi Abbas, dressed in a white evening jacket, walked in looking like a jovial tomcat, complete with a sleek, expectant smile. The smile did not last past the alcove and the view of Touch Lathrop stretched out on the carpet. He glanced sharply at Catherine. At that point the man with the mirrored lenses stepped out smartly, placed the muzzle of the gun against Abbas' temple and pulled the trigger. The tiny noise of the gun sounded hollow and ineffectual, as though children were playing cowboys and Indians with an air pistol. But Mehdi Abbas hurled toward the floor. The rear of his head seemed to lift off and launch itself into the air, splattering the far wall.

Abbas twitched once and lay still. The silver-haired man was abruptly beside the body. Mehdi Abbas lay sprawled face down. The silver-haired man bent over and pointed his gun at the back of Abbas's neck. He pulled the trigger. The body jumped.

"Jesus Christ," Tom said.

Catherine turned away and began weeping.

The end of the bright-red tie worn by the silver-haired man had fallen out of his jacket. He calmly replaced it and straightened the knot.

"All right," he said quietly. "It's done." He gazed down at the body. "He was an old and miserable enemy," he said, seeming to speak to the corpse. "Prepare a nice place in hell for me, will you, Mehdi? I will be along soon enough."

The man with the mirrored lenses nodded with satisfaction. "We have been a long time dragging this asshole out into the open."

"Now we have complications." The silver-haired man lifted his eyes off the body and cast a glance at

Tom. "This rescue of yours, Mr. Coward. How was it to be accomplished?"

"There's a car downstairs," Tom said. He was still trembling, and his voice sounded strained and foreign. "We were going to drive her to Paris."

"A great rescue plan, if I do say so. A work of genius. All right. Let's proceed with it. I presume you have no objections to making sure Catherine reaches Paris safely. It's probably just as well if she is not seen with us."

"What about Touch?" Tom asked

"An unexpected bonus," the silver-haired man said. "He stays."

"They'll think he shot Abbas."

"For a little while. Long enough to slow things down. He'll be all right, Mr. Coward. I wouldn't worry."

"Oh, you'd be surprised at the things I worry about," Tom said. "Rakko, for instance."

The silver-haired man lifted bushy eyebrows above opaque eyes. "What of him?"

"Suppose he's outside?"

"Then perhaps we all will be dead, and we will never have to worry about anything again. And I will be joining my old friend Mehdi Abbas in the furnace room of hell much sooner than I intended."

20

But Rakko was not outside. When Tom and Catherine emerged, the corridor was empty, except for an ancient roué wearing tassled white loafers. He had on a wine-colored jacket and his face was red. He was diligently attempting to get his key into a lock. His smile as they passed was not dangerous, just appreciative of the sight of a beautiful woman in a gorgeous evening gown. They found the service elevator and took it to the ground floor, then went out the back.

Shree was behind the wheel of the Renault. He wore Walkman headphones, and Tom could hear the thin whine of Huey Lewis singing "The Power of Love." Tom walked over and yelled in his ear,"Bang, bang, you're dead." The Shree uttered a scream so high-pitched it should have attracted all the dogs in the neighborhood. Then he bounced out of the car in a white rage.

"You scared the hell out of me. We were starting to get really worried."

"We know. You were afraid you were going to run out of Huey Lewis tapes before we got back."

"We don't even want to talk to you. Where is Touch?"

"Upstairs mopping up," Tom said. "Let's go."

"We won't leave without him," Shree said obstinately.

Catherine carried an overnight bag with her. She opened it up and pulled out a small, nickel-plated revolver.

"Everyone's got a gun," Tom said.

The Shree moved off a few paces, his arms at his sides, a good little soldier obeying orders. Only his face suggested that mutiny was in the air. "If any harm comes to Touch, we will visit you, Tom Coward, and we will bring death with us."

"That sort of witty talk probably charmed Shirley MacLaine no end, Shree, but to me you're just another chauffeur turned guru. The woods are full of them."

"Why don't you fuck yourself?"

"That's what passes for guru talk in the eighties," Tom said to Catherine as he climbed behind the wheel. She squeezed into the passenger seat and Tom sped off down the alley. He looked into the rearview mirror in time to see the Shree Ramana eating the Renault's exhaust fumes and shaking a raised fist.

They climbed out of Cannes and got onto the A-6 autoroute headed north to Paris.

"Quite a night," Tom said.

She passed a hand across her eyes. "I wish you hadn't seen that."

"Who are your friends?"

"The older man is called Ygal Ben-Josef."

"The gangster?"

"He might not appreciate the description. He prefers to think of himself as a retired gentleman who sits around sampling couscous in various Jerusalem restaurants. He and Mehdi Abbas were enemies for a long time."

"So it was his people who hit the yacht yesterday."

"They thought they would find Mehdi there. At the last moment, he changed plans. He had a habit of doing that. It kept him alive. Anyway, Rakko showed up to take me back to the hotel. We had to improvise a little. I'm sorry you had to see that, Tom. It wasn't intended, honestly."

"It wasn't intended?" The anger spilled out of his voice. "What the hell was intended?"

There were tears in her eyes. "I don't know, anymore. I don't know what I wanted. I had some hazy idea of revenge, I suppose. Not all this, Dieter dead, Mehdi, Jerry Alt. It's so terrible, and I'm responsible."

She began the story as Tom whizzed along the highway, keeping the Renault in the passing lane and the speedometer hovering around the 160-kilometer mark. Clustered dots of light signaling the presence of slumbering villages were occasionally thrown up into the night sky. Otherwise, there was only Catherine. And her story.

She had only vague recollections of her mother, she said. Most of what she knew came much later, from the platoons of friends and acquaintances mommy kept on constant alert around the world. Catherine merely recalled a vibrant honey-colored beauty, all laughter and gorgeous clothes. Estée was from Montreal, launched into the world from a Victorian mansion atop Mount Royal. She spent her life being silly and frivolous and careless with just about everyone who crossed her seductive path. Her life was largely expended searching out the next good time and the next lover. The former, likely as not, led to the latter. She found her first husband, Pierre Bujold, in Beverly Hills. He was a renowned plastic surgeon who liked to tell people at parties that he kept Jack Benny looking thirty-nine for forty years. The couple had a daughter, Corinne, before Estée left the surgeon and headed for Paris, where she met the most divine French novelist. She moved out of Beverly Hills and into the Faubourg St. Honoré in such a hurry that she neglected to take one of her belongings: her daughter.

Let the plastic surgeon have her, she decided. He was no longer interested in parties. The French novelist also got tired of the parties. He lasted a surprising seven years before becoming a total bore. Then there was the expatriate American muscleman who starred in sword and toga movies and was the worst actor she had ever met. It did not take her long to decide American musclemen were even more boring than French novelists. The French painter, Robert Verneuil, was not so boring. He had the stamina for the parties and the charm to outlast his predecessors. Verneuil was as close to love as she ever got. During a couple of free moments between soirees, Estée, to her amazement, became pregnant again. Catherine was the unwanted result. By that time, Verneuil was hustling Estée off to Jerusalem. Catherine was just ten years old when her parents died. She thought later that there should have been something much more romantic about their death. Terrorists. A bomb. No such luck, though. A new car hit an old wall late one drunken night.

The couple expired, naturally, without a cent to their names. Not long afterward, a young woman appeared in Jerusalem and was introduced to Catherine. Corinne, at the age of twenty, was the half-sister Catherine never even knew she had. Catherine had never seen anyone quite so beautiful. It was a dazzling experience just to watch one of Corinne's smiles light up a room and warm everyone within range. She would take little Catherine back to Montreal, she announced to the authorities, try to give her the home and the security she required. The authorities were delighted. So was Catherine. Who could resist anyone as beautiful as Corinne?

That began a magical time in Catherine's life. Corinne focused entirely on Catherine. She was sweet, gentle, loving, everything a young girl could desire. Catherine even took the name Bujold. Corinne was now both mother and sister. The two were inseparable. Well, not quite inseparable. Corinne every so often would have to go off to California "on business." She told Catherine that she modeled professionally, and although she preferred Montreal, most of her assignments came out of California. As Corinne grew older she wondered vaguely why she never saw photographs of Corinne in the fashion magazines. But she assumed Corinne worked for American publications they did not see in Montreal. Besides, life was perfect; she was content. In those years, she said, she could not remember a single unhappy moment. Then one day in 1975, seven years after her parents died in the car crash, Corinne came home from California. She was radiantly happy. She was in love, she told Catherine. There was a wonderful man, a movie director. His name was Welles Carpenter. Not only did he love her, he also wanted her to play a part in a movie he was making in Egypt. Catherine, who was by now seventeen, was delighted. Her sister the movie star, she joked. Two weeks later Corinne was off to Egypt. Shortly after that, a stuffy, mustached representative of the Canadian External Affairs Department was uncomfortably explaining to her that a woman with a Canadian passport bearing the name of Corinne Bujold had been found dead in the desert outside Giza, near Cairo. Foul play had been suspected, and an arrest had been made. The suspect, however, had been released, and there was now increasing suspicion that the woman had committed suicide. There was also, the representative added, some confusion. The passport said the dead woman's name was Bujold. But she had checked into the Mena House under the name of Ginger Shane. Everyone connected with the production of the movie shooting at Giza was under the impression that her name was, in fact, Ginger Shane, and that she was an actress from Los Angeles. Could Catherine do anything to clear up this discrepency? Of course, she couldn't. And suicide? The sunny, beautiful woman she loved so dearly had killed herself? It just wasn't possible.

In this way, then, Catherine's safe, secure world was shattered. It took took her more than two years to pull herself back together. By this time she had discovered that Corinne had left close to six hundred thousand dollars in various bank accounts. In her will, she had left everything to "her beloved sister." Catherine used some of the money to go to California where, dumbfounded, she began to discover the truth about Ginger Shane and the astonishing double life she was leading.

After that she journeyed to Egypt and arranged to have her sister's remains shipped back to be reburied in Montreal. On a whim she went around to have a chat with the young Egyptian police inspector who had investigated Corinne's death and had insisted on making the arrest. At first, he was reluctant to talk to her, but they ended up conversing for hours. Over dinner that night in Cairo, the inspector unveiled his doubts and suspicions about the case. Yes, the case was closed, and yes, officially, Ginger Shane had committed suicide. He had been told by his superiors to dispose of the matter as quickly and quietly as possible. The government was interested in attracting more international film production to the country. That would not be possible if policemen went around throwing noted producers into jail. The woman was obviously a drugged lunatic. Her death was a suicide. Leave it at that.

But the inspector was convinced there was more to it. He had discovered that Ginger spent the night with

Dieter Voss and Welles Carpenter. The hotel staff reported finding drug paraphernalia in their rooms. He was convinced that one of the men was responsible for Ginger's death. It was even possible that the two of them, strung out on drugs, had participated in some sort of ritual murder. Whatever happened, Ginger Shane had not killed herself, and her murderer or murderers had gone free.

"So you decided to do something about it," Tom said, keeping his eyes on the road.

"I'm not sure if I ever made a conscious decision," she said after a moment of silence. "It just seemed to flow naturally. I went from one thing to another, and it began to happen. It was an automatic reflex, really. The person I loved most was dead. My life was shattered. The only thing left was to find who killed her, and why."

"Welles Carpenter had disappeared," Tom said. "But Dieter couldn't have been too hard to find."

"The Egyptian police inspector knew he was in Paris. I flew there, assumed the name Corinne Verneuil and began taking the odd modeling assignment, while I played hard at the nightlife and waited to meet Dieter."

She lit a Gitane. The acrid smell filled the car.

"I didn't realize you smoked," Tom said.

"I started up again." Her voice was hard and hollow. She exhaled blue-gray cigarette smoke. "Cigarettes are awful, but they are wonderful at the same time. Anyhow, it was not hard to arrange a meeting. Dieter was quite well known around Parisian society: a movie producer who played hard and liked the ladies. We were introduced at a dinner party. I could tell immediately that he was interested in me. Let's say I made sure he remained interested. I was very sexy and coquettish for him, even the first time. I immediately gave him the impression I thought he was pretty hot stuff. He liked that. Men." Her mouth was not pleasant to look at when she said the word. "You pet their cocks or their egos, and you can have anything from them." She looked at him in the darkness. Her face was defiant. She was expecting him to ask about how she snared him. The cock? Or the ego?

It was not a question he had to ask. He already knew the answer. He tightened his grip on the wheel and said nothing.

Eventually, she turned away and stared out into the darkness. She began to talk again.

"I met Ari when I was in Paris. He was dark, very handsome, very strong and secure in himself. It turned out that he worked for an organization called the Mossad. That is the Israeli secret service. They knew of my Israeli background, minimal as it was, and they had had their eye on me for some time. They thought I could be useful to them. It was Ari who introduced me to Ygal Ben-Josef. He and Dieter had been partners of sorts years before. Dieter would make terrible movies; Ben-Josef would put up the drug money for them. It was through Ben-Josef that Dieter was introduced to Mehdi Abbas. Abbas and Ben-Josef had collaborated in the drug trade between Israel and Egypt. What Ben-Josef didn't know, however, was that Abbas was using the proceeds from the marijuana and hashish, to finance certain Palestinian terrorist elements. The Mossad knew this and made sure Ben-Josef found out. He was furious and immediately broke off the partnership. After that, a nasty war broke out between the two men. One of the skirmishes involved Dieter.

"Abbas set out to woo Dieter away from Ben-Josef. It didn't take much. Abbas offered to provide budgets that would allow him to do more important films. Dieter was very excited. Here was his chance, finally, to become a big-time independent movie producer and to get away from the cheap schlock he had been making. Dieter became heavily involved with Abbas. The Mossad had been after Abbas for some time, without much success. Abbas was very elusive and very careful. He seldom appeared in public. No one knew where he was at any given time. Now, however, there was a new possibility. Perhaps if they worked it right, the Israelis could get get at Abbas through Dieter Voss."

"And you were the bait."

"I could lead them to Mehdi Abbas and at the same time destroy Dieter Voss for what he did to my sister. It was good for them. And it was very good for me. But the Mossad could not become directly involved. At least that was Ari's story. Ben-Josef, the gangster, acted as the middleman, the conduit."

"He also agreed to pull the trigger," Tom interjected.

She inhaled deeply on the cigarette and shook her head. "I was naive, I really was. The little girl who wanted revenge, but didn't want to get any blood on her hands. What a fool! I was dealing with killers. Mehdi Abbas never had any intention of allowing Dieter to live. He had Jerry Alt killed at the Palais simply because he had been talking too much. Besides, he wanted to throw a scare into Dieter. And by the time we cornered Abbas in that hotel suite tonight, I suppose I knew that Ben-Josef would never be satisfied to take him back to Israel for trial. The best way to ensure he never caused any more trouble for Ben-Josef or the Mossad was simply to execute him. It 's the way these people work." She finished the cigarette and tossed it out the window. "I didn't know it then, that's all."

"Did they know why you were so interested in getting Dieter?"

"Ben-Josef knew. But they weren't concerned about my motives. They were only concerned about Abbas."

"So you had an affair with Dieter."

"I was Corinne Verneuil, the model and passionate tart who could not keep her hands off the handsome, sexy Dieter Voss. We were married a year ago, midway through production of *Saudi*, the movie that was to be his crowning achievement. My God, what a cosmic joke that was. By that time Dieter had introduced me to Mehdi Abbas. In fact, Abbas was at our wedding, oozing a great deal of charm."

"And, of course, you were smitten."

" 'I love Dieter. But, oh, Mehdi, there is just something so irresistible about you.' " Her laughter was bitter. "Abbas was as much the arrogant ladies' man as Dieter. Perhaps more so. Women, for Abbas, were prizes to be won. Trinkets that one collected and placed on display. He wanted very badly for me to be one of his trinkets. How could I ignore such a powerful, attractive man?"

As the shooting of *Saudi* was completed on location in Egypt, not far from where her sister had died, Catherine began to play a most dangerous game: manipulating two powerful, dangerous men while seeming to be manipulated by both of them. One night they all got drunk, and Dieter suggested they make love together. He entered his wife from behind, while she made Mehdi Abbas come in her mouth.

It was after the affair with Mehdi, that Catherine discovered the secret that would destroy Dieter Voss. As the filming of *Saudi* ended, she found that her husband was taking millions out of the production and transferring the money to Sir Cecil House in the Netherland Antilles. In turn, Sir Cecil quietly set up a front company, hired a local agent to act as the company's offshore manager, and began to reinvest the stolen money in American real estate.

By the time she and Dieter arrived at Cannes for the festival, Catherine had all the proof of embezzlement she needed. What she didn't realize was that Abbas had already hired Rakko to kill Sir Cecil. Now he was taking a ruthless delight in concocting a plan to eliminate Dieter. The plan gained momentum as Abbas came to understand what a disaster *Saudi* truly was.

"And Dieter never suspected anything was wrong?"

"He knew Mehdi was angry, and suspected it was because he had stolen five million dollars from him. That's why he was desperate for *Saudi* to be accepted. If he could make it a hit, perhaps Mehdi would forgive and forget. When he could no longer lie to the world about *Saudi*, he tried to sign Lacy Bergen to a long-term contract. He was hoping he could appease Mehdi Abbas that way. Abbas already knew Lacy's mother. One night he invited her for dinner at his yacht, and Dieter decided that with her out of the way for the evening, he could put into action a plan that would ensure Lacy's commitment to his production company. He enlisted my help, of course. But he didn't count on you being there and screwing everything up for him."

"Where did Jerry Alt come into this?" Tom asked.

"Jerry acted as a kind of go-between. He was a *poseur*, constantly announcing projects he could never make, always in financial trouble. A bit of a joke, really. Years before, he had borrowed money from Mehdi that he had never been able to pay back. Mehdi used him. I gave Jerry information about *Saudi*, and he got it back to Abbas. That way I would not be directly linked to Abbas. It was Jerry who rented the apartment in Le Suquet so we would have a place to meet."

"So after he had Jerry killed at the Palais, Abbas thought he'd better clear away any evidence of your presence in that apartment. That's why he sent Rakko around."

"Yes, that's right."

Headlights leered into the rearview mirror, very close. For a moment Tom thought it might be the police. But it was only a BMW, impatient for the slower Renault to get over. Tom moved into the right lane and the BMW lunged by. Its taillights blinked insolently and it was gone in the darkness. Catherine began to cry, weeping quietly. Her head was turned away from him. He wanted to reach out, touch her, reassure her that everything was all right. But nothing was right. Everything, as usual, was all wrong

Just before dawn there was a nameless village with cobblestoned streets, red tile-roofed houses and an ancient bridge running over a bubbling stream. There was a medieval inn with wood-beamed ceilings and a big brass double bed. He was dreadfully tired. The bathroom would have scared hell out of the medieval French. It featured a cathedral ceiling and gold fixtures. Floor-to-ceiling mirrors everywhere. His image repeated itself dozens of times as he stripped off his clothes, started the water gushing into the marble bathtub. As the room began to fill with steam, he pulled out his shaving kit and began to smear thick cream over his stubble. A shave, a drink and bed. Try to put the whole mess away for a while. Fat chance of that. The door was open and the *auteur* of the mess was allowing the chiffon and silk to slip down those endless show girl's legs. She came into the steam and the gold. The mirrors were beside themselves with ecstasy as they threw around her naked image. She went over to the bath and turned off the taps. Then she ran her fingers lightly along the back of his neck. There was a chair beside the sink. She turned him around and sat him down in it. Then she plucked the razor from his fingers. "Let me," she murmured.

He was going to object but he was mesmerized by the dozens of Catherines now bending over to run the razor through the shaving cream along the side of his face. The blade scrapped gently against his skin. She kissed his mouth. The blade moved against his skin. Then she rubbed the tip of her breast against the shaving cream. The fingers of the other hand slipped around his cock.

"Don't," he said.

She smiled. "You don't mean that," she whispered. "Say only what you mean."

His penis was a hard mast propped up into her stroking fingers. She shaved. Stroked. Shaved. Stroked. He groaned loudly.

"There's something that still confuses me," Tom finally managed to say.

"What, darling? What confuses you?"

Shave. Stroke. Shave. Stroke.

"You had become Corinne, a great part. You played it brilliantly. You fooled everyone. But in the midst of a great performance, you discard your costume and go back to being Catherine. Why?"

She withdrew her hand from his penis, held his chin while she brought the razor around it. "A ridiculous thing, perhaps," she said. "But the more I was Corinne for Dieter and for Mehdi, the more I hated her."

"Did you do this with Dieter?" he asked. "Or Mehdi?"

Her smile was enigmatic. She swung one leg up and straddled him. The razor rasped against his skin as she eased down onto his penis.

"Oh, there," she said. "How did you get in there?"

She began to move up and down on him, very slowly. At the same time she continued with the shaving, running the razor down his neck. The sound of skin against skin. Steel against skin. Dozens of Catherines fucking and shaving in the gold and the mirrors.

As she worked, she began to talk again.

"Dieter loved the idea of me sleeping around. With men. With women. It excited him very much. I did it, of course. I was very compliant and enthusiastic and all that. But I was disgusted with myself. I was trying to avenge my sister's death, trying to come to terms with what she had done with herself and her life. Now, ironically, I found myself becoming exactly what she had been. Maybe even worse, in a way. She had become me. I even had her name."

"And Ginger," he demanded. "Did Ginger do this in her movies?" He was excited – and angry. He wanted to love her, and to hurt her. His feelings were as complex as the multitude of images swarming around him.

She put the razor to one side, wrapped her arms around his neck and kissed him. Her breasts tossed against his chest. When she pulled away, her face and mouth were covered with shaving cream. She ran a hand across her lips.

"I had to get away from Corinne, even if it was for a little while. Dieter gave me plenty of freedom, in Paris and then in Cannes. So it was easy to escape, wear a wig, different clothes and just become – well, become me for a few hours. I should never have gone into the Carlton that night. But I didn't think anyone would be there, and I wanted a drink. I met you, and you were quite fun. You didn't know Corinne, the little sex object. You only knew me, Catherine, a woman at the bar. That was so nice, Tom." She shuddered against him. "Almost as nice as this."

"Until Rakko made his appearance."

"Yes. Rakko. Terrible Rakko. He is the only man who makes me truly afraid. He spotted me going into the Carlton and came in to find out what I was doing there alone. He was very suspicious and angry."

"Why didn't he kill me on the beach?"

"I wouldn't let him," she said.

"Oh? Why not?"

"How could I?" The smile was softer, less enigmatic; the smile of a woman you could love so easily. "It is as I told you before, Tom. You are my knight in shining armor." She giggled. "My beautiful, clean-shaven knight." Then she bit her lower lip and her eyes closed, and she began to buck against him so that everything else was forgotten. The images loomed up and enveloped them.

Late in the morning, he found the razor where she had dropped it as they made love. Bits of shaving cream still clung to it. The smell of her still hovered in the air. But the evening gown was no longer on the floor. And his was the only image reflected in the mirrors.

She was gone.

21

The police are looking for you." Lacy Bergen's voice over the phone was accusatory.

"Why would the police be looking for me?"

"They say you're an accessory to the murder of Mehdi Abbas. They found him dead in his suite at the Carlton Hotel. They're holding Touch Lathrop. Apparently he was in the suite. Only Touch has a concussion, so he's in the hospital. Tom, they spent an hour and a half questioning me and my mother."

"Why would they question you?"

"Because when they came to search your room, there I was in your bed, with my stuff all over the place. That's why they questioned me. They think I'm your moll or something. I'm really upset. There are reporters snooping around. They're all asking questions about you. They even found out you got kicked out of the hotel. My mother is having fits all over the place. She's afraid it's all going to get into the papers. About me and you, I mean." She lowered her voice to a conspiratorial whisper. "Tom, you didn't kill anybody, did you?"

"Of course not. What do you take me for?"

"That's what I told Mother. But she's a little down on you right now. She knows I'm crazy about you."

"How does she know you're crazy about me?"

"Because I told her."

"Oh, great."

"Listen, Tom, I'll stick by you. Honest, I will. I am very loyal and true blue. I mean if you need money for your defense or anything like that, I can provide it. I've got lots of money. I'm rich as all get out. Incidentally, where are you?"

"I don't think it's a very good idea to tell you."

"You mean you think the cops will sweat it out of me?" she asked melodramatically. "Tom, they'll never make me talk, I swear. They could stick bamboo shoots under my fingernails and everything and I wouldn't talk. I'd be pretty pissed off, though, if they ruined my nails."

"I just don't want you implicated in this any more than you are," Tom said. "Look, Lacy, I appreciate everything, I really do. It's just that there isn't much you can do right now. I'll be in touch as soon as it's all clear, I promise."

"Tom, I love you. Just remember what I said before, okay? I'm in for the long run."

"I'll remember," Tom promised as he hung up.

There was nothing to do but go on to Paris. Catherine, thankfully, had not taken his Renault. But then why would she? Now that she had disappeared, he and Touch were neatly left to hold the bag for the murder of Mehdi Abbas. Maybe the staff at the Carlton would recall a woman in the top-floor suite. But then again, maybe not. If no one saw Catherine, then there were only Touch and Tom and the corpse of Mehdi Abbas.

"God, you're a smart fellow, Thomas," he said aloud as he got behind the wheel of the car. "How the fuck did you get so smart? "

He turned the Renault onto the autoroute. During the drive to Paris he tried hard to hate Catherine Bujold. He did not succeed very well.

Paris intoxicated him. Victor Hugo called it "the ceiling of the human race." Precisely. Paris was reason enough for life. Walks along the Seine. Afternoons at the Jeu de Paume museum. Sipping espresso in outdoor cafés on the Champs Elysées. The lamb stew at La Coupole. The tarte aux fraises and the crème glacé on Ile Saint-Louis. Kir royale at the Closerie de Lilas. The underwear ads in the Paris Metro. This was why you lived. Everything else was inconsequential window-dressing. He would sit at La Selecte in Montmartre and know Hemingway and Fitzgerald and Morley Callaghan once sat there. He would eat the cold lamb salad at Brasserie Lipp, wash it down with a bottle of Rouge d'Alsace Pinot and know that not long ago Jean-Paul Sartre had done the same thing for lunch. Paris and its triumphantly overblown sense of its own grandeur exhilarated him, excited him. Paris was the most beautiful, the most seductive city in the world. He would die thinking, "Oh, shit, this means I will never see Paris again." Therefore, he would live forever; he could not leave Paris.

Of course his view of Paris was entirely romantic and idealized. Someone once had suggested that if he loved the city so much he should live there. The idea appalled him. The city was the place of his dreams. It was a lovely woman who could rejuvenate his spirits. If he lived there, then Paris would be the woman he lived with, not so lovely, perhaps, not so special. So he was selfish about the city. He used it and gave nothing back, except ceaseless love and gratitude.

At the moment, as he turned off the Boulevard St. Germain in the midst of the rush-hour traffic, his idealism about Paris was held in check. Today, as he searched for Rue Madame, Paris was a gray and dangerous place, a background against which he huddled, praying that some gendarme would not leap up and arrest him for murder. He was, this time, not a rapturous visitor to Paris but a rather frightened fugitive.

The radio was full of reports about anti-American demonstrations. As summer approached, Ronald Reagan was the mad cowboy and the American flag was good only for burning in the streets. There had been a huge demonstration that afternoon outside the National Assembly. Eventually it had been broken up by riot police. More trouble was expected that night.

He found that most unusual of things in Paris, a parking spot, in front of the fortress-like building on Rue Madame where Touch Lathrop had his apartment. There was a private school across the street and from behind a high stone wall, as he locked the car, he could hear the exuberant cries of children. He dodged the dog shit in front of the heavy wooden door and went into the cement courtyard that led to the apartments. An elderly woman in a black dress, carrying a fluffy white poodle, passed him without so much as a suspicious glance.

The apartment was large, a vault-ceilinged place with high, draped windows, fire places, *faux-marbre* walls. There was a frescoed drawing room, Louis XIV furniture, Vermillion lamps. Given Touch's proclivities, Tom had expected something with Navajo throw rugs and cowboy paintings. There was either more to Touch than initially met the eye, or else he had given a good interior decorator his head. Tom suspected the interior decorator.

Now what? he wondered. If Touch was talking to the police, then it was only a matter of time before he told them about the apartment. They would certainly come here looking for him. He couldn't stay. Not for long, anyway.

The telephone rang. In the regal emptiness of the apartment, the sound was jarring. He debated for a moment whether to answer it. What if it was Catherine? He picked up the receiver.

"*Oui?*"

"So. You are there," the caller said.

"I'm here," Tom said.

"Are you alone?" the caller inquired.

"Yes."

"She isn't with you?"

"I don't know who you are talking about."

"Catherine. She's not with you?"

"No."

The voice said: "We must talk. Meet me tonight at the Café Deux Magots. Eight o'clock."

Then the line went dead.

Paris was a nervous town. The omnipresent battleship-gray vans of the CRS once again lined the back streets, this time behind the Boulevard St. Germain. As Tom walked along Rue de Rennes, he could peer inside the vans and through the grillwork in the windows. Inside stony-faced riot police sat quietly, staring straight ahead. Waiting.

Battalions of kids swooped along the street past him, their faces alive with excitement. The air was clear and chill and the night was full of danger. At the wide intersection where Rue de Rennes bumps into Place St. Germain, the numbers of students and police abruptly multiplied. For the moment the area was a kind of good-natured demilitarized zone. The demonstrators jostled past the cops, festive in spirit. The police in turn showed nothing.

Traffic had been rerouted in anticipation of trouble, so that St. Germain was oddly empty as Tom crossed to the Deux Magots. Ordinarily the tables that littered the street would be crowded with customers trying to get the attention of the bustling waiters.

But not tonight. The tables were mostly empty. The few patrons dedicated enough to the drinking of Cinzano and Pernod, and willing to brave the police and the demonstrators, huddled self-consciously over their aperitifs, keeping a nervous eye on events unfolding up the street. Ordinarily, there were any number of street performers plying their trade – singers, acrobats, unicyclists, jugglers. This evening there was a single fire-eater, a human torch. He was a long-haired lad, stripped to the waist, showing off a perfect torso, as he sent a sheet of fire off into the night. Actually, the fire-eater blows a fine mist of kerosene out his mouth toward a lit torch that he carries. Thus, the fire doesn't burst out of his mouth, but instead rushes toward it from the torch. The effect however, is quite dramatic, as the human torch looks as though he is literally spitting fire. It is a dangerous business, but for once the fire-eater was not the focal point of the street show, and he knew it. The demonstrators had the starring roles. Nonetheless, his show went on.

An old waiter, his hair pushed straight back from a high, liver-spotted forehead, eyed Tom with sad suspicion as he entered the restaurant. The walls were waxen; the red leather of the banquettes was fading faster than memory. The mirrors along the walls held onto the past, made it smoky and unclear. The circus was outside. In here, Deux Magots showed off its age quietly. Tom gave the waiter a determined smile and ordered a Kir Royale.

The waiter had just set the drink down when Tom heard a door at the back of the restaurant open and close. Tom turned with the drink in his hand. The Director stepped toward him, raising his cane in a gesture of welcome.

22

The Director was dressed like a native Parisian. Or at least the way the Parisians dressed in old American movies about Paris. He wore a rumpled gray trench coat and a beret, which was shoved on his head at a jaunty angle. The dark glasses complemented the look. Tom half expected Gene Kelly to appear behind him, singing something by Cole Porter. The Director leaned heavily on the ivory-handled walking stick, and he moved with the lumbering magnificence of a float in an Easter parade.

"*Bonsoir,* Tom," he said. "Did you have any difficulty getting here?"

"Not really," Tom said. "But I'm afraid there may be some trouble tonight."

"Yes," said the Director, "it looks like it. The demonstrators don't like America. But then nobody over here likes the Americans these days. They think Ronald Reagan commits international crimes that end up being paid for on European soil."

"Can I get you something?"

"No, nothing for me, thanks, Tom. I must keep my wits about me for the next while. That means no alcohol, alas."

"How did you know where to find me?"

The Director leaned his awesome weight against the bar. The very act of moving across the room seemed to have drained him. His face was puffy. "A little guesswork, actually. I read in the papers that

Touch Lathrop had turned up in the hands of the French police, and that the authorities were looking for you in connection with the murder of Mehdi Abbas. I figured you might be headed this way. And I've known about Touch's Paris apartment for years. It was worth a phone call, anyway. *Voila*! Here you are."

"It's too bad I couldn't bring Catherine along with me," Tom said. "Then you could have told her the truth – that you are Welles Carpenter."

The Director removed the dark glasses, as though they were a disguise he no longer needed. He blinked in the yellowish light.

"Yes," he said. "That's what I would like to tell her. It's ironic. When she first arrived in Cannes with Dieter, we were actually introduced one day on the Carlton terrace. She didn't recognize me. No inkling of who I was. She didn't know how close she was to the man who supposedly killed her sister. But then I've changed quite a bit." He slapped at his enormous belly. "Welles Carpenter was swallowed up long ago inside the body of a very fat, sad old man."

"Oh, I don't know," Tom said. "I think you thoroughly enjoyed the role of the Director."

"It was a great part, actually. This mysterious old lizard in the noonday sun on the Carlton terrace, dispatching wisdom. I enjoyed it immensely. So did everyone else. They didn't want to know who I was. That would have spoiled it. They preferred the mystery. Cannes is all illusion, anyway. I fit in very well."

"But now there is no more mystery. We are all revealed for what we are. The part of Corinne the slut was played by Catherine Bujold. And for this engagement, Welles Carpenter essayed the role of the Director. The dead are buried. You can disappear into the woodwork again, Welles. The play is over."

"Not quite. Catherine still believes Welles Carpenter is a killer."

"At this point, I'm not sure what she believes. I'm not sure what I believe."

"I did not kill Ginger Shane."

"Then who did? Dieter?"

"I don't think so. I was being fairly honest when I came forward to provide Dieter with an alibi. The circumstances we concocted were a lie. We most certainly did not spend the night discussing production problems. But I'm all but certain he wasn't responsible. Who killed her? To be honest, I'm not sure. I'm not sure anyone killed her. Look, I was dreadful with Ginger. I used her. I brought her to Egypt for reasons of the flesh. I thought she was beautiful and that she was a great lay. I did not think she was anything else. I thought it would be fun to have Ginger on the set. She could play a small part, and I would have someone to keep me warm each night. It's hard for me to say that now, but it's the truth. I must say it.

"When Dieter came along to dinner, I thought, well, a threesome might be fun, and there was a lot of dope and wine, and she seemed to be playing along just fine, until we got back to my suite. Then she had a fit when Dieter attempted to, uh, include himself in the proceedings. He left. I calmed her down, and then I told her something that is absolutely dreadful, and that in retrospect I regret a great deal."

"The threat is as old as show business," Tom said. "You told her that unless she went to Dieter's room, she wouldn't get the role, and she would have to get back on the plane and go back to being a porn actress."

He wagged his head almost imperceptibly. "And off she went to his room. I knew then that something had broken inside her. The tiny mechanism that supports self-esteem had snapped. But I let her go. I was arrogant and angry. I was also worried and drunk."

"What happened then?"

"She was back in an hour. Tears, awful hysteria. Dieter had told her she couldn't have the role. She wanted to die, she said. I gave her Nembutal, which was a mistake. She wanted to leave the hotel at that point, wanted to go out on the desert and meet what she called the father of terror. I was drunk enough for it; she was hysterical enough. Next thing we were in a car, speeding out to the pyramids. I had a bottle of Wild Turkey with me. I was really gone by that time. We got to the pyramids, under the moon, and stumbled around a bit. She took off her clothes, yelled and screamed at the sky. Then I passed out. When I awoke about an hour or so later, she was gone. So was her clothing. I figured she must have returned to the Mena House. When I got back, there was no sign of her in the room. No sign of her anywhere. The next day, they found her body a couple of miles away."

A clamor rose from outside. Tom could hear the crack of teargas guns. The old waiter hurried over.

"*Messieurs, s'il vous plaît.* We are about to close. It is becoming very bad on the street."

"We'd better be going," Tom said. "This is leading nowhere. There's as much confusion in here as there is out there."

Welles Carpenter stared at his dark glasses for a moment, then, as though climbing once again into his disguise, slowly placed them back on the bridge of his nose.

Tom asked, "Why did you get in touch with me? Why did you want to meet me here?"

"You stuck your nose into this," Welles said. "Initially, I was somewhat amused. A welcome respite from reporters wanting memories of Cannes past. Ten years had gone by. I was secure in my new identity. It was like a second skin. If you wanted to ask certain questions about Dieter Voss and his new wife, I could handle them. I, of course, knew who it was Dieter had married, and I suspected that she did it to get at him. After all, Dieter had been arrested for her sister's murder. But then you started to cut closer to the bone, and it became irritating – and worrisome. By that time, I had come to understand what it was Catherine was up to. If she believed Dieter to be a killer, then perhaps she believed Welles Carpenter to be a killer as well. I became concerned enough that I left the festival and returned to Paris. But then it got very messy. Dieter was dead. I was worried that perhaps the people who murdered him were coming after me. I was hidden, but I was not that hidden. I thought if I could get to you, then perhaps you could help."

"How can I help?"

The old waiter approached again. "*S'il vous plaît, messieurs.* Please! You must leave it is very dangerous to stay here. We must close. *Tout de suite!*"

Welles shifted the cane into his right hand and used it to pivot his incredible weight in the direction of the door.

"Set up a meeting between me and Catherine. I want to tell her my side of the story. Look, Welles Carpenter disappeared a long time ago, not because he was guilty of murder but because he was responsible for the destruction of a beautiful young woman who only wanted to love him and change her life. Welles Carpenter could not live with that knowledge. Therefore, Welles Carpenter was destroyed. I died in Egypt a decade ago. My life and my career died with me. I did not escape the suffering, believe me. If I can make that clear to Catherine, she may be able to find it in her heart to forgive me."

"I'll see what I can do," Tom said, as he followed Carpenter's laborious progress toward the door. "But I have no idea where she is or whether I will see her again. My suspicion is that I won't. I think she just wants to get away and forget that this ever happened."

"If that's the case," Welles said, "she will find the forgetting difficult. I know. I couldn't do it."

They were finally outside the café. The old waiter slammed the door behind them and locked it. Welles turned to him.

"Anyway, I thank you for lending an ear. Maybe I never will meet Catherine. Maybe it's just as well. It was only an idea, perhaps faulty, but an idea. Besides, Tom, I like you. I admire your spunk and tenacity. Didn't think you had it in you. So, if the truth is to be known, maybe it's just as well you know it."

"Except," Tom said, "everyone seems to have different versions of the truth for that night."

Out in the intersection, a car, thrown over on its side, was burning furiously. Dark shapes danced against the flames. Demonstrators streamed past the café shouting, setting fire to tires they had piled in the street. Wisps of teargas trailed through the night air. Out of the smoke moved helmeted riot police.

"They're pushing the demonstrators out of the intersection," Tom said. "They're trying to break them up into smaller groups and drive them into the side streets."

In front of them, on the edge of the curb, the young man who played the human torch seemed oblivious to the commotion unfolding around him. He tipped a plastic bottle to his mouth, and exhaled a fine mist of kerosene toward the flaming torch. A three-foot long tongue of fire lept into the air. He looked around, his eyes alight with glee.

"*Comment ça va*?" he called out.

Welles Carpenter turned slowly to him, as though expecting to engage the man in conversation. The fire-eater lifted the bottle and suddenly sprayed kerosene across Carpenter's face and chest. Carpenter dropped his cane in horror, and stumbled back a couple of feet. The fire-eater exhaled again, drawing the torch away from his mouth, the tongue of flame dancing in its wake. The flame brushed against Welles Carpenter's shoulder, and suddenly the upper portion of his body was engulfed in fire. He waddled into the boulevard like some comical special effect called in to relieve the tension of the riot. Nearby, demonstrators began screaming. Tom knocked the bottle of kerosene from the fire-eater's grip. The man retaliated with his foot, kicking Tom savagely in the groin. Tom sank to the curb.

A black Peugeot whipped around the corner. Pain lunged through Tom's body, blurring his vision. He vaguely noted that Welles Carpenter had fallen on one knee on the boulevard. The Director lifted up his arms, imploring the heavens. The heavens were closed for the night. His arms were on fire.

A moment later, the Peugeot slammed into the burning body, sending it flailing through the air. By that time, Tom was on his feet, ignoring the pain. He managed to reach Carpenter, threw his jacket over him, trying to smother the flames. Tom bent down. The fire had burned away most of his beard. His blackened lips moved.

"Didn't," he mumbled. Tom bent closer. "Kill her. Didn't..." Then Welles Carpenter was dead.

The Peugeot screeched to a stop a few feet away. The rear door opened and Catherine Bujold reached out, motioning frantically to Tom.

23

"Tom," she called to him. "Get in!" He caught a glimpse of Ygal Ben-Josef behind the steering wheel. Her voice again: "Get in!" The voice was tough. Not the voice of seduction or of love. The voice of the last chance. Tom ignored it. He dodged up the street, away from the voice. The overturned car was still smouldering. Figures loomed out of the clouds of teargas and smoke, coughing, holding handkerchiefs to their noses and mouths. Tom's throat was on fire. He began to choke. He kept running. In the distance was a searing white light, as though someone had turned on the houselights at the end of the world. Alien forms loomed up from the light. The riot police, clearing the area with a mechanical savagery.

For Tom, safety lay in the direction of the danger. He glanced behind him. Catherine had got out of the car and was running after him. He started for the far side of the street. A group of students, bloodied and panicky, tore past him, knocking him spinning. Directly behind them were helmeted riot police, clubs raised. A high-tech monster shielded by Plexiglas erupted from the smoky haze swinging a club. Tom dived away. The riot baton caught him a glancing blow off the side of his head. He tumbled forward, holding his head. Everything was tipping at crazy angles. He hit the curb, tripped and fell, facedown, on the sidewalk. The police line broke, cops running pell-mell through the intersection. Catherine emerged through the remnants of the line, calling out to him. He rose to his knees. He could feel the blood, damp and sticky, on his head, his hands. He tasted blood in his mouth.

He somehow got to his feet and staggered into a side street. And suddenly, as though someone had closed the door on the colossal French production of *A Riot in the Streets*, everything was deathly quiet. He leaned against a wall, groaned loudly. A big black rat sauntered across the street perhaps twenty yards away. Oh, Jesus, he thought, all the evil in the world was out tonight. He turned and started along the street, his footsteps echoing off the grim dark walls on either side.

"Tom, Tom please." Catherine's voice. "Don't run away. It's all over. It's finished."

His legs were refusing their marching orders. Some son of a bitch had attached heavy iron weights to his feet. Was this someone's idea of a joke? He would stop. Just for a moment. Then some great unseen force pushed him to his knees, and the gravity of the universe conspired to keep him there. The blood was running down the back of his neck, onto his shirt.

She reached him then, knelt down and took him into her arms. She wore a vermilion-colored leather jacket with a high collar. Her eyes glistened in the night, and her mouth was as inviting as desire itself. Christ, he thought. he really was the fool of the world. He still longed to kiss that mouth. She was saying something that he couldn't make out. She held a handkerchief to his head.

"Well," he mumbled, "is it my turn now? How are you going to do it Catherine? How are you going to kill me?"

"Shh," she said. "You talk too much. Did anybody ever tell you that, Tom Coward?"

"Constantly," he said.

"Don't talk now, my darling. We are going to get out of here. We are going to get out of this and live happily ever after."

"Sure," Tom said, "and waiters at expensive French restaurants will smile. And peace will come to the Middle East."

She got him to his feet. "Can you walk?"

"On water," he said.

The black snowflakes marring his vision began to clear.

"How did you find out about the Director?" he asked.

"Ygal Ben-Josef. His people found Welles Carpenter's address in Paris. They followed him to Deux Magots. I had no idea you were to meet him there, Tom."

"Oh, shit. Why did you have to bother with him? He was a broken old man. He had already done the job. He destroyed himself."

"Please, darling, please let's not talk about it now...."

"But you don't understand."

"We will talk later, I promise. Once we are away from here."

"But...."

He couldn't finish. Ahead of them, a long black shadow, beautifully backlit, fell on the street. The shadow moved, the backlighting shifted and Rakko raised the machine pistol. Catherine pulled Tom into a doorway, and suddenly the street clattered and echoed with gunfire.

She was no longer holding him, and he fell back against the wall. She tried the door. Locked. Of course. He heard her say, "*Merde*."

"Don't you have a gun?" he said.

"No." She frantically jiggled at the latch. Nothing.

"Christ, you don't have a gun? What the hell kind of a killer are you, anyway?"

Then – footsteps. Lots of them. Rakko coming, with a small army? A moment later, a squad of riot police were racing down the street toward the Boulevard St. Germain. Catherine grabbed Tom, dragged him out in the street in the wake of the police. No sign of Rakko.

"Come on," she said into Tom's ear. They trotted after the squad of police. The gendarmes seemed to have no inkling that directly to their rear, two civilians were scurrying for their lives.

Then suddenly the police were gone, speeding up and disappearing around a corner. The god of fucking everything up, a god that closely monitored Tom's life, had made them evaporate. The street loomed empty. They turned a corner onto a narrow side street. There was a low stone wall topped with wrought-iron spikes. Abruptly the long shadow cascaded across those spikes, a graceful, free-floating thing that landed a few feet in front of them. What passed for a smile in Rakko's emotional makeup was pulled across that pale undertaker's countenance.

What the hell, Tom thought. He lunged at the smile and somehow got hold of Rakko. He knocked him back. The machine pistol clattered to the street. Tom's hands closed around that long scrawny neck. He felt the bob of an Adam's apple. He was all-powerful now, the adrenalin pumping, possessed of the sense that he had better not ever, ever give up his grasp on that neck. Rakko's dark glasses fell away. Tom's face was inches from that ghastly hollow eye. It stared at him as he tried to end Rakko's life with a squeeze of his hands. He smelled Rakko's breath. Garlic, for Christ's sake. Just before going out for an evening of murder, he had eaten garlic. Tom tightened the grip.

But then Rakko lifted him up and shrugged him off like a minor irritation. Tom was thrown backwards, flying through the air for what seemed like seconds before the pavement reached up and pulled him down. He landed with a painful grunt and saw Rakko spring at Catherine just as she raised his machine pistol. She fired as he knocked the gun from her hands. Then he grabbed her by the hair. Suddenly there was steel flashing in the darkness, and Tom realized that Rakko was raising up the long, curved Kukri knife, and he had only a millisecond to get the machine pistol. He lunged for it. Saw the blade swooping up. His fingers closed over metal. He had the gun in his hands. Where was that blade? The knife was nowhere in sight. Blood was everywhere. Oh, shit. *Shit!* He fired blindly. Rakko threw the bloodied rag doll he had been holding to one side, stumbled back, sank against the fence. The knife was still in his hand. Tom was on his feet now. He did not take his eyes off Rakko. The killer raised the knife. The blade dripped blood. Tom squeezed the trigger. The machine pistol jumped in his hands. He heard the sound of it, a deafening, unrelenting clatter. It seemed to go on forever.

24

On the final day of the Cannes Film Festival, Jacques, the head bartender at the Carlton Bar said, "At least this year the weather was not so bad."

"Christ," said Alvin Jarvis, "most years it rains like shit. This year the sun is out. But everything else is shit."

Jacques shrugged. "It is Cannes, *monsieur*. Everyone arrives with great expectations. Everyone goes home with a hangover."

"I don't know why I come to this fucking place, I really don't," Alvin lamented. "My wife has left me, I didn't get laid and the deal for *Buns II* fell through."

"At Cannes, only the gays get laid," someone else said. "They're chasing each other up and down cobblestoned streets having a whale of a time. The few heterosexuals remaining in the world are left to beat their meat and dream."

"The movies were crap this year," another person said. "Nothing sold in the marketplace, I hear. Of course, it was all crap. The same crap that was here last year. The same crap that is here every year. I come to Cannes, and I think, Jesus Christ, it's the end of movies."

"The movies never die," another patron observed. "Only the people who make them."

"Thank God. That's what saves the movies."

"Well," said Alvin Jarvis, "there is one good thing. I hear everyone's running around trying to negotiate rights to *Saudi*."

"Yeah," someone said, "I hear Cannon's anxious to have it, and so are the De Laurentiis people."

"Dieter Voss died so that the world would not be robbed of the awful experience of sitting through *Saudi*. What a sacrifice."

Alvin Jarvis turned to Tom Coward. "What do you say we go out on the terrace and have a talk?"

Tom nodded, picked up his beer and followed Alvin out the glass door. On this final day of the festival the terrace was almost empty. You could actually attract a waiter with a wave of the hand. Paul Wheeler, the movie critic, hurried by, his face filling with horror when he spotted Tom.

"Oh, dear," he said, "I've been reading all about you in the newspapers. Tsk, tsk. I suppose this means you haven't been attending the screenings."

"What with one thing and another," Tom said.

"Well, we don't expect members of the popular press, anyhow. It was all *merde* this year. You heard, I suppose. They gave the Palm d'Or to that perfectly dreadful Jacques Noiret film. Gawd! Spare me. I understand it was a political compromise. But it's always a political compromise, isn't it? Oh, well, at least they didn't give the best-actor award to Clint Eastwood. That was the big rumor around here yesterday."

"Who did they give it to?"

"Jerry Lewis," Wheeler said. "A consummate artist. Anyway, I have to meet a cute Polish director. I said to his publicist, 'I didn't know they made cute Polish directors.' He said, 'Well, look at Polanski.' I said, 'I rest my case.' "

Wheeler hurried off, and Tom spent about twenty minutes telling Alvin the story. Alvin kept shaking his head, and muttering, "Jesus Christ, *Jesus* Christ. So you killed the fucker? Right there on a goddamn Paris street? *Jesus* Christ."

"Not exactly," Tom said. "Rakko is still alive. For the moment. They don't expect him to make it. He's hanging on by a thread. It's amazing, really, considering the number of bullets in him."

"*Jesus* Christ. But what made him come after the girl?"

"He thought Catherine killed Mehdi Abbas."

"How are the cops reacting to all this?"

"The Sûreté is delighted to have Rakko in their hands. He solves a lot of problems for them. They don't doubt I was defending myself when I shot him. They do seem a little surprised that I was able to shoot him."

"Well, shooting people isn't exactly your forte, Tom. And, Christ, that guy Rakko sliced the poor woman's head right off. Jesus. That must have been something to see."

"It's something I'm trying very hard not to think about."

"Yeah, right. Sorry, Tom. I wasn't thinking. I know how you felt about her."

"Have you heard from Lea?"

Alvin moved his beer glass around on the tabletop. "I hear she's back in Los Angeles. But that's all I hear. She's probably fucking some guy who swears he's gonna turn Saul Bellow novels into movies. Well, I hope she's happy. I know I'm not. Those fucking Canadians. Pulling the financing out from under me. Can you believe it? At the last moment, as usual."

"So there's no *Buns II*?"

"I didn't say that. I just said the Canadians pulled out. I'm talking to the guys over at Cannon. They seem interested. In this business, you never say die."

"Unless, of course, it's art."

"If it's art," Alvin said, "you say die real quick. Course, if you say art loud enough, you get to ball my wife. There are compensations."

Tom drank some of his beer and watched as a couple of workmen began to dismantle the oversize cutout of the gun-toting Touch Lathrop. Touch wavered for a moment, as though reluctant to leave such a favored perch on the terrace, then gave up and cascaded gently down.

Alvin said, "I just want you to know I care about you, you asshole. Are you gonna be all right?"

"Well, I won't be going back to the Hotel du Cap anytime soon, but otherwise, yeah, I think I'll make it."

There was a copy of *Screen International* on the next table. The banner headline on the front page practically jumped into his lap: "Despite Tragedy Festival Ends On A Positive Note."

"Why did you come back here, anyway?" asked Alvin.

Tom reached over and grabbed the paper. Beneath the headline was a photograph of Lacy Bergen. She was smiling into the camera and looked very happy. Beside her, sitting very close, was Touch Lathrop.

Tom looked up from the paper. "I'm sorry, Alvin. What did you say?"

"I wanted to know why you came back here. I mean, the festival's over, isn't it?"

"Yeah, it's over," Tom said. "But the Cannes police want to ask me a few questions. And there's something else. There is someone I have to see." He put the paper to one side. "Any idea what you're going to do about Lea?"

"I'm going to see if I can't find that Italian starlet I met at that party. She could make me forget my troubles, I'm sure."

"Alvin, love is making a commitment. It isn't constantly running away and finding something better. You have to stick it out. It's for the long run."

"Where the hell did you get that stuff from?" Alvin said irritably. "You can't tell me you actually believe that shit."

"It must be true," Tom said. "It's right here in this edition of *Screen International*, underneath the photograph of Lacy Bergen. She says that's how she feels about Touch Lathrop."

The villa turned out not to be very far away from the one in which Tom had discovered Lacy Bergen being photographed in flagrante delicto. This one had been built at the turn of the century by a Frenchman who wished he lived in Italy. There was much more Tuscany than Cote d'Azur to the place. Tom strolled along the mosaic walkway. Beyond the loggia with its Florentine vaults and red Italian marble columns, he found the pool. Lacy Bergen, in a yellow bikini, was stretched out on a chaise longue. When she saw him approaching, she sat up quickly, looking as though she had been caught cheating on a high-school physics exam. She removed her sunglasses and presented Tom with a nervous smile.

"I bet in all your born years you didn't expect to find me here," she said.

"On the contrary, this is is exactly where I expected to find you. After all, you and Touch are in all the newspapers."

"God, so are you," she said. "In the newspapers, I mean. Are you all right?"

"I couldn't be better. Actually, that's not true. I could be better."

"Oh, Tom, I know how you feel. I mean, you must have loved her so, and now she's dead. I'll bet you're terribly distraught. I'm sorry. I really, truly am."

"That's very nice of you," Tom said. "But tell me. Just how it is that you know what I'm feeling?"

"Because I'm feeling the same thing, don't you see? I'm in love, too. I would be just overcome with grief if I ever lost Touch."

"Never mind losing him. How did you find him in the first place?"

"Actually, you're responsible for us meeting."

"I'm delighted to hear it," Tom said in a brittle voice.

"I went to see Touch in the hospital to find out what had happened to you. We started talking and – I don't know, he sort of swept me off my feet. There was all this incredible electricity between us. He said he was a real big fan of mine, Tom. And that he had always admired me. And he's so different from what he's like on the screen. So much more soft-spoken and gentle. Warm and gentle, Tom. That's how I would describe him. And he cares about me. He really cares."

"And here I thought I was the true love of your life. That you were in for the long run."

She bit her lower lip and her eyes studied the inlaid mosaic of the pool deck. "I guess I'm just a kid," she said sullenly. "I guess I don't know what I want."

Tom patted her on the knee. "Don't worry about it, Lacy. I'm not here to give you a hard time. I just need a word with the warm and gentle Touch Lathrop. Incidentally, where's your mother?"

"How come every time you see me you ask about my mother?"

"I worry about her when I can't see her. I'm always afraid she's going to spring out from behind some bushes."

"She's checking us out of the Hotel du Cap. We're flying back to Los Angeles tomorrow. Touch has got some things to do in Spain for a couple of weeks, then he's going to meet me in L.A."

"How does your mother feel about Touch?"

"She likes him a lot, Tom. She thinks he's just great."

Shree Ramana glided into view wearing a taupe-colored caftan edged in pink. His face was beaming with the wonder of life. Then he saw Tom, and life was not so wonderful. He came to an abrupt halt by the poolside.

"And what are you doing here, please?" he demanded. The guru's eyes blazed with hostility.

"We are here, please, to see Touch," Tom said. "Is he around?"

"He's inside," Lacy said. "I'm so glad you two know each other. Shree has been so much help to me. He calls it illuminating the self."

"Oh, I know what he calls it," Tom said.

"I've learned things about myself. Shree thinks I was once a great queen of Egypt. He says that would explain, well, you know, my movie-queen status in the eighties. We don't really change our status in our reincarnations. We just keep reinventing ourselves."

"I'm sorry to hear that," Tom said. "I was hoping to come back the next time around as Shirley MacLaine."

"Look, Coward. We've had just about enough of your shit." The Shree blocked Tom's path into the house.

"You see," Tom said to Lacy, "that's eighties guru talk."

"Get the fuck out of here!" Shree screamed.

"You know what, Shree? I'm getting tired of your guru talk."

Tom grabbed him by the front of his caftan and tossed him into the pool. The Shree fell backwards, landing with a great splash. He disappeared under the aqua-blue water. A moment later, his head bobbed above the surface.

"For Christ's sake," he called out in a high, sputtering voice. "I can't swim!"

"Tom! How could you?" Lacy yelled.

"It wasn't hard at all," Tom called back. "I hope he drowns."

He went up a flight of orchid-decked stairs and found Touch on the phone in a salon full of chintz sofas and French windows. The windows opened onto a sumptuous garden choked with wisteria and olive trees. Touch started a bit when he saw Tom. He put down the receiver and got to his feet. He was every inch the movie-star cowboy: carefully pressed blue denim shirt, open to reveal reddish-blond chest hairs. Tight jeans. Rattlesnake-skin boots. He shook Tom's hand and said, "Tommy, I didn't expect to see you back here."

"I'll bet you didn't." Tom gazed around him. "Nice place."

"Yeah, say, isn't it? After I got out of the hospital, what with all the press and everything, I needed a place to get away for a couple of days. They came up with this for me. Just luck, I guess. Say, what was all the commotion outside?"

"I just tossed your guru into the pool," Tom said. "Apparently he can't swim. For all I know he might have drowned. Not that it matters. He's going to be back for the next life."

He sat down on one of the chintz sofas, while Touch managed one of his disarming all-American smiles. "Hey, Shree's not such a bad guy, Tommy. You and him just never hit it off very well, I guess. Of course, you think he's a fake, and Shree senses that. He's very sensitive, you know."

Tom said nothing. He sat looking at Touch, who perched uncertainly on the edge of another sofa.

"Sorry to hear about Catherine, Tom, I really was. She shouldn't have bopped me on the head at the hotel. Maybe I could have done something." He shrugged and cleared his throat. "I don't know. It's hard to say what might have been. What's past is past. I've spent years trying to deal with the past. Time now to look to the future. I must say that since all this broke, things have been going kind of crazy for me careerwise. There is talk about me and Chuck Norris doing the movie version of this whole story. You know, the rescue and everything."

"There was no rescue," Tom said.

"You know what I mean, Tom. It would be movies. Happy endings and all that stuff. I think Chuck wants to play your part, although I don't think he likes the idea of an entertainment journalist. Thinks that's kind of sissy. I think he'd prefer to be an ex-Green Beret. Anyhow, the whole project is very interesting."

"It sounds very interesting indeed," Tom said. "And it would also be a bit of a departure for you, Touch."

Touch's eyes narrowed. "How's that, Tom?"

"For a change, you'd be playing the bad guy."

"I'm not sure I understand what you're getting at."

"I think you do, Touch," Tom said. "I think you know why I'm here. So let's cut the gentle, soft-spoken bullshit, shall we?"

Touch's face began to harden, the way it hardened in the movies when he decided it was time to kill a couple of Commies. "All right. Let's cut the bullshit."

"You killed Ginger Shane. Not Dieter Voss. And not Welles Carpenter. The last thing the poor son of a bitch said before he died was that he didn't kill Ginger.

You've starred in enough movies, Touch. You know when a man makes a statement with his dying breath, it's a true statement. In all the furor, you somehow got missed. What really happened in Egypt, Touch? I've heard so many lies and half-truths, it would be nice to hear the true, no-bullshit story. Wouldn't she come across for you? Here was this porn actress who fucked everybody. And she wouldn't fuck you. Was that it?"

Touch's baby-blue eyes shone with anger. He took a couple of deep breaths, settled back against the cushions of the sofa, trying to calm himself down. "The true story. Shit. The true story. I've reworked so many variations over the years, I'm not sure what the truth is anymore. It's pretty simple, actually. The simplest goddamn thing you could ever imagine. At the time, I was having all these weird nightmares, the sort of crazy stuff you get from hanging around places like Nam and East Africa too long. I'd been collecting the ears of the bastards I killed, stringing 'em together. Real barbaric stuff. That's how I saw myself then. A warrior-barbarian. All blood and hell. Even when I got out of it, got to Egypt, there was a lot of that shit still locked inside me. So I can't sleep this one night, and I decide to go for a drive in the desert. I take one of the Jeeps and off I go. Out to the pyramids and back, that was it. Just enough to clear my head, settle myself so I could get some rest.

"The headlights picked her up. She was just squatting there, naked in the sand, like some beautiful apparition. I thought I was hallucinating or something. Then I saw Welles Carpenter lying beside her. At first I thought he was dead. But it turns out he's just stoned out of his mind. Meantime, she's all hot and crazy, wanting to ride in the Jeep. Sure, I say, cute girl like you wants to ride in my Jeep, why not? So off we go into the moonlit desert, me riding with this crazy beautiful, naked blond. I kiss her as we drive, and she kisses me back, really gets into it. I think, wow, we are going to have some fun tonight. "

He spoke steadily, without interruption, as though reading from a script he had written a long time ago. "Then she found the gun I was carrying with me in the Jeep. A Colt .45 that some guy sold me in Saigon. No big deal whatsoever. I'd carried it all through Africa. Kept it under my pillow at night. When she started waving it around, I stopped the Jeep. She leapt out and ran away, still waving this damned gun. I got a blanket out of the back. I was figuring we could do it right there in the desert under the stars. But she wasn't having anything to do with that. Just kept waving the gun around and saying weird things. I started to get really pissed off, frustrated. There was a lot of anger in me in those days, bubbling just beneath the surface. It didn't take much to bring it out, not in Nam, not in Africa. I grabbed the gun away from her. By then the rage really was building. But I wasn't planning to hurt her. Then she began taunting me, really ugly stuff. Kill me, she yelled. Do it. Do it. She was begging me to kill her, for Christ's sake. Said she wanted to go to the father of terror."

He closed his eyes and rubbed his hands across his face before continuing. "I put the gun to the side of her head, cocked the trigger, a shell in the chamber, everything set to go. It wasn't like I hadn't pulled this stunt a few times in my life. 'Is this what you want?' I remember yelling that at her. 'Is this what you want?' She said, yes, yes, do it. Do it. And in the midst of her yelling, I started to scream, and Christ, my finger tightened on the trigger –"

His face was stony. His eyes were brimming with tears. "It had become too easy to pull the trigger." He spoke so quietly now Tom had to lean forward to catch his words. "Then I picked up the gun, got into the Jeep, drove back to the hotel and fell asleep. The next morning I woke up feeling just terrible. I couldn't believe what had happened. For a while, I thought for sure it must have been one of my nightmares. Then everyone was running around looking for this actress named Ginger Shane. I didn't know her name, but I knew where she was. I knew she wasn't coming back, and I knew that it was no goddamn nightmare. I had the .45 with the spent chamber as proof."

"But then they arrested Dieter," Tom said.

"Yeah." He couldn't help a crooked grin. "But then in a day or so they let him go, and everyone started convincing themselves that Ginger had committed suicide. It was just that some Arab had stolen the gun. In a way, they were right. She did commit suicide. I just pulled the trigger for her."

"But it didn't end there, did it?"

"How do you mean?"

"You still needed Welles Carpenter to make you a movie star."

"I don't feel very good about that, Tom, I honestly don't. But a few days passed, and I thought it might be interesting to shake Welles up a bit, see what fell out. So I took him aside and said, 'Listen, Welles, I don't know what you were telling the police, saying you were with Dieter all night. Hell, I saw you leave the hotel with that girl and drive off into the desert. Now it was probably nothing. But if I told the police what I saw, they might start to think you killed this Ginger Shane.' Welles got all flustered and nervous. He was begging me not say anything, and saying that if I kept quiet he'd make me a star. The next thing I knew, I was on my way to Hong Kong."

"Tell me one more thing," Tom said. "Did you really want to rescue Catherine? Or did you just want to get to her before she got to you?"

"Are you kidding?" The all-American face looked offended. "I figured it was the least I could do in memory of her sister, Ginger Shane, and what she meant to me."

"A lot of people are dead because of you," Tom said.

"I'm sorry about that. But they all had a part in it. Welles and Dieter fucked Ginger over. They drove her toward suicide. Not me. I happened to be there at the end, that's all. You think there wouldn't have been an end if I wasn't there? Don't kid yourself. She was a death looking for a place to happen."

He rose to his feet and stretched. "Anyway, it's all water under the bridge. There's nothing I can do about it now. Nothing any of us can do. Tell you what, Tom. Go out tonight with your friend Alvin, have some champagne. You seem to like champagne a lot. Tomorrow we'll all go home and forget about this as best we can."

"Is that what you plan to do? Forget about it?"

"I plan to make a movie with Chuck Norris, Tom. I plan to become a big star, you know, just like Sly and Clint and all those other guys who didn't have to go through half of what I've gone through. I've come too far to turn back now. This is my moment. I'd be a fool not to take it."

"You don't deserve your fucking moment." Tom was on his feet.

The Shree came into the room. He had changed into a peach-colored caftan. It apparently came with a gun. The Shree pointed the gun at Tom.

"Don't do it, Shree," Tom said icily. "We'll just meet in the next world and I'll wring your neck."

"I don't think the gun is necessary, Shree," Touch said calmly. "Tommy here is going to leave quietly. This is finished and he knows it."

"It's not finished," Tom said. "I'm going to get you."

Touch produced a lovely smile. He was the golden, baby-faced boy, comfy as hell in his Mediterranean villa. "No, you're not, Tom," he said. "I'm afraid there isn't a damn thing you can do."

"Oh, yeah? Just watch me. Keep an eye peeled, Touch. You never know when I'll be coming."

"I should be jotting down this dialogue," Touch said, still grinning. "We can use it in the movie."

25

The doorman decked out in the top hat and red coat perked up as soon as he saw Tom emerge from the taxi. "Mr. Coward, good to have you back with us again."

"Its good to be back, Fred." Tom handed the doorman his bag and they went into the richly appointed lobby of the Beverly Wilshire Hotel. The desk clerk seemed even more pleased than the doorman.

"I can't tell you how delighted we are to see you, Mr. Coward."

"Well, it's delightful to see you, too, Pierre."

Even the porter was overjoyed. "Meester Coward, you weeth us for a long time, or what?"

"Or what, José," Tom said as the elevator doors closed.

José laughed uproariously. "Oh, Meester Coward, you are one funny guy. I tell you."

Tom glanced at him suspiciously. "Why is everybody so friendly?"

"You great guy, Meester Coward. A real great guy."

"It seems to me the last time I was here the assistant manager was threatening to impound my luggage."

José unlocked the door to his room and stepped aside so that Tom could pass into the room.

There was a pair of nylon stockings on the floor. A large Louis Vuitton suitcase was open on the bed.

Satin underthings spilled from it. A fragrance, foreign and expensive, clogged the room. Tom turned to José. "I think we're in the wrong room."

José put the suitcase down and gave Tom a knowing wink. "I don' theenk so, Meester Coward. You enjoy your stay now." The wink was followed by the sort of broad Latin smile that accompanies invitations to Tijuana whorehouses. Tom handed José a five-dollar bill.

"What the hell is going on here?"

José's answer was to slip out the door, closing it discreetly behind him. The bathroom door opened and Lacy Bergen stepped into the room. She wore one of the hotel's robes. Her long, dark hair was damp and slicked back behind her ears. Her face was as clean and bright as a new plate.

"Tom, darling," she announced. And flew into his arms.

Tom gently pushed her away. "How did you get in here?"

"Let's say that I had the cooperation of the hotel's entire staff."

"So I noticed."

She hugged him. "Oh! It's so good to see you again. I thought you were never going to get here. I've been waiting for days."

"How did you know I was coming at all?"

"Alvin told me. I think he's going to produce my next movie. His wife has this lovely script and they're anxious to do it together."

"Alvin and Lea?"

"I think they've had a reconciliation. I had dinner with them last night. They were very lovey-dovey. They told me all about you. They both love you very much, Tom."

"Isn't that wonderful? What happened to Touch Lathrop? Remember him, warm and gentle Touch?"

"Oh, God. Him. Yuck. He turned out to be really weird. I mean with that guru and everything. I was so glad when he went off to Spain to scout locations for some movie he's doing. I got tired of him real fast."

She put her arms around him once more. "Besides, when you walked into that villa, I mean there was just this electricity. Didn't you feel it? And then when you said about me being your true love, and being in for the long run, I felt so awful. I didn't say those things to be frivolous. I said them because I meant them. I just got confused for a moment, that's all."

"Lacy, you miss the point. You didn't have to say those things. You don't have to make a commitment to me."

"Why not?"

"Well, for starters I can't make a commitment to you. "

"Alvin and Lea said you might say something like that. They say you have this trouble with commitment. But I don't care, Tom, I really don't. I'll make you commit yourself to me, I really will."

They were saved from further discussion by a knock on the door. At least Tom thought they were saved, until he opened the door and Maddi Bergen stormed in.

"I knew I forgot to ask something," Tom said.

"And what was that?" Maddi snapped.

"I forgot to ask about you."

Maddi launched the special glare she reserved for Lacy. It was the one that managed to suggest disappointment, rage and superiority all in one. "I cannot believe you actually are in this man's room again," she growled. "Have you no shame, young woman? Have you taken complete and total leave of your senses?"

Lacy struck her obstinate pose, the one that included the graceful toss of the elegant head. "I wanted to be with Tom, Mother. That is my prerogative. I exercised it."

"Listen, will you two go somewhere else to fight?" Tom pleaded. "As usual, I just got off a plane. As usual, I am very tired. And, as usual, I don't need this."

"Get dressed," Maddi said to Lacy. "There's been a terrible accident."

"Accident? What accident?" Lacy demanded.

"You are going to have to be brave, Lacy, darling. It's Touch Lathrop." Maddi's voice had fallen to an appropriately mournful timbre. "He's been killed in Spain. Some sort of car accident. I haven't the details. It happened late yesterday. On one of those terrible mountain roads, I suppose."

Lacy looked solemn. "That's horrible," she said. "Even if he was kind of creepy, I didn't want anything to happen to him."

"Don't call him creepy. Touch was not creepy," Maddi Bergen countered. "You hang around this –" she flung a hand in Tom's direction "– and then you dare to call Touch Lathrop creepy? God, young lady, we're going to have to have some discussions about your judgment concerning men."

"My judgment? What about yours? What about you and that awful Arab who got himself killed and turned out to be some sort of drug-peddling gangster?"

"Look, we don't have a great deal of time to discuss this now. You must get dressed. An *Entertainment Tonight* crew is downstairs in the lobby. Miss Rona wants to interview you about Touch. The Touch Lathrop you remember. That's what Rona wants."

"Mother." Lacy stamped her foot angrily. "What am I going to say to Rona Barrett? Isn't she the one who did that report on how I don't wear the goddamn jeans I advertise?"

"Never mind about that."

"I didn't even like the guy."

"Don't be silly. You two were romantically linked."

"He was real weird. He kept a gun under his pillow."

Maddi looked alarmed. "How do you know what was under his pillow?"

Lacy realized she had gone too far. "I'll get dressed," she said with resignation. "I'll talk to Miss Rona."

But Maddi was not to be put off. "We have just signed a six-figure book contract with one of the biggest publishing houses in New York, young lady. You are not going to stand there and tell me you aren't a virgin? You are not going to tell me that and throw the entire contract into jeopardy."

Lacy closed the bathroom door in her mother's face. Maddi looked as though she had just been slapped with a dead flounder. She turned on Tom, fists clenched, teeth gritted. "I don't know what the hell it is you think you're up to here, Coward."

"Oh, Maddi, shut up, I'm tired of this, I really am. I checked into the hotel, that's all. My crime is that I checked into the damned hotel."

She came close enough so that he could watch the blood rushing into her face. It was not a pleasant sight. "I warn you, Coward. There will be terrible consequences if you do not stay away from my daughter. You know nothing about wickedness, believe me. But you will, you will if you don't leave Lacy alone."

He grabbed her by the elbow and hustled her toward the door. "You're in my room, Maddi, and you're a pain in the ass. Now get out."

"You have not heard the last of me, Coward, I promise you that!" For the second time in as many minutes a door was slammed in Maddi Bergen's contorted face.

Lacy peered hesitantly out a partially opened bathroom door. "Is she gone?"

"She's gone."

She swept out. Full movie-star entrance. "Oh, Tom," she gushed. "I'm so proud of you. Kiss me. Love me. Hug me."

"Not so fast," Tom said. "How did you know it was there?"

"What do you mean? What was where?"

"The gun. How did you know Touch Lathrop had a gun under his pillow?"

"Oh, Tom!" She stamped her foot in exasperation.

When Lacy left a few minutes later, Tom picked up the telephone receiver and got the front desk. "Hello, Pierre. Listen, I appreciate this. But I think you had better move me to another room. That's right. No, just a misunderstanding, that's all. I'm like Garbo. I want to be alone."

He opened the tiny refrigerator. Just as he suspected, there was a bottle of Mumm's. He opened it, poured himself a glass and went to the window. It looked out across Wilshire Boulevard at Rodeo Drive. He wondered if fate killed Touch Lathrop. Or perhaps Ygal Ben-Josef somehow found out about Touch, and made sure Catherine had her final moment of revenge. Not that it mattered. He sipped at his champagne and thought of beautiful women and dark rainy nights and how the good things always end so badly. He thought of the loneliness of the world. He thought of these things and he drank the champagne. Down on Rodeo Drive, mad dogs and rich Americans were shopping for Gucci loafers in the midday sun.